HIGHLAND HERITAGE

HIGHLAND HERITAGE

Rowena Summers

Pan Books

First world edition published in Great Britain 1991 by
Severn House Publishers Ltd of
35 Manor Road, Wallington, Surrey SM6 0BW

Simultaneously published in the U.S.A. and Canada 1991 by
Severn House Publishers Inc of
271 Madison Avenue, New York, NY 10016.

This edition published 1997 by Pan Books
an imprint of Macmillan Publishers Ltd
25 Eccleston Place, London SW1W 9NF
and Basingstoke

Associated companies throughout the world

ISBN 0 330 37014 6

Copyright © Rowena Summers 1991

1 3 5 7 9 10 8 6 4 2

A CIP catalogue record for this book is available from
the British Library.

Printed and bound in Great Britain by
Mackays of Chatham PLC, Chatham, Kent

For Ann with love

Chapter 1

Even before she was fully awake, the wine-clear air had infiltrated into the unfamiliar bedroom and begun to enliven Annie's senses. But it still took a few minutes for her to remember exactly where she was. She turned her head sideways on the pillow. At some time a maid had drawn back the brown velvet curtains from the long windows, and motes of dust danced in the beams of sunlight streaming through the glass.

And then she remembered. She was at Blairfinnan. The tediously long journey from the far west of England to Scotland was behind her, and it was the start of a new life. And however strange, she knew that she owed her gratitude to her dour Uncle Dougal who had offered her a place in his home.

Annie swallowed hard, knowing she must look forward now, not back. She flung off the bedcovers and went across to the window on bare feet. She stood motionless for a moment then, caught by the sheer beauty of the purple and gold heather-clad mountains surrounding this idyllic area of the Highlands. It was truly a glorious day, and without warning, she suddenly felt the glory of it in her soul.

She turned away from the window, feeling a spurt of happiness that took her by surprise. This land of her ancestors was not so alien after all, and these people who were her distant kin wouldn't be strangers much longer. She told herself so with renewed determination.

There was a pitcher of fresh water on her wash-stand, and she washed and dressed quickly, and a little later she sought out her Aunt Morag in the dining-room. She had met her aunt for the first time yesterday, but she had liked her immediately. She was as pert and friendly as her uncle was large and blunt. Aunt Morag was a real homemaker, though to Annie it was still a little unreal to think of this vast pile of granite stone that was Blairfinnan as a home. It couldn't be more different from the cosy Devonshire cottage she had left behind . . . and she regretted now that her father had told her so little about the ancestral home he had left so long ago. . .

'Come and sit yourself down, my dear,' Aunt Morag greeted her now. 'There's porridge or kippers, or both if you've a hearty appetite in the morning. And Maisie will pour you some tea.'

Annie accepted the tea but declined any breakfast other than fresh-baked bread and preserves.

'You should eat more,' Aunt Morag observed. 'You could do with a little more flesh on your bones, Annie. A man likes to see a well-rounded lass.'

Annie would normally laugh off such a remark, if it weren't for the less than subtle suggestions from her uncle on the journey here regarding his son and herself.

'Aunt Morag, I've no interest in what any man thinks of my shape! I'm not looking for a husband –'

'But at your age you should be, dear. It's the natural way things for a lovely young woman to find a man of her own,' she said more gently.

'And for that I'm supposed to fatten myself up like a cow ready for market?' she said, wanting to defuse the situation before Morag too could mention the son of the house as a prospect for Annie. At least he was away in Edinburgh in practice as a junior lawyer, she thought in some relief, so she wouldn't have to see him constantly.

Aunt Morag laughed. 'Aye well, many a young lass has changed her mind on that score soon enough! Rob comes home as frequently as he can, and he sometimes brings friends with him. But I don't want you to feel lonely here, Annie. I'm thinking we could arrange a short visit to Edinburgh soon. The city has a history going back hundreds of years. We could stay at lodgings near Rob and he could show us the sights. Would you like that?'

'It sounds very nice,' Annie murmured. History had always fascinated her, so she would be intrigued to learn about Edinburgh's background. It also sounded like a contrived way to throw her into her cousin Rob's company, she thought dryly. But she could hardly say so, when Aunt Morag was clearly doing her best to make her feel at home.

'I'd be interested to know about our family history too, since my father told me very little of it,' Annie went on.

'Your father was always keen to make his fortune elsewhere,' she said sadly, and they both knew such hopes had come to nothing. 'But there's mebbe more of an interest for you than just looking at old books and portraits, Annie. Rob's been saying for a while now that we should have a proper written record made of our history. I don't have the head for it, and Dougal doesn't have the patience, but mebbe you'd be keen to do it, since I understand you've become quite a scholarly lass.'

'If I am, it's all thanks to Uncle Dougal's generosity in seeing to it,' she said quickly.

She admitted that she would always be grateful to him for paying for the kind of tuition her parents could never have afforded. She already owed him a good deal, and it was Dougal's strong sense of fealty that had made him insist on bringing her here to Scotland when her parents had died so close together. Any suspicions she had about him trying to throw her and Rob together were best kept to herself for the present.

Aunt Morag went on briskly. 'Och, it was never his intention to make you feel beholden to him on that account, my dear! But the idea interests you then?'

Annie began to realise how much it did interest her. 'It does enormously! And I shan't feel I'm here on sufferance if I've a definite task to do.'

She blushed as she spoke, seeing the genuine distress on her aunt's face at the words.

'I don't want you to feel like that at all, lamb. Blairfinnan belongs to us all, and you're most welcome. I was fond of your father, Annie, and distressed when he left Scotland all those years ago to venture so far south. But you've got many of his ways to remind me of him.'

Annie felt she'd be bursting into tears if Aunt Morag wallowed in too much more of this. Her loss was too recent, the pain of her gentle mother and then her father dying, all to sharp. She finished her breakfast and folded her napkin.

'Thank-you for saying that, Aunt Morag,' she said. 'But I don't want to start immersing myself in history right away, not even family history. Is it all right if I wander about by myself today? It's too lovely a day to stay indoors.'

Morag patted her hand. 'You're to do just as you wish. Dougal's gone off to settle some arguments with the tenants, and I've my own tasks to see to, so you just get to know your new home in whatever way you choose.'

Annie had been walking for more than a hour before she paused to take a rest. By then she had come a good way from the house itself, and she sat down on the banks of the loch to view Blairfinnan with an objective eye. It was truly breathtaking, set in its own verdant glen, all turrets and curves, the kind of place that reeked of a turbulent past. Yet, for all that, it was still a house that could truly be called a home, a place where you could sense there had been love and closeness and passion over the centuries.

There had assuredly been bloodshed and intrigue too, she guessed . . . for a moment she was thankful that in this year of 1854 both these present surroundings and the wider world seemed to be at peace. And she felt a real stirring of interest at knowing she would be finding out more in her researches for the family records.

There was also something else she wanted to know about. Something her uncle had referred to briefly, but in undeniably strong terms on that interminable coach journey from Devon. A feud had existed for generations between the Blairs of Blairfinnan and a neighbouring family called the Mackintys. On their arrival here, Uncle Dougal had said shortly that only the lovely meandering loch she was approaching now separated their two properties. The loch was still and beautiful, reflecting the glorious colours of the surrounding mountains.

Annie admitted that she loved a mystery, and until now she hadn't even known that a mystery existed in her own family. Certainly her father had never mentioned it, and since her mother had been a Devonshire girl, her father had settled happily into the country life of his choice with little reference to his Scottish heritage. It was only the regular payments from Uncle Dougal for her education that had kept the knowledge of Blairfinnan alive in her mind.

But perhaps in her researches into family history she would find out what really lay behind this intriguing feud, since her uncle had obviously been reluctant to tell her.

Annie half-lay back on the soft summer grass, closing her eyes against the glare of the sun and revelling in its warmth as she leaned back on her elbows. She felt the soft caress of her hair against her shoulders in the light summer gown she wore, and was surprised to discover how much she was enjoying these moments of solitude as well as finding pleasure at the welcome of her new family. The welcome had been given without question, and she'd been foolish to be apprehensive of what she would find here.

'Do we have trespassers on Blair land now then?'

The blissfully warm sunshine had lulled her into a momentary doze, and she jerked her head around with a start at the male voice so close by. It seemed to come right out of the waters of the loch, and now she saw the rowing-boat near to the bank. Its owner was dark and very large in the small boat. His face was strong, the muscles in his bare arms powerful as he sculled the oars gently, his dark hair unconventionally longer than normal. Hardly registering why the thought flitted into her head, Annie had the odd sensation that anything this man did would be in defiance of convention. . .

'I assure you I'm not trespassing, Sir,' she said haughtily, and before she could say anything more he had laughed softly, and drew both oars inside the boat to assess her.

She wasn't sure she cared for the way his gaze moved over her in so leisurely a fashion, as if he would imprint everything about her on his memory. Her too-slender shape, her tumbling red hair that she hadn't bothered to pin up that morning, her vivid blue eyes that must assuredly be flashing at him now at his insulting laughter.

'Then you must forgive my clumsy way of speaking to a young lady. We Highlanders are not over-blessed with the social niceties, though your cousin Rob will be the exception to the rule, of course.'

Her eyes had widened at this apparent knowledge of her status at Blairfinnan, and he went on easily. 'Oh aye, I know exactly who you are, Annie Stalwart Blair, and why you're here.'

She was still drawing breath to answer him when his voice softened a fraction. 'And I'm fair sorry to hear of your bereavement. A lassie of your tender years needs a mother.'

She gasped, outrage overtaking her confusion at his sudden appearance and knowledge of her affairs. 'Tender years! I'll have you know I'm well past eighteen years old, Sir. I'm hardly a babe in arms!'

'That you're not.' He had folded his arms across his chest now, and she could see the teasing look in eyes that were so dark they looked almost black. She felt a strange heat rippling through her at that look, as if all her nerves had been touched by a flame.

'So how do you like your new home, Miss Annie Stalwart Blair?'

She sat bolt upright now, folding her own arms in some exasperation and in a strangely compelled manner, as if she needed to hide her shape from his too-knowing eyes.

'Do you know everything about me?' she asked in annoyance. 'You have the advantage of me, Sir –'

'For pity's sake stop calling me Sir in that ridiculous way. My name is Stewart Mackinty –'

'Oh!' she said, her arms falling to her sides in surprise, even though she knew in a flash that she should have guessed . . . she recalled her uncle's words in the coach last evening when she'd asked about any other young folk living hereabouts.

'None but the Mackinty lad, and you'll have nothing to do with him,' he'd stated baldly.

'Why not?' he sounded so serious she'd begun to smile until he saw his black look.

'Aye well, you may as well know first as last. We shun the Mackintys for good reason. They've always been a wild clan, and years ago they tried to rob us of some of our land and there was considerable blood spilled because of it. It goes back to the time of the Uprising of '45, lassie –'

'But that's over a hundred years ago,' she'd echoed, wondering how long anyone could reasonably hold a grudge.

It's no matter. The hurt still lingers, and you'll obey me in this, Annie. You'll no be speaking with the Mackinty lad, you hear?'

And here she was now, at the edge of the glitteringly beautiful loch in the morning sunshine, in the company of the most charismatic young man she had met in her life . . . she caught herself up short, wondering what she was thinking about. But she had to admit he certainly had the edge on the rough young farmworkers she had known in Devon. And almost certainly on her cousin Rob, whom she had yet to meet, and towards whom she was already feeling defensive, hoping he didn't see her arrival as a *carte blanche* invitation to court her. . .

Her chin tilted. Her old life in the farming community among the rolling hills of Devon had been free and easy, and no-one had ever told her whom she could or couldn't speak to before, and she wasn't about to let it happen now.

Stewart Mackinty gave a faint smile. 'I see that my reputation has gone ahead of me.'

'Not at all. I know nothing about you personally, except that my uncle mentioned some sort of ancient feud.'

She stopped now, remembering that he was the enemy. And just as quickly dismissed such an absurd idea. They might have been any two neighbours chatting amicably at the water's edge . . . or meeting on a lovers' tryst . . . she felt the colour rise in her cheeks, and saw that Stewart Mackinty was all too aware of it. He laughed quite naturally, and she couldn't help thinking what a welcome sound it was, reverberating in the peacefulness of the glen, with only the quiet lap of the loch to disturb it.

'Aye, a feud that's long overdue in the passing,' he said with the kind of dry comment she was learning to associate with these highland dwellers. 'Perhaps you and I can help to dispel it, Miss Blair.'

There was no mistaking the blatant sexuality in his mocking smile now, making her heart leap with a feeling she couldn't begin to analyse.

'I hardly think so.' She scrambled to her feet, realising how disloyal she was being to her uncle by conversing with the Mackinty lad in this way . . . and half annoyed to know how easily she was absorbing the new patois. *Lad* indeed. There was nothing of the lad about Stewart Mackinty, not in the way she interpreted the word. . .

'You disappoint me, Annie. I'd hoped I might have found a kindred spirit to settle these old differences for good and all. Did you know that your father and mine were once as close as brothers until your bombastic uncle raised this stupid feud again over fishing rights in the loch? And your dear cousin's managed to keep it alive all these years –'

'Of course I didn't know. I've only been here five minutes,' she snapped, beginning to find his superiority irritating, and registering that there was obviously no love lost between him and Rob Stalwart Blair. 'Who does the loch belong to then?'

'Well, if you want to be strictly accurate, the dividing line of the two properties runs down the centre of it, but since we can hardly control the flow of the water it's always been taken that the loch belongs to the Mackintys and the Blairs on equal terms.'

'Don't you mean to the Blairs and the Mackintys?' Annie retorted, a glint in her eyes.

He laughed again, retrieving his oars as the faint sound of another voice called him from the opposite bank.

'It's easy to see which side you're on. But I've enjoyed our little spat, and we'll meet again, wee Annie, I promise you.'

She shaded her eyes from the sun as he rowed effortlessly away from her, covering the distance across the loch with an easy rhythm, and leaving a triangular wake behind his boat. On the far side of the bank Annie could see a small girl skipping up and down as she waited for him. Her thoughts returned to the name he'd just called her.

Wee Annie indeed! How dare he sound so patronising! She stood up and shook the grass from her skirt as she turned to march away from the loch – except that it was difficult to march over the soft springy ground with its high waving grasses and still keep her dignity. Especially when she couldn't resist glancing back to where the man had reached the opposite bank by now, tied up the rowing-boat and gone ashore with the child in his arms. Was it *his* child? she wondered with an unexpected little shock.

As if by some intuition, he glanced back at that exact moment and waved to her. Without thinking, Annie waved back. Drat the man, she fumed. Now he'd think she was a party to his hope of ridding the families of their long-standing feud . . . maybe their thinking did travel the same lines, she acknowledged, but she had no intention of giving Mr high-and-mighty Stewart Mackinty the satisfaction of thinking she was agreeing with any of his plans!

By the time the family sat down together for their evening meal, Annie was consumed by curiosity about their near neighbours. She'd had plenty of time to think over what Stewart Mackinty had said, and what stuck in her mind the most was the fact that their two fathers had at some time been as close as brothers. It wasn't hard to imagine that such a friendship in these isolated areas would be valued, and the loss of it something of a disaster.

What intrigued her more was that she had never heard her father speak of a family called the Mackintys, and knowing his sensitivity, she guessed that something in the break-up had gone very deep with him.

Over the tasty bowl of steaming cock-a-leekie soup she ventured to ask a question.

'Are there any other people living near Blairfinnan, Uncle? Apart from Stewart Mackinty, that is?'

He spluttered into his soup, angrily dabbing at his mouth with his napkin, his face turky-red.

'I'll thank you not to upset my digestion by bringing that name to the dinner table, Annie,' he snapped.

11

'For pity's sake, Dougal, the lass didn't mean any harm!' her aunt intervened at once, throwing Annie a warning glance. 'It's only natural she'll want to meet other folk –'

'Well, as long as it's not the likes of that one,' he growled, and then looked at Annie sharply. 'Or is it too late for that? Have you already had words with the scum?'

She flinched. 'I don't know why you think so badly of him. He seems a perfectly pleasant young man –'

'Then you have spoken to him, after my express orders that you were to have nothing to do with him!' Dougal thundered, flinging his napkin away from him and pushing the bowl of soup aside while the maid hovered nervously nearby to remove it.

'I didn't know I was to be a prisoner here, Uncle,' Annie said heatedly. 'If this is what you call Scottish hospitality, then I'd be better off making my own way in the world. I can always teach, or be a ladies companion, or a skivvy –'

'No Stalwart Blair was ever a skivvy, and I'll thank you for not insulting us by suggesting it,' he said, though in less aggressive tones now as he saw the determined blue sparkle in Annie's eyes.

'You must allow Annie some freedom, Dougal,' Aunt Morag said gently. 'She's not a child.'

It was the second time that day someone had made a comment to that effect. Without warning, Annie remembered the appraising look of eyes as dark as coals, and the strange way it had made her feel. More aware of herself than ever before, because a man had looked at her as if she was a woman. . .

'Aye, I can see that,' Dougal grunted. 'And mebbe you're right. We must introduce the lass to some young folk to keep her mind busy. It'll be good when Rob comes home to amuse her.'

Annie kept her eyes on her bowl of soup as she finished it. Whatever her uncle said, he was still thinking of her as a child if he could refer to his son coming home to amuse her! She wondered what Rob himself would have to say about that.

For the first time, she began to wonder about him as a person. She'd already formed some opinion of him from the small snippets of information she had heard of him. He'd be suffy, for sure; dogmatic, probably; very like his father in his appearance and manners; and maybe considering Annie as a convenient marriage partner without too much effort on his part. . .

She was jolted by her thoughts, and irritated to find she was judging her cousin before they had even met. Part of her assessment was based on the disparaging way Stewart Mackinty had referred to Rob, and for that reason alone she decided she must be doing Rob a grave disservice.

'I'm looking forward to meeting my cousin,' she said to appease her uncle, as the empty bowls were taken away, and a great side of venison placed on the table for Dougal to carve while the ladies helped themselves to carrots and parsnips.

'Why don't we invite a few people while he's home at the weekend, Dougal, and make a small party of it?' Aunt Morag said.

Dougal shook his head decisively. 'I'm sure the two young ones would prefer to get to know each other in a more leisurely way than by having too many people about –'

'Oh, but it would be so nice to have a party,' Annie said. 'Please Uncle. I don't know anyone else here yet, and if I'm to be part of the community, I should be seen to be sociable, don't you think?'

She spoke artlessly, disregarding the fact that she already knew one other person. She saw his eyes narrow a little as if assessing this niece with the quick wit and the soft way of speaking in an accent so different from his own. He wasn't sure of her yet, Annie thought, and was perhaps only just realising that his annual generosity in sending money south to educate her had made her more than a match for him when it came to verbal clashes.

She was already certain that Stewart Mackinty wouldn't be invited to any party here. It didn't matter to Annie. He was just one man in the length and breath of an entire country . . . but she was honest enough to know he was a man who had already intrigued her, and whose image she couldn't quite get out of her mind no matter how hard she tried.

She hoped she would sleep better than on her first night here. She had quickly become accustomed to the sounds of the house and the unearthly quiet of the glen now. That morning she had walked until she was too tired to walk any more, and had a healthy glow in her cheeks long before she returned to the house.

She had spent the afternoon in cosy discussion with Aunt Morag, touching on anything and everything but the one fact that intrigued her the most, the feud between the Blairs and the Mackintys. Her aunt was a dear, but Annie sensed that even here, she must tread warily. Aunt Morag was nothing if not loyal to her husband, and Dougal's antagonism to the Mackintys seemed invincible.

And now she lay in her bed for the second night at Blairfinnan, and annoyingly, sleep simply wouldn't come. Remembered words kept slipping in and out of her mind, and none of them were words she had heard in this house. She remembered not only the words, but the voice too, deep and rich and almost caressing . . .

it was the kind of voice it wasn't easy to forget, making her shiver now as it had done then. . .

. . . 'I thought I'd discovered a kindred spirit . . . your father and mine were once as close as brothers . . . I've enjoyed our little spat . . . we'll meet again, wee Annie. . .'

There was assurance in his manner, boldness in his speech, and an undeniable attraction in the man himself. Annie moved restlessly in the large bed. She didn't want to think about Stewart Mackinty at all, least of all to feel herself attracted to him. It would be the most disastrous thing to lose her heart to a man in the very family her aunt and uncle apparently hated most of all. Especially one who was most probably married, since it seemed reasonable to suppose that the child she had seen belonged to him.

With a little shock, Annie realised the way her thoughts were going. She'd hardly met the man, yet here she was, weaving dreams about him – or more accurately, trying *not* to weave dreams about him! But it seemed impossible to keep her thoughts away from him, no matter how hard she tried, and the memory of his words kept infiltrating her mind.

Did he perhaps remember how close the fathers had been, and possibly other members of the Blairs and Mackintys too? Perhaps there had always been a kind of affinity between them, that Uncle Dougal meant to squash well before it emerged once more in another generation.

Annie pursed her lips together in the soft darkness, knowing she was allowing herself to become fanciful. In the silent hours of the night it was easy to let the imagination roam where it would, and to indulge in reckless dreams where no-one else could intrude.

She knew it was complete folly to dream about Stewart Mackinty at all. It was virtually forbidden . . .

besides which he was no more than an irritation that had already got beneath her skin, and the sooner she rid herself of it the better. It was nothing more than sheer devilry on that part of her that could still be attracted to him, that made his mocking smile seem to float in front of her eyes even when she closed them tight.

'Aunt Morag suggested I might try to put together a historical record of the family,' she said to Dougal on Friday morning. 'I know she'll be busy today preparing for Rob coming home, so are you agreeable to my browsing in the library, Uncle?'

'As you like, lassie.'

'Have you any suggestions where I should begin?' she asked, assuming he'd be flattered at being asked.

'You must please yourself. There are plenty of books relating to our past, and a stack of old papers and documents stuck away in cupboards in the library. I could never be bothered with it all, though I know Rob had a mind to go through them some time. He'll no doubt be interested to help.'

Perversely, Annie didn't want Rob to help. This was a project that appealed to her greatly, and she wanted to accomplish it alone. She also wanted to prove that she could contribute something to the family, even though her uncle seemed singularly uninterested what she did now that she was here, Annie thought resentfully. His duty had been done in bringing her to Scotland, and from now on it seemed she could fend for herself – until his son came home. She still sensed that Dougal's sights were set on matchmaking between the two of them.

'Then you won't mind my poking into private papers?' she pursued, hardly knowing why she was trying to provoke him.

He shrugged impatiently. 'There's nothing private that need be kept from you, lass.'

Except for the way he avoided the subject of the Mackintys, and seemed in danger of throwing an apopletic fit whenever their name was mentioned.

But today she decided it didn't matter, and she pushed the forbidden name out of her head. She had her own purpose now, and having explored most of the house, she found her way to the library that morning. It was an enormous room, its walls lined with bookshelves from top to bottom. It would have been a very oppressive room but the huge windows that ran almost the entire length of one wall with a fine vista of the sloping grounds that ran towards the loch.

A shimmering heat haze rose from the grasses in the glen, and for a moment, Annie longed to be outside in the wine-clear air of the Highlands, and not become immersed in the heavy task ahead of her. But only for a moment. She was intrigued at finding out about her ancestors to put it off any longer. Later, when she was in need of a change, she would take a stroll and clear her head.

In front of the window there was a desk with writing materials at hand, and comfortable chairs for reading. For all its remoteness there was nothing lacking in comfort at Blairfinnan. There were bound catalogues on the desks, and she opened one at random to find with faint surprise that all the books in the library were catalogued according to subject and shelf number. It was going to make her initial task much easier, she realised.

She had no idea where to begin until she remembered that there would surely be a family Bible. It was no trouble to find it, but if the catalogues were neat and tidy and obviously dusted by the household maids, the Bible on its high shelf was not.

It was musty and dust-covered, and looked as if it hadn't been opened in years. It was also so heavy she could hardly carry it to the desk, but once there she opened the cover carefully, placing a block beneath it as she had been taught to do in preserving old books, to save the binding from cracking by too much bending.

The list of names dazzled her eyes. Births, marriages and deaths had all been recorded faithfully for generations. The list extended for several pages of fly-leaf, and the names of various clans that she recognised were mingled with her own. There were the Blairs and Finnans, the occasional Macdonald and Argyll and Fraser, and some less usual names, even the occasional English one, or one that seemed likely to be of Scandinavian origin . . . and then the name of Mackinty seemed to leap out at her.

Annie stared at it, totally bemused for a moment, but there it was, as clear as the fading spidery writing of more than a hundred years ago could be.

James Andrew Mackinty, espoused of Miranda Stalwart Blair, married in October 1745, died in April 1746.

Annie stared at the entry, trying to make sense of it. There was no explanation such as there was in most of the other entries, where family deaths were recorded in somewhat gory detail. Several had died of raging consumption, another of knife wounds inflicted by a felon, one ancient had died of the arthritics, a younger man had drowned, a wife had died in childbirth after a tortuous labour, and so it went on.

But the names of the two people arousing most interest in Annie were recorded together and they had seemingly died together with no further explanation.

'How very odd,' she breathed aloud, as she was wont to do when something troubled her greatly. 'So it's not such an unheard-of thing for a Blair to be connected with a Mackinty!'

'Does it surprise you?'

She whirled around, her heart in her mouth at her foolishness at commenting aloud and the indignity of being overheard. She hadn't heard the door open, but the stranger standing near it had a strong family resemblance, albeit with her uncle's fleshy features. This was a handsome young man, nonetheless, and he moved towards her now with a grace belying his prematurely paunchy size.

'I thought I was alone,' she stammered.

'So I observed, Annie,' he said. 'It is Annie, of course? I can't imagine my father would have given anyone else permission to delve into our family secrets.'

She looked at him uncertainly, unsure whether he was being censorious or not. And then he smiled slightly, extending his hand to her as he came nearer.

'Don't look so anxious! Haven't you guessed who I am?'

'My cousin Rob,' she said at once, for who else would have such an air of ownership as this one! He caught her hand in his with a firm handshake.

'The very same,' he said, his accent more modified than that of his father or Stewart Mackinty, she noted. All the rough edges had been smoothed out by the university education and the career into which he had now entered. He sat down in one of the other chairs, and Annie sat down too, a little wary, but finding him not in the least stuffy after all.

He was stocky to Mackinty's powerful build. He was not as dark either, and his eyes were a light hazel colour compared with those gypsy eyes of the Mackinty man . . . his laughter was not quite as free, his voice not as resonant . . . and she was quite infuriated to find herself comparing everything about Rob with the other one.

Chapter 2

'We didn't expect you home so soon,' she said inanely. 'Your parents are both away from the house –'

'It's no matter. It gives me more of a chance to get to know you without other people around. I've no doubt I'll be interrogated soon enough on my every move in Edinburgh. It's the usual thing.'

The thought of being interrogated, as he put it, by parents who cared, was poignant enough to make her speak more sharply than she intended. But she had already deduced that there was little formality among these highland folk. They spoke as they thought, so she did the same.

'There's not much to know about me. I'm just the poor relation, which I'm sure you know already!'

'And one who's already become interested in our troubled past, I see,' Rob said coolly, indicating the Bible. 'Have you met our roisterous neighbour yet?'

'I've as much right to know about our so-called troubled past as anyone here,' Annie ignored his question. 'My father and yours were cousins, however distant, and there's a blood link between us all.'

'Even though the blood link is at its thinnest between you and me,' Rob said. 'Quite thin enough for it to be no bar to matrimony if we so desired. I wonder if your astute little mind didn't see that as an added incentive in coming so far north?'

Annie gasped at the pompous words. He definitely had all the makings of a lawyer, she thought keenly. If this was a sample of shock methods in extracting truth out of a client, she didn't care for it.

'In other words, you take me for a fortune-hunter, is that it?' she said, just as bluntly.

'Are you?' he said, his eyes unblinking and sharp as an eagle's.

'I most certainly am not,' she spoke vigorously at this inquisition. 'I have no intention of marrying anyone, least of all someone I've never met until this minute! And since you don't have me in the witness-box, *cousin*, I'll thank you for leaving me to my browsing.'

She turned her back on him. She didn't care whether she was being rude or not, even though she was the interloper here. She braced herself for yet more scathing remarks, or to hear the door slam behind him as he went out.

Instead, she heard him laugh, and at the sound she twisted round. He was seated now in one of the leather-covered chairs scattered about the library, and his good-looking face had lost its former aggressiveness.

'Have I said something to amuse you?' Annie said, not prepared yet to consider whether his baiting had been a joke or not. If so, she thought it in very bad taste, but to her ears he had certainly sounded serious enough.

'No, just reassuring,' Rob said. He took her by surprise again, but this time she felt a stab of intuition. Her lips twitched into a half-smile.

'Do I understand from that remark that you're not so keen on the thought of marriage either?'

'Mebbe. At least, not to someone my father plans for me. I prefer to do my own courting to a lady of my own choice.'

'And have you already chosen her?' She could be as direct as he, and she flashed the question at him.

He laughed again, not with the same dark richness of Stewart Mackinty's laugh, but a friendly laugh all the same.

'That's my business, and the less you know, the less you can tell,' he said. 'I don't deny that I never particularly wanted you here, but if you want to play a small charade with me, I see no harm in letting folk think we've a fondness for each other, do you, wee Annie?'

Her heart jolted. Was this the usual way for a young man to speak to a woman in these distant parts? *Wee Annie* sounded so patronising . . . and yet she wasn't so offended by it coming from Rob Blair as she'd been from Stewart Mackinty. The reason for that eluded her for the moment, but in any case it hardly mattered. She need never come in contact with him again. Mackinty land was on the other side of the loch, and from all that she'd heard, he'd do well to stay there.

'Have I startled you into silence?' she heard Rob say now. 'I'd a feeling you always had plenty to say for yourself!'

'So I have,' she answered promptly. 'And I'd like to know why you think I should agree to pretending anything for you, and why you say you never wanted me here! I don't know you, and I don't like the thought of deceiving my aunt and uncle when they've been so kind to me.'

'Och, it's only a small deception, lassie. 'Twill keep them happy, and it's not as if you've a beau already, is it? You'd hardly have come all this way and leave some

22

heart-broken swain in deepest Devon! You're not the sort.'

She sat down again now, intrigued. He was a highly intelligent young man, she conceded, and a catch for anyone . . . though not for her. And he'd managed to avoid her other question neatly. That was the lawyer in him, of course. . .

'And what sort am I, since you seem to know me so well!'

'Aye, well, that goes with the job,' Rob commented. He looked at her through lazy eyes. 'Let's see now. You've an adventurous spirit, otherwise you'd never have travelled to an unknown destination so readily. From the way you rounded on me, you don't suffer fools gladly, and you're not afraid to speak your mind. You're defensive and proud, but for all that, you're a bonnie lassie, and a man could do worse than hang his trews over your bedpost.'

The instinctive gasp she gave at this candid character assassination was tempered by laughter at the wickedness of his last remark.

'Is this the way all Scotsmen speak to young ladies?' she grinned, feeling the heat in her face and knowing she must be blushing furiously.

'Och, this is nothing,' Rob said carelessly. 'You'll not have come up against the Mackinty lad yet –'

'Oh, but I have,' she said, and felt the blush deepen.

'Then you'd do well to keep away from him –'

'Tell me something, will you? Is he married? I saw a child with him –' she stopped abruptly, knowing she sounded far too interested in the man. But she was burning to know.

Rob spoke shortly. 'No, he's not married. The bairn is his niece, his sister's lassie, the poor wee thing. And it's no fault of hers the Mackintys have a bizarre notion of revenge.'

23

Annie stared, willing him to continue. When he didn't, she burst out in annoyance.

'Well, go on. You can't leave it there! What kind of revenge, and what for?'

Rob shrugged, and indicated the Bible, still open at the fly-leaf Annie had been studying.

'It's all there in the two names you were commenting on when I came into the library. James Andrew Mackinty was Stewart's ancestor, of course. He was besotted with one of ours, the luscious Miranda Blair, and they fled away together one dark night to be secretly married –'

'Did it happen over the anvil at Gretna Green?' Annie said, remembering the romantic tale of runaway lovers getting wed at the smithy that her uncle had recounted to her on the journey here, and too enchanted by the romance of it to notice the anger on her cousin's features. It was family history after all. It had happened over a hundred years ago and had surely been relegated into legend. . .

'It did not. The smithy hadn't been established as the marriage place for runaways at that time,' Rob said shortly. 'They were wed in some hole-and-corner affair at an inn, and took to following the fortunes of the Bonnie Prince. They died together because of it.'

'Oh!' Annie said. Though she realised now that she should have guessed something of the sort, from the relevant dates in the family Bible.

Married in October 1745 . . . Died in April 1746 . . . she remembered from her history books that the second Uprising to be called the Jacobite Rebellion had happened in 1745. She realised something more. Even now, to these obviously hot-blooded Highlanders it was far more than an episode in a history book. . .

'So what has all this got to do with some Mackinty idea about revenge?' she prompted, forgetting the wider

24

aspects of history for the moment, and seeing that Rob was about to leave the library, seemingly bored with the whole subject.

He turned when he reached the door. 'It was accepted in our family that Miranda was always a wild one, but the others have always maintained that the Mackinty lad was bewitched by her. They say that but for Miranda, their James Andrew wouldn't have been slain by a bunch of Butcher Cumberland's men who were searching the glens for rebels and ended up by cutting them down in their little love-nest. The Mackintys of the time made a vow that one day another Mackinty lad would take a Blair lassie from Blairfinnan and tame her. There's never been one of a suitable age and nature – until now.'

She felt the colour leave her face as quickly as it had appeared.

'You're not going to tell me this is the only reason you might have objected to my coming here? Do you really expect me to believe I'll be seduced by Stewart Mackinty because of some ridiculous ancient vow?' She couldn't stop the incredulity in her voice, and she saw Rob's face harden.

'It's not your place to mock something that's been ingrained in the Blairs for generations, lassie. I'm surprised your own father told you none of this –'

'My father made his own life,' she said, defensive at once. 'Maybe I can understand the reason for him wanting to get away from here now, if you're all so narrow-minded that you can't forget old hurts.'

'And mebbe you'll see why my father would be keen for us to marry, since it will thwart any Mackinty notions that may be brewing now that the Mackinty lad's seen you,' Rob said.

Annie could hardly credit what she was hearing. Stewart Mackinty probably hadn't known of her existence until she'd been brought here, though the gossiping servants would undoubtedly have pre-empted the fact. She still truly believed it was family duty that had made Dougal Blair offer her a home. But now that she was here it seemed that if he intended manipulating her and his son into marriage, it was mainly to stop this ancient Mackinty vow being enacted! She burned with rage and exasperation.

'Nobody's going to tell me who I'll marry either, Rob,' she snapped now. 'And if you want us to play a little game with your father, why not? When he finally realises he can't force us into marriage, it will serve him right for interfering in other people's lives.' She paused as a thought struck her. 'I do have your word that you're not playing a game too? You're not trying to push me into something I can't get out of, are you?'

Rob laughed, his good humour restored.

'I am not. I have my own reasons for it, as you rightly suspect. But since you appear so mistrusting, I'm quite willing to draw up a document for each of us to sign, to the effect that you and I have no fondness for each other, apart from that of family connection, and no intention of marrying. Will that suit your ladyship?'

Annie was caught by the idea.

'Yes, I like the sound of that! It will be something to wave under your father's nose if it ever became necessary!'

She doubted that it ever would. It was too ridiculous a thought that Uncle Dougal could force her into anything. Except, of course, for the undeniable fact that she *was* dependent on him now, and she *was* the poor relation. . .

Once on her own again, her spirits began to droop. It wasn't a comfortable thought to know she had no-one in the world but these people who all seemed to have devious reasons for wanting her here. Her heart gave a sudden lurch. And what of Stewart Mackinty? Did he have a reason for wanting her too?

There was a sick feeling in the pit of her stomach. All her life she'd been so removed from her Scottish family that she could still think that the old turmoils of these quarrelsome neighbours were petty and had nothing to do with her. She hadn't even known the squabbles existed, and her father hadn't thought it necessary to mention them . . . but not she was drawn right into the middle of them.

And she saw very clearly that if the Mackintys really took this need for vengeance very much to heart, then Stewart Mackinty could see in her the means to save his family's honour. Which meant she must be constantly on her guard whenever there was a danger of seeing him. It was hardly flattering to know that if Mackinty ever did pay court to her, it would only be in a spirit of revenge, and not because he was enamoured of her at all! She would be the Blair lassie a Mackinty would tame. . .

She brushed a hand across her forehead to push the unruly strands of hair from her eyes, and asked herself what kind of idiot she was being to let these old feuds have such an effect on her! She was still her own woman, capable of choosing her own fate. And since she'd already decided that any further contact with Stewart Mackinty was to be avoided, she dismissed all thoughts of him.

But however much she tried, they wouldn't leave her. Nor would the memory of his face and his eyes and his voice. The memories came rushing back as if to haunt her, and the image of the man seemed to swim in her senses just when she thought she was successful in getting him out of her head.

In the end she simply gave up worrying and wondering, and turned back to the family Bible instead, remembering that she was supposed to be sorting out facts and dates to put together on the block of paper for the interest of the family. And not even her Uncle Dougal could deny how much the Mackinty family history seemed to be intertwined with the Stalwart Blairs. . .

She walked down to the loch again that evening. Her uncle and cousin were ensconced in men's talk, and Aunt Morag liked to be alone after dinner. The weekend party idea hadn't transpired, but a few friends were to be invited to Blairfinnan for supper and a game of cards the following evening.

Morag was thinking of a much grander topic now, and was presently deciding whether or not they should have a costume ball in a few weeks' time to celebrate the beginning of summer. The weather was already balmy, and would be a good way of introducing her niece to the community.

It appealed to Annie as well. She had never in her life been to a costume ball, let alone one held in her own family home. The Devon cottage had hardly been a place for such grandeur, she thought with a rueful smile. The Stalwart Blairs might be considered by some to be almost hermit-like in their highland stronghold, but they certainly had style.

Across the still waters of the loch, rose-soft with sunset now, she caught sight of a tall figure striding along the far banks. She made to slip away at once, not wanting Stewart Mackinty to think she was spending all her time curiously watching his property and the small landing-stage where his boat was tied up. But there was no escape. As she turned to flee, he called to her, his voice as uncannily close as if he was standing right beside her.

'Have they forbidden you to speak to me yet, Annie Blair?'

Her pulses throbbed with annoyance, and she couldn't resist a retort.

'Even if they had, I might not listen. I don't hold with neighbours being at odds with each other, nor family feuds to which I'm no party.'

She discovered she hardly had to raise her voice to be heard. The highland air was so clear and pure that it easily carried their voices across the distance of the loch.

She heard him laugh. At the same time a dragon-fly skimmed across the motionless water, rippling its surface. It seemed to echo the way her heart was behaving. This was forbidden territory and she knew it, but the fact only added a certain spice to talking with the Mackinty lad. If she was defying her uncle's wishes, it was only because she could see no sense in them. And not for any other reason.

'Stay there. I'm coming across,' she heard Stewart say.

Annie felt sudden alarm. It was one thing to have the waters of the loch between them. It was quite another to have him rowing across to her in the small boat, while she stood waiting as if this was an arranged meeting.

'You'd better not –'

But obviously when Stewart Mackinty made up his mind to do something, he simply went ahead and did it. And he was already stepping into the flimsy craft that still looked far too small for him, and rowing towards her with powerful strokes.

In a matter of minutes he was beside her, tying up the boat to a nearby stump and sprawling down on the grass to scrutinise her even more thoroughly than the previous time. His dark eyes seemed peculiarly unwavering, unlike most people's whose eyes shifted about when they stared at a person for too long. It was Annie who finally looked away.

'So. They've already spread the word, have they? I thought I saw your pompous cousin arrive home earlier. Are they matchmaking for the two of you?'

She felt a great sense of impatience.

'Do you know everything that goes on at Blairfinnan?'

'A good deal of it,' he grinned. 'And what's your answer to the arrogant Robert?'

She was about to snap that it was no business of his. Or to repeat that she wasn't marrying anyone, least of all any of the quarrelsome men she'd met so far since coming to Blairfinnan! Which included Stewart Mackinty of course . . . and she wouldn't give him the satisfaction of letting him know she'd even noticed him in such a way.

Feeling as awkward as a bird poised for flight, she glared down at him as he sat on the sweet summer grass a few feet away from her. Then she remembered the little pact she and Rob had made. It gave her an odd little edge of protectiveness, she thought, while hardly knowing why she needed it. She tilted her head more provocatively.

'Why should I tell you whether or not I find my cousin attractive enough to be my husband? It's no business of yours –'

She gave a sudden cry. One minute he was assessing her through narrowed eyes, and the next he had jumped to his feet and crossed the small distance between them. Without any warning, she was in his arms.

'It was always my business from the minute I heard you were coming to Blairfinnan, my lassie.' He breathed the words close to her mouth, and before she could utter a sound he had blotted out the sky with his kiss, and it was impossible for her to break away from his embrace.

Not that she wanted to . . . For wild sweet moments they were locked together, and all the dormant womanly feelings in her eighteen-years-old body seemed to burst out of her in new and shivering sensations. Her arms wound around him and held him tight, for if they hadn't she would have lost her balance and been sprawling on the ground in the Mackinty lad's arms. . .

The shock of her own thoughts made her push against him so hard it was Stewart who had to steady himself. Furiously, Annie rubbed at her mouth as if to deny that the kiss had ever happened. She was enraged at her own stupidity, and for acting as if she had never been kissed before. But neither had she . . . not like this. . .

'Don't ever do that again,' she said in a low vibrant voice, willing her fast-beating heart to slow down, and knowing he was very aware of the way her nipples had hardened against the thin fabric of her gown.

'Never is a long time, Annie,' he said softly. 'And you and I have a lifetime of unfinished business together.'

He didn't touch her now, but it made no difference to the effect he was having on her. She had never known anyone like this. The men of her acquaintance had been Devon farmers. Most were gentle men, married and comfortable, or else too young and boisterous for her to ever want to take their playacting seriously. This man was different. She felt a shudder of something she didn't understand run through her veins, a mixture of excitement and fear and anticipation. . .

'*We* have nothing at all,' she said tightly.

'Then why don't you go?' He sat down again, leaning back on his elbows, taunting her. His shirt was open at the neck, displaying the tanned skin of his throat and the thick shadow of hair on his chest. Beneath it, the plaid of his kilt was spread out around him, the strong legs carelessly splayed. Annie felt a blush begin, knowing she was staring at the fine figure he made.

31

In the softer south of England, there were still some who ridiculed the highland way of dressing, calling it women's garb, but now she knew how short-sighted that was, for no-one would ever dare to call Stewart Mackinty a woman. . .

'I'll tell you why you won't go,' he leaned forward now, teasing her with his eyes and the curving smile on his sensual mouth. 'You're as impatient with this old nonsense as I am, and you want to know what I intend to do about it –'

She stepped back a pace as if to ward him off. 'You think a lot of yourself, don't you! I've no interest at all in your intentions, now or in the future. The only thing we agree on is that an ancient feud is nonsense, and a waste of friendship. That is, if I'm to believe that the Blairs and Mackintys were once good friends.'

She stopped, seeing the smile widen, and realising she was playing right into his hands.

'Some were more than friends, and could be again –'

'How? Do you intend coming to steal me away in the night in an enactment of that other pair?' she said witheringly. 'Oh yes, I've already learned about that, and I promise you I'm made of stronger stuff than Miranda. I've no intention of being charmed away just to serve your vanity!'

'I see how quickly you've learned of our past history, lassie, or had your father already told you?'

'He had not. And it's hardly *our* past history.'

She stopped, because from what she had learned so far about the Blairs and Mackintys it was obviously difficult to separate one past from the other.

But he wouldn't be put off. It incensed her to see that the angrier and more confused she got, the more amused he became.

'Just as long as your adamant refusal to be charmed includes your cousin, lassie. I'd hate to see such fire being quenched by your becoming a lawyer's wife. They say Edinburgh's a fine town if you've the stomach for its smells and debauchery. I daresay your man is making his fortune there, since there can be no lack of business.'

Being so used to the country, towns had never enchanted Annie overmuch, but she saw no reason to let Mackinty know that she agreed with him. He didn't conjure up a very savoury image of the town Annie still had a fancy to see because of its past, but she spoke pointedly.

'If my aunt and I decide to visit Rob in Edinburgh, I'm sure he'll make us very welcome, and it will good to be among civilised folk. Now I'll bid you good-night, Mr Mackinty, and thank you not to bother me again.'

She swished away from him with her head high, and his voice echoed after her.

'I'll be bothering you in your dreams, sweet Annie, and on many another night, I promise you. When I see something I want, I never give up until I have it.'

She felt the pulses beating in her neck. He was impossible. Uncouth, arrogant . . . and yet for all that she had a swift image of the way he had scooped up his little niece in his arms and carried her tenderly across the Mackinty land. Could anyone who was obviously so adored by a child be all bad?

She pushed the memory out of her mind, remembering more shrewdly that if he pretended an affection for herself, it was only to emerge triumphant in his family vengeance. To tame a Blair lassie . . . she couldn't get the words out of her head now, any more than she could forget the touch of his mouth on hers, nor the way if felt to be held so close in his arms. . .

'Where have you been, Annie? We were getting worried about you.'

By the time she reached the house she heard her cousin's voice as if through a mist. She had been so wrapped up in her wanton images of Stewart Mackinty she hadn't seen him standing on the outer steps watching her approach. He noted her shoes, damp with dew, and the way her luxurious hair had come unpinned from its carefully curled style, giving her an unconsciously wanton look.

'I walked as far as the loch. I didn't realise the evening had gone so cool. There's quite a dampness on the grass now.' She spoke in short sentences as if she couldn't quite catch her breath. Rob looked at her suspiciously, and she felt suddenly thrust into a world of intrigue she didn't want to know.

'And if you want to know if I met Stewart Mackinty, then yes, I did!'

The words were so defiant in her head she wondered if she had actually said them aloud. But apparently not, for Rob was merely saying that she could get a chill if she wasn't careful, and that would put a stop to all his mother's plans for tomorrow night's occasion, and the grander one of the costume ball later.

'It's going ahead then?' Annie said, glad to divert him from whatever thoughts he'd been harbouring. And even more glad to divert her own from the disturbing Stewart Mackinty.

Rob tucked her hand through his arm as if he owned her.

'You'll soon discover that when either Mother or Father get an idea in their heads, it very quickly becomes a reality, Annie, and there's little anyone can do to stop it.'

She didn't dare ask him whether Morag too was doggedly determined to see the two of them married. If so, it was one plan that was doomed to failure. She was cheered by remembering that Rob had his own ideas on that too, although he seemed to take to the role of charmed cousin extremely well, she thought later, and she must remind him of the document he'd promised to draw up.

In the withdrawing-room, the four of them sat amicably over shortbread and cocoa, laced liberally with whisky for the men, while Morag launched enthusiastically into her plans.

'We'll hold the ball in the great hall, Annie,' her aunt said. 'We'll hire musicians and caterers, and it will be a splendid affair. There's no need for us to hire costumes, since we'll find something to suit us all in the Blairfinnan treasure-house of family attire. I'll show it to you tomorrow, and you shall choose what you wish to wear.'

'You sound quite carried away by the thought of it all, Aunt Morag' Annie said, smiling at such enthusiasm.

'Aye well, mebbe I am,' Morag said. 'It's not so often we have occasion to celebrate things in style, and the Lord willing, this will only be the first of many.'

Annie sobered at once. She didn't want to suspect that her aunt referred obliquely to possible nuptials between herself and Rob, and to even more far-off events, which would include their offspring, ensuring the future of Blairfinnan . . . but it was all becoming crystal clear now.

Instead of feeling cosseted at being welcomed so lovingly into this family, Annie felt certain she was being manipulated. She was no more than a – a prize heifer, who would eventually produce fine new stock for Blairfinnan – with Rob Blair's help, of course!

She was tense at the thought. Never in a million years . . . he might be a very personable young man, and now that they'd come to their own secret understanding, she could freely acknowledge that. But he was not the man for her!

Especially not now that she had met another man, taller and broader than Rob, crossing the loch with as much dash as if he crossed oceans to be by her side . . . aghast, she dismissed the image as quickly as it entered her mind, because he was the last person in the world for her. She must never forget that Stewart Mackinty would have his own reasons for turning a lassie's head . . . a Blair lassie, at any rate. She felt an unexpected stab of pain at the thought.

'You seem just as taken by the idea of the ball, Annie,' Aunt Morag said. 'You've been staring at Rob for a full five minutes, and you two will make a fine pair on the dance floor.'

Annie hadn't even realised she was staring at Rob. There had been no-one in her vision except the one man who shouldn't be there at all. She forced a smile as she saw Rob's teasing look.

'I'll have to wait until he asks me until we know that for certain,' she said dryly. 'I'm afraid I haven't had much practice at dancing. It was not considered much of a necessity in a farming community!'

Rob spoke easily. 'We'll practise together tomorrow, Annie. We can't have you letting Blairfinnan down, though I shall undoubtedly be claiming most of your dances for myself.'

'Won't that be seen as favouritism if I'm meant to be meeting people?' she said lightly, suddenly enjoying this meaningless teasing. Especially as she could see out of the corner of her eye how Aunt Morag was approving the way they seemed to be getting along so well.

'Oh, I'll allow you the occasional turn with one or another,' Rob said.

'How many will be invited to the ball?' Annie said to Aunt Morag. 'Are there many friends and neighbours hereabouts?'

'Friends, aye,' she replied with a certain emphasis.

'And what of those across the loch?' Annie said with great daring. 'Wouldn't it be a gesture of friendship to ask any of them? I'd like to meet everyone –'

She saw how Rob's brows had drawn together. His face had darkened almost as much as his father's, but it was Dougal who answered crossly from his comfortable fireside chair.

'Am I to be plagued by folk who won't listen to me! I thought I'd made it clear, Annie, that the Mackintys are no friends of ours –'

'But why shouldn't they be friends of mine? They've done nothing to me,' she said, resentful of his attitude and finding the whole situation farcical. 'Where's the sense in continuing a feud over something that happened so long ago?'

'It'll mebbe seem like nonsense to you, my dear, but it's a case of family honour, and it's clear that your father omitted to instil any in yourself.' Dougal's voice was hard as iron now, and Annie felt her face flush.

'Forgive me, but I'd be obliged if you didn't criticise my father when he's not here to defend himself, Uncle!'

'Let's leave it for now, Father,' she heard Rob come to her defence. 'Annie doesn't know all our ways yet, but she's got plenty of time to learn.'

Morag spoke firmly. 'Rob's right, Dougal, so come down from your high horse and don't fluster the lass. Annie, I know you'll be missing folk of your own age, so next week you and I will take a carriage-ride into the town and meet my friend Fiona Moray and her daughter Catriona.'

Annie's thoughts were diverted at once. 'I didn't even realise there was a town nearby.'

And people, and civilisation? And a young lady about her own age who could possibly become a friend. . . ? Once she'd crossed the border into Scotland and travelled steadily into the Highlands, it had seemed to her as if she was in a barren land of soaring mountains and beautiful glens, and very little else. She had felt an almost terrifying sense of isolation. . .

Morag laughed. 'Well, mebbe it's more of a village than a town! Did you not know how near we were to Earnlie? I thought you'd have looked to your geography books to know that!'

Annie had never heard of a place called Earnlie, and she'd become so disorientated during the weeks of travelling and overnight halts to rest horses and themselves to reach Blairfinnan, she'd had no idea that the house was near anywhere at all.

'You'll know of our Highland Games, no doubt?' Rob put in. 'Every August the local Games are held near the village of Earnlie, Annie, and we always attend them – providing the earth doesn't choose that moment to shift, of course –'

'What?' Annie said, startled.

'He's teasing you now, lass,' Morag chided her son with a fierce look. 'But it's true that Earnlie lies on what's called the Highland Boundary fault, and once in a while there's a wee bit of earth movement, but it's no more than bothersome. The last earthquake to be called such was fifteen years ago in 1839.'

'Even that didn't stop folk from miles around attending the Games,' Dougal said. 'As well as being a great social occasion, it's a great test of strength among the young men.'

That didn't surprise Annie at all. She was quite ready to believe that the entire population of Scotland thrived on some kind of contest. Everything here was seen as a challenge, man against the elements, and man against man.

She wondered if Stewart Mackinty took part in these Games. If he did, and if he were to compete against Rob, she wondered too just who would be winner. . .

Chapter 3

'Will you tell me something without snapping my head off?' Annie asked Rob the following morning when they had practised the rudiments of dancing until they were both exhausted.

He looked at her quizzically across the summer-house where they were both sitting out of the breeze now.

'Why do I have the strongest feeling this is going to have something to do with the Mackintys?'

'Do you promise?' Annie persisted.

But he was not a lawyer for nothing. 'I'm not promising anything until I know what it is you want to know.'

'You said the child was Stewart Mackinty's niece, and you also called her a poor wee thing. Why is she a poor wee thing?'

She was beginning to realise how attractive she found the rhythm of the highland speech. It was her father's tongue, of course, so she felt quickly at home with it.

She waited impatiently for Rob's answer. He had folded his arms and looked at her stubbornly.

She gave an elaborate sigh. 'If you won't tell me, I can easily ask Stewart,' she said. 'It makes no difference to me who tells me –'

'All right,' he said shortly. 'Stewart had a married sister whose husband died in an accident, and then the girl herself died in childbirth soon afterwards. The bairn is hers, and old Callum Mackinty fair dotes on her. She's even known by the Mackinty name, as if her own father never existed. She's brought up in the Mackinty house with just the two men and a handful of servants.'

'And that's why you call her a poor wee thing?' Annie couldn't see that there was anything so wrong in having two grown men care for a child so lovingly.

'Not exactly. There's also her affliction.'

He was so infuriating. Annie felt as if she had to drag everything out of him he didn't want to tell her. It would be his lawyer training, she supposed, this ability to tantalise her as if she was a victim in the witness box until she was too demoralised to care what happened to her any more or what indiscretions she emitted. Well, she wasn't one of his victims.

'You seem to know a great deal about what goes on at the Mackinty house, considering you're such enemies.'

Just as Stewart seemed to know all about the doings of the Blairs, she remembered. 'And what is this affliction you're talking about?' she went on edgily.

He gave a slight smile. 'Servants gossip, Annie, and my mother's not above listening to them when it suits her. Besides which, Maisie's cousin is a skivvy at Craggan, the Mackinty house, a fact which can be quite useful at times. Anyway, it's said the wee bairn was difficult from the day she was born, crying constantly and taking no notice of anything. Old Callum thought she was no more than a wee bit daft at first, and went about bewailing the fact that it was yet another cross he had to bear. Then a doctor told them young Kirsty was as bright as the next one except that she was most likely deaf.'

'Oh, but that's so sad,' Annie said softly, instantly imagining what it must be like never to hear the sounds of birds singing, or water trickling over a stream, or laughter, or the sound of a lover's intimately caressing voice . . . she, who had never heard such a thing in her life yet, had no difficulty in imagining that it must be something very special. . .

'Aye, but apparently it's not as bad as was first suspected. The deafness is only in one ear, and I gather the Mackinty lad has taken some pains in teaching her to speak. I doubt that she'll learn much though.'

'If she's only partially deaf, then of course she can be taught, Rob,' Annie said immediately. 'It would need time and patience, but it would be so worthwhile to enlighten the child.'

Rob leaned back in his summerhouse seat and looked at her thoughtfully. It was just as if he sensed the sliver of excitement than ran through her at that moment.

'I trust you're not thinking of applying for the post then. It would be a sore point indeed with my father if you thought to instal yourself in the Mackinty household.'

Annie knew she must tread carefully.

'My parents left me with very little money, Rob, and before your father so kindly offered to bring me to Blairfinnan, I hardly knew what I was going to do next. Thanks to Uncle Dougal's generosity in providing my education, a governess post was one of the few options open to me, and my tutor always said I was a born teacher. It didn't really appeal to me, but I confess that this little Kirsty does. Would it be so very alien to everyone if I thought I could help her? What about you?'

She held her breath. If she could only get Rob as an ally . . . She hardly knew why this was becoming so important to her, except that if she did take on young Kirsty's education, at least she would be doing something useful. She wouldn't be a useless burden on her new family, and time wouldn't hang so heavily on her hands as it threatened to do here.

He shrugged. 'I don't suppose it would matter that much to me. I'm sorry for the bairn, even more so with having to live with those two hot-heads. But I wouldn't be in your shoes if you suggest it to my father, Annie.'

'What about Aunt Morag's feelings on it?' she persisted. 'I sense that she's not so taken with the importance of an old family feud.'

'You sense right. My mother has no patience with it,' Rob said. 'But she's loyal to my father, and wouldn't go against his wishes. Don't upset the harmony of the house, Annie.'

He had a quaint way of putting things that seemed exactly right, she supposed, though when Dougal Stalwart Blair was in one of his rages, she doubted there was much harmony for anyone within hearing. As if by mutual understanding though, they spoke of other things after that, and spent the day amicably together.

And that evening there were guests in the house for the supper and card-playing, and Blairfinnan seemed to come alive with their chatter. People whose names Annie found quite splendid, with personalities to match.

The bewhiskered Donald Macdonaldson and his wife Dora, with their gauche twins Angus and Fergus, like peas in a pod with their fiery hair and matching faces and adolescent squeaks whenever anyone spoke to them. The autocratic white-haired Mairi McWilliams who had lived for a time in fashionable Edinburgh and whose skirts had the widest hoops of any lady present to prove it. The skeletal octogenarian Alex Jackson, who remembered Annie's father and instantly endeared himself to her despite the wreaths of cigar-smoke he breathed out between sentences. It had been a good evening, Annie thought later, and they were good people, who did their best to make her feel at home.

But long into the night her thoughts kept returning to Kirsty Mackinty. It was one thing to be told the subject was banned, and quite another for her to keep her mind off the intriguing family next door. Even though 'next door' was a fair distance away, and didn't remotely resemble the close-knit community on the Devonshire estate she had left behind.

By now she was inexorably curious about the entire clan. The older Callum Mackinty – apparently as stubborn and steeped in tradition as Dougal Stalwart Blair; the child – clearly loved and protected, but without the help needed to aid her normal development, or the softness of a woman's care; and Stewart Mackinty. . .

His image was instantly in her mind, as if it never lurked far beneath the surface of her consciousness. She moved restlessly in the stiff calico sheets, feeling their chill against her limbs. He disturbed her far more than he should. Far more than any man had ever done in her life before. He was a man any woman could fall in love with, and the devil take her if that woman was Annie Blair! The memory of her father's one blasphemous saying swept into her mind. And with it her mother reprimanding him, but with such love in her eyes, because for her Sutherland Stalwart Blair could do little wrong.

How would they see this situation? Annie thought now. Those two, who had fallen instantly in love from

43

the moment the fiery young Scotsman had arrived in Devon and set eyes on the pretty daughter of a Devonshire farmer . . . Annie knew instinctively that if they had been faced with convention or old feuds, they wouldn't have let them stand in their way. How often had Annie heard her mother say in her romantically soft Devon accent that love was the most important thing in the whole world?

'What in heaven's name am I thinking about?' she spoke aloud into the silence of the June night. 'Who ever said anything about love! I'd be completely mad to fall in love with Stewart Mackinty of all people. Especially when I know now just why he's flirting with me.'

To tame a Blair lassie. . .

She closed her eyes tightly for a moment, not wanting the thought of being 'tamed' by those powerful masculine arms to deter her from her resolve to repulse him at all costs. Nor to remember for a single second that she already knew the thrill of being held close in those arms . . . or the tenderness with which he'd scooped up little Kirsty Mackinty. . .

And here she was, back where she started, thinking about Kirsty again. But this at least was safer ground, she thought. Poor baby, never knowing either parent, and without skilled help to bring her out of her half-silent shell. Annie was no expert, but her tutor had often said she'd be a natural teacher, with her patience for children and animals. Which she cheerfully admitted was in total conflict to her impatience with certain adults, especially males!

Her cousin Rob had said she didn't suffer fools gladly, but she would never call Stewart Mackinty a fool, just misguided, perhaps, in not seeing that the household in which she lived wasn't stimulating enough for Kirsty's needs.

A sudden tap on her bedroom door made her jump. For a moment she wondered sickly if it could be Rob, and that all his fine talk about drawing up a document for their mutual benefit was a sham after all. She called out huskily.

'Who is it?'

With a flood of relief she heard Aunt Morag's voice.

'Are you all right, Annie dear? I thought I heard you call out.'

The door handle turned and Aunt Morag was illuminated in the voluminous nightgown, the candle held high above her head revealing the hedgehog-style tortuous rags into which she'd twisted her hair. Aunt Morag was not above a little vanity then, even if it pained her to attain it, Annie thought with a hidden smile. She moved across the room as Annie sat up in bed.

'Did I disturb you?' she said in dismay. 'I didn't realise I was talking so loudly. Talking to myself is a habit, I'm afraid. They say it's the first sign of going mad, so I'd better stop it!'

She spoke lightly, but in reality she was trying frantically to remember what she'd said. It wouldn't do for anyone to hear her blathering Stewart Mackinty's name into the night! The delicious Scottish word came easily to her mind.

'I doubt there's any fear of that, Annie. You seem a sensible enough lassie to me.'

Aunt Morag took her seriously as she perched on the end of Annie's bed. 'The walls here are plenty thick, but there are air vents in this wing and sometimes there's a peculiar rumble if people are talking and I wondered if anything was wrong.'

'Not a thing,' Annie said. Nor do I have a lover tucked away in my room! But surely Aunt Morag didn't suspect such a thing. There was only Rob . . . and she suspected that her aunt wouldn't have bothered investigating if she'd thought Rob and Annie were together. . .

'I find it hard to sleep, to be truthful,' she went on. 'I'm sure I'll get used to the quiet in time, but it's so different from Devon, you see.'

'And I daresay you're a bit homesick yet,' Aunt Morag said understandingly. 'But you're a country girl at heart, so I wouldn't have thought it was so different, Annie.'

'It is though.' For a moment the sweet nostalgia of Devon was almost too much to bear. The soft rolling hills, the abandonment of wild flowers everywhere, the homeliness of the cottage and the scent of the wood-fire on winter evenings. . .

And the quiet here was so different, so absolute. She was used to the whispering night sounds of a farming community on the edge of the sea, with its accompanying cries of sea birds and the rush of waves over shingle and sand.

She was lost in her memories, and hadn't realised the tears were running down her cheeks until she felt Aunt Morag's comforting arms around her.

'There now, my lamb, you'll be mourning your father still, and we've been the short-sighted ones not to see it.'

'I'm all right,' Annie mumbled. 'I'm sorry to be so feeble, Aunt Morag. I never cry. Well, hardly ever, anyway.'

'It does a body no harm to give in to their emotions now and then, dearie. Will you take a wee drink of water to calm you, or shall I fetch you something stronger, mebbe?'

'Oh no, just water will be fine. But I'll get it myself, Aunt Morag. I'm so sorry for disturbing your sleep like this,' she said as she scrambled out of bed to go to the pitcher where a drinking cup stood ready for her convenience.

'Och, I wasn't sleeping yet,' Aunt Morag dismissed the idea as if sleep was of no consequence, and then she paused as she saw that Annie's attention was caught by the clear moonlit night through the window. She had thrown back her own curtains tonight, not wanting to be shut in by the dense velvet drapes. And she stood motionless now, gazing out at the panorama beyond.

She drew in her breath sharply, and spoke in a low voice. 'My father once told me there was a magic about the highland night that could only be experienced with the heart and not with words. I didn't understand it then, but now I know exactly what he meant.'

'Your father always had a way with words,' Aunt Morag commented, but Annie was no longer listening to her.

One of his words that had so enchanted the childish Annie had been the gloaming, that strange twilight period when day hovered into night as if reluctant to leave the daylight hours.

That time had long passed, and the brief blackness of night had gone with it, so that there was already a peculiar pre-dawn pearliness about the sky. The moonlit garden stretched away below, and beyond the darkness of the copse from where the scent of pine permeated so evocatively, was the meandering loch, silvered now to glassy perfection.

The circle of mountains soared towards the sky, their heather-covered slopes picked out in soft shadows, their outlines edged in moonlight. Even though it was the beginning of summer, there was still a brush of lingering snow on their peaks, caught by the moonlight like a dusting of white icing on a cake.

'It's so beautiful,' she said in a small voice, as if afraid to break the spell of such perfection. 'I wonder how my father could ever bear to leave it?'

She heard her own words as if she was completely detached from them, and something seemed to settle very firmly into place inside her heart.

'Welcome home, Annie Blair,' Aunt Morag's voice said softly behind her. The next minute she heard the click of her door, and she was alone.

Rob had gone back to Edinburgh, and Annie was looking forward to the journey into the nearby town or Earnlie. Today she and Aunt Morag were going to take afternoon tea at a tea-room with Morag's friend and her daughter Catriona. It would be almost like going into one of the south Devon coastal towns with her mother, Annie thought, when they would browse about the shops and end up taking tea and fruit buns in the small tea-room overlooking the bay. It wouldn't be *quite* the same, but almost.

She remembered being told that this town of Earnlie lay on something called the Highland Boundary fault, and while she and Aunt Morag rode together in the small family dog cart which Annie aknowledged that the lady handled very well, Annie asked her about it.

'You needn't let that worry you, lass. When folk have lived with the threat of an earthquake for decades and nothing ever happens, it becomes no more than a bit of legend.'

'But it could happen, couldn't it?' Annie persisted, imagining for a moment that every rumble beneath the wheels on the stony track was a sudden earth movement.

'Oh aye, it could happen, and sometimes folk do think they feel a slight ripple, though I suspect it's more in the imagination than in the earth beneath their feet. Blairfinnan's too far away from the area to let it concern us, Annie. Anyway, I doubt that anything but an Act of

God could upheave that solid mass, even though we did feel a wee shiver in 1839,' she added casually as if it was of no importance.

Privately, Annie had always thought that an earthquake could be nothing less than an Act of God. Not that she'd ever really thought of it at all until now.

'So folk go about their business and don't consider the danger?' she went on. 'Even in Earnlie itself?'

Aunt Morag glanced at her. 'I didn't think you were the kind to scare so easily, Annie –'

'I'm not scared! I just don't particularly want the table in front of me to start tipping up!' she said, trying to make a joke of it.

'It won't, I promise you. And it's only foolish folk who let such things rule their lives,' she said with mild admonition. 'Look ahead now, Annie. We're coming into the outskirts of Earnlie now.'

Annie looked. It wasn't so much a town as a large village, she thought, whose main feature was a church that she must now think of as a kirk, which Aunt Morag said they must be sure to attend next week, having neglected it this week in the excitement of herself and Rob coming home.

There was a long straggling street of cottages and shops; the bakery that exuded the familiar, wonderfully enticing smells of hot loaves and pastries; the saddlery, with its pungent scents of leather; the blacksmith's shop, whose ringing sounds of hammer striking anvil could be heard the whole length of the street; the small fashion emporium and milliner's combined, with its display of hats and ribbons and a beautiful blue silk gown with a triple flounced skirt taking pride of place in the centre of the window; the haberdashery with its assortment of bits and pieces to suit every requirement. . .

'It's not so very different from any other small town, is it?' Annie said, her spirits lifting more by the minute at the recognition of so many familiar sights and sounds. Civilisation was not so far away after all . . . and she felt guilty at even thinking such an ungrateful thought when she had been shown such generous hospitality.

Aunt Morag laughed. 'Did you think it would be, love?'

'I didn't know what to expect,' Annie said. 'When Father's lawyer said it would be in my best interests to take Uncle Dougal's kind offer and come to Scotland, it felt as if I was going into a strange new world.'

'And instead of which, you find that we're not heathens or barbarians after all,' Aunt Morag said with dry humour.

Annie hugged her arm affectionately. 'You're anything but that, and I know I'm very lucky to have you!'

Especially when the alternatives were to work as a skivvy at worst, or a Ladies Companion or governess to impossibly spoilt children at best. . .

'Here we are now,' Aunt Morag said, reining in their horse as they turned into the yard of the tea-room. A young lad appeared as if by magic and offered to water the horse and mind the vehicle while the ladies were engaged in tea-drinking.

'All right, wee Jamie,' Aunt Morag said, ruffling the boy's hair. 'And if you do a good job, there'll be something for your trouble when we come out.'

'There's really no need to have the horse attended,' she confided to Annie as they unruffled their skirts before entering the establishment. 'But the lad's family is a poor one, and they need every copper they can get.'

Annie was touched by her generosity, and her thoughtfulness for the young lad and his family gave her fresh heart if it ever came to the question of herself becoming involved in the teaching of Kirsty Mackinty.

Inside the tea-room the tables were set out with fresh
lawn cloths and sparkling tableware, and in the centre of
each one was a pot containing a few sprigs of mountain
heather. The freshness of it teased Annie's nostrils
as much as the smell of currant buns and oat-cakes
obviously fresh from the bakery along the street, whose
family name she had recognised as the same of that
above the doorway here.

Aunt Morag was already moving into the room to
greet two ladies seated at a window table.

'Annie, I want you to meet my old friend, Fiona
Moray, and her daughter Catriona. And this is Annie,
whom I've told you all about. She's still feeling a little
strange in her new surroundings, but we're doing our
best to make her feel at home.'

'And succeeding very well,' Annie said quickly,
taking each proffered hand in turn. The older Moray
lady was as comfortably matronly as Aunt Morag.
Catriona was slender and dark-haired with dark eyes
and a mouth that was rather too full of teeth for her
to be truly pretty, but Annie soon discovered that her
frank vivaciousness more than made up for that.

'Thank goodness you're not what I imagined,' Catriona said, when they had been talking for five minutes
and the tea and pastries they ordered had been brought
to their table. 'I was so afraid you were going to be
stuffy, and instead of that you're blissfully ordinary.'

As her mother gave a resigned sigh of reproof, she
put her hand over her mouth at once, and spoke
mournfully.

'Oh dear, now you'll think I mean you're plain, and
you're nothing of the sort, Annie! You're very pretty
indeed! But my stupid tongue's always running away
with me, so do say you forgive me.'

'Of course I do! I'm just delighted to make your
acquaintance, Catriona –'

'Call me Trina. Everybody does. Catriona's such a mouthful, don't you think?'

'But it's such a lovely romantic name.'

Mrs Moray smiled knowingly. 'I can see your father in you, Annie. That's just the kind of remark he would have said.'

'Then you knew him too?'

'Oh aye. We were all much of an age, you see.'

Annie did see, and she felt warmed anew that these people who were strangers to her, had known her father all those years ago, and obviously remembered him with affection. It made a link between them all, and the links were getting stronger all the time. But right then her attention was caught by something else. From her window seat she could see the length of the long street, and a tall figure was striding along it in the direction of the tea-room at the end. A masculine figure, whose strides were having to be shortened to match those of the small child dwarfed beside him, and almost running to keep up.

Her heart began to beat faster, and as if drawn to what she was seeing, Trina Moray followed her stare as the man and the girl drew nearer. To Annie's dismay, Trina waved a greeting to him, and he waved back. She drew back a little, hoping he wouldn't see her, but it was too late.

The next minute the door had opened and the doorway seemed filled with the tall figure of Stewart Mackinty.

'Trina, I thought it was you. How are you – and your mother too? This is a rare meeting.'

'Hello Stewart,' Trina said warmly. 'It's good to see you again. We're both fine, and how's wee Kirsty today?'

'Good,' he nodded. 'We're in Earnlie for her regular visit to the doctor, and all's well.'

Until then he had purposely ignored the Blair ladies, but now he nodded towards Aunt Morag's flushed face, and then fixed his gaze on Annie.

'I trust you're settling in well enough, Miss Blair?'

'I am, thank-you, Mr Mackinty,' she said evenly, wondering if she had ever really been held in this man's arms and kissed so passionately. He was the soul of correctness now, and just as before, it was she who dropped her gaze first. She felt a little easier as she smiled at the solemn-faced child.

Close to, there was a strong resemblance between Kirsty and her uncle in the dark gypsy eyes and curling hair, but there was something more in the troubled way the child glanced around the busy tea-room with its chattering clientele.

It occurred to Annie that the noise could be worrying her. Ever since Rob had told her about Kirsty's condition she had thought about it often in the quiet of her sleepless nights, and came to a possible explanation now. If Kirsty only had half her hearing, she could be off-balance in deciding just where a noise came from. If too much came at her all at once, it must be quite bewildering and even frightening, to a little mite like this.

'Hello Kirsty,' Annie said to the child who was standing silently beside her now. She mouthed the words carefully, discreetly putting her fingers near her mouth as she spoke so that the child automatically followed the movement.

'Hello,' the child said after a moment's hesitation.

'Say hello Miss Blair,' Stewart corrected, but this was all too much for her, and she hid her face in his kilt.

'She's not good with strangers,' he said directly to Annie. 'But since we're near neighbours I'd like to think we'll not be strangers for ever. I'd like to invite you to supper one evening if your uncle would allow it –'

53

Aunt Morag suddenly spoke up, having sat stiffly through the social exchanges between Trina Moray and Mackinty, in which she could hardly intervene. But she was clearly not prepared for Annie to do the same.

'You know very well that he will not, Mr Mackinty,' she said pointedly. 'And if you'll excuse us, we'd like to finish our afternoon tea.'

'Of course,' Stewart said genially, and it was clear to Annie he'd expected no other response. 'Kirsty and I are about to do the same.'

And there was nothing at all that Morag could do to stop him taking his niece to the opposite side of the room for their refreshment, where he and Annie had a perfect view of each other. The two matrons had resumed their conversation, and were greeted by a mutual friend at another table. While their attention was distracted, Trina leaned towards Annie.

'I was forgetting all about your family feud with the Mackintys, but he obviously knew exactly who you are!' she said in a low voice.

'Quite honestly, I don't feel this feud has anything to do with me,' Annie said. 'I didn't even know it existed until I came to Blairfinnan, but I've heard plenty about it in the short time I've been here.'

Enough to know it might have very much to do with her, if Stewart thought she was the Blair lassie to be tarned.

'Isn't he a handsome man though?' Trina sighed with a dreamy smile. 'Do you know, I've been trying for months to make him look at me the way he looked at you just now? I suppose I should just thank my stars you're not attracted to him.'

Annie was just as thankful that Trina couldn't read her mind just then. But the other girl's words had got her attention.

54

'You mean that you are?'

Trina laughed. 'Myself and every other red-blooded lassie from here to Edinburgh, I should think. Stewart Mackinty could have his pick of a dozen that I could name without giving it a second thought! Surely you could guess as much!'

Annie supposed she could. Watching him surreptitiously now as he cut across the fruit bun for Kirsty, there was no doubt that he'd be a good catch for any designing young woman. Fiona Moray probably wouldn't be averse to thinking the same for her daughter Catriona.

'I don't really want to think about Stewart Mackinty at all,' she said quickly. 'The mere mention of his name at Blairfinnan is enough to give my uncle a near-heart attack.'

Trina laughed.

'Och, your uncle's bark is worse than his bite, Annie. Give him an ultimatum and he'd back down at once. He did so over Rob, didn't he?'

'Did he? You forget I'm a stranger here and know very little about my family, Trina. What did Rob do that annoyed my uncle so much?'

It took her by surprise. Rob seemed so set in his profession, and not the kind to go upsetting apple-carts. . .

'He went away to Edinburgh, that's what. Your uncle wanted Rob to settle down and become the laird in waiting, instead of which he wanted a career of his own. Once it was a *fait accompli*, of course, your uncle was as meek as a lamb, and boasting to anyone who would listen about his clever son.'

'That's interesting,' Annie said thoughtfully, noting the facts for any future occasion. 'But I still don't imagine he'd be too pleased if I said I was interested in trying to teach the Mackinty child her letters.'

'*Are* you?' Trina said, staring. 'Well, I suppose it's one way to court the company of Stewart Mackinty.'

'I didn't mention it for that reason,' Annie retorted, beginning to sense that likeable as she was, the other girl's head was full of little else but the attractions of the male sex. 'It's probably a foolish idea anyway. This family feud seems as potent as it ever was, so why should I expect to be allowed to go into the enemy camp – and why would the Mackintys welcome me? Forget everything I said about it, Trina, please.'

'It's a shame, though.' Trina Moray was obviously not a girl to let it go that easily. 'You'd have found Stewart an interesting man to talk to, but for this old feud.'

'I didn't say I hadn't talked to him,' Annie was forced into saying. The other girl's eyes widened.

'Then you have! And without your uncle's knowledge, I'll bet. How did you manage it?'

To Annie's relief, the intervention of Trina's mother took away the need for an answer. The friend she and Morag had been speaking to had left the tea-room now, and Fiona turned towards the two girls, seeing the way they were leaning towards each other and evidently intent on some extremely interesting topic of conversation.

'Now then, you lassies, is it young men you're discussing as usual? Tell me how you found your cousin Rob, Annie dear?'

The temptation was very strong to say glibly that she just turned around and there he was. . .

'He's very pleasant,' she said, keeping straight-faced at this confirmation that the Moray women were two of a kind when it came to likeable feather-headedness. Fiona Moray laughed. She had a loud, almost masculine voice, and was seemingly quite unaware of its carrying power.

'No more than that? Fie on you, Annie Blair. Your aunt Morag tells me you and Rob have been practising the dancing for the costume ball at Blairfinnan. Such an activity is bound to make a young girl's heart beat faster.'

'Perhaps, but only because I'm not used to dancing. There wasn't much call for it among the young Devon farmers.' Annie smiled, adding her own bit of teasing.

'All that will be changed by the end of the ball, my dear,' Fiona declared. 'You and Catriona will be much in demand from the young bucks on the night.'

'Is it to be a masked ball?' Trina said eagerly, and Annie looked to her aunt for guidance. Before Morag could open her mouth, her friend had spoken up.

'But of course it will be a masked ball! You can't have a costume ball without the added excitement of unmasking at the end of the evening! It's such fun to discover who you've been behaving a little indiscreetly with during the dancing – and always under the watchful eyes of your older chaperones, of course!' she added.

But the implication was that a young lady knew very well with whom she was making these little indiscretions under cover of the mask, and that it was all part of the deliciously innocuous flirtations such dancing allowed. Annie, who had never been involved in any of it before, felt a sudden tingle of anticipation.

'Oh aye, of course it will be a masked ball,' she heard Aunt Morag say with quiet dry humour as her friend took over.

But by then Annie was watching Stewart Mackinty guiding his niece out of the tea-room, and as he passed their table he gave a small nod of farewell in their general direction. That was all, but somehow she had the distinct impression he'd been listening very intently to all that had been going on at the window table in these past minutes.

Chapter 4

Annie had done little more about collating the family history. There didn't seem to be any urgency, and she guessed that the idea had only been suggested as an afterthought to give her something to do in the first bewildering days in her new environment. Privately, she thought Rob was far better suited to doing it anyway, since she still felt more of an outsider than a true Stalwart Blair.

But she had at least discovered in the old documents why the house was called Blairfinnan, through the marriage of a Blair man and his Finnan bride who wanted to link their names forever when the house was built for them by a rich and indulgent father.

She had discovered something else too. The kirk at Earnlie, at which the Blairs regularly attended morning service, was just as attentively visited by the Mackintys, and it had been thus for as long as anyone could remember. On the next Sunday morning after meeting the Morays in Earnlie, Annie had glanced across the aisle of the kirk at the arrival of folk in the opposite pews, and with a little shock had encountered the dark eyes of Stewart Mackinty. She had turned her head forward at once, but she remained conscious of him all the way through the service.

Afterwards, when the minister was greeting his flock outside the kirk, she saw that the Mackinty group was standing nearby, the small girl held firmly by Stewart's hand. He stepped forward, once the minister had welcomed Annie into the community.

'You'll forgive this intrusion into your privacy, Sir,' Stewart said with exaggerated formality to Dougal.

'Aye, if I must,' the old man replied, so distantly that to Annie it was almost farcical.

'My father would extend the normal courtesies of bidding your niece welcome to the Highlands,' Stewart looked directly at Annie now, and his mouth curved into a half-smile. And she remembered instantly the warm pressure of that mouth on hers, and the way it had made her feel, like she had never felt before, nor since. . .

Callum Mackinty held out his hand to Annie, and she almost felt her uncle flinch as she could do no other than accept the welcome.

'I'm pleased to meet you, Miss Blair,' the older Mackinty said gravely. 'And I trust you'll be happy among us –'

'The lass is not among *us*, man,' Dougal said bluntly. 'She's a Blair, and lives by Blair rules. I thank you for your courtesy, but now we'll be on our way –'

'Thank-you, Uncle, but I'm capable of speaking for myself,' Annie heard herself stung into replying.

She had never needed anyone to speak for her, she thought indignantly, and didn't intend to start now. Nor did she care for what her uncle was implying. She wasn't a captive in some ancient Blair stronghold, and wouldn't be treated as such. She smiled at Callum

Mackinty, noting the family likeness between himself and the other two in the odd-looking little family; old man; young man; and the diffident child hanging back behind them both.

'*I* thank you for your welcome, Mr Mackinty, and I'm happy to know you.' She dared to say it because this old feud was none of her doing, and she decided now that the sooner she made it plain to both sides how she felt, the better.

Stewart broke in as Dougal's face darkened. 'The bairn's taken a fair liking to you, Miss Blair, and would appreciate a bit of female company. Perhaps you'll come and take tea with us one afternoon.'

'That she will not,' Dougal snapped, loud enough for the minister to glance in their direction and frown.

'Am I not free to choose my own friends, Uncle?' Annie said, but less aggressively now, for this was no place to start an argument, and on second thoughts, wasn't she playing right into Stewart Mackinty's hands if he thought to tame her?

She wished she could get that ridiculous phrase out of her head, but it kept coming back to torment her. And perhaps it was just as well that it did, she reminded herself.

Before her uncle's face could go even blacker with rage, she spoke more sharply to Stewart.

'I think we both know that it's better if I decline your invitation,' she said. 'But I appreciate the offer.'

She turned away to take hold of her aunt's arm and follow her uncle to the Blair carriage. She was annoyed to find that her legs were shaking. She hadn't realised she'd be virtually a prisoner here, but it was becoming clear now that as far as the neighbouring family was concerned, it was precisely what her uncle intended. The thought was at once alarming and absurd, when she had this whole vast, beautiful country to call her own.

But she didn't, not as long as Uncle Dougal thought he could dictate whom she could and could not meet.

'I promise you we'll meet again soon, Annie Blair. I thought you'd be living up to your Stalwart name better than that!' she heard Stewart call mockingly after her, but she dare not look around as she sensed that her uncle's temper was about to explode.

While they were in the kirk she had seen the names of past Stalwart Blairs emblazoned on rolls of honour in past battle glories, and partly to escape her uncle's irritation, she went to the library on returning home to trace the reason for the family name in one of the old documents.

She found that Stalwart had been adopted as a family name through countless acts of bravery by members of the clan in battle. It had been instigated by a Duke, who had once said the Blairs were nothing if not a stalwart breed of loyal Highlanders. They had become Stalwart Blairs from that day onward.

Annie found it all as romantic a tale as any born out of legend. She forgot Stewart Mackinty's mocking voice, finding a pride in her background she hadn't known existed. It was good to know she was part of a heritage that went back hundreds of years. She remembered Aunt Morag's reference to the costume gallery that apparently held such treasures to choose from for the forthcoming ball and anticipated examining them with pleasure.

The costume ball was arranged for the end of June, when the nights would be long and sultry, and doors could be flung wide to let in the subtle scents of heather and glen, and the headier and more sophisticated aromas of roses and woodbine and honeysuckle from the arbours beyond the house. Aunt Morag had declared that Blairfinnan was to be *en fête*.

The ball was to be an extravaganza to be remembered long after it was over, and no expense was to be spared regarding food and drink for the guests, and the hired group of musicians to play for the dancing. A team of helpers would be employed at Blairfinnan for a week before the event, to make sure everything ran smoothly.

There would be games and charades as an interlude from the exhaustion of the dance, and prizes for the best costumes, both ladies' and gentlemen's. At midnight there would be a grand unmasking of all present to add to the fun.

'You promised to show me the Blairfinnan costumes, Aunt Morag,' Annie reminded her, a few days after they had encountered the Mackintys at Earnlie kirk.

By now she was swept up in a fever of organisation, and her enthusiasm was sweeping everyone else along with her. Annie was more than happy to be involved in the preparations, though her uncle kept well away from what he called women's doings.

'Do we really have such a selection of costumes here, Aunt?' she went on.

Morag laughed. 'You've learned a little of our history by now, haven't you, my dear? You've seen the family portraits in the gallery, and you'll know that the Stalwart Blairs have bred some of the handsomest men and women in the Highlands. Something one of them wore might appeal to you. One of our ancestors was also a keen collector of fashion, even to those of the Far East and Egypt. If you have a fancy to appear as Cleopatra, such a garment is as your disposal. Blairfinnan has been quite famous for its costume balls over the years, and I'm quite sure we shall find something suitable for you to wear.'

And once she was shown the glass cases that held the gowns in the special costume gallery, Annie knew she would be spoiled for choice. But splendid though some of the well-preserved silks and satins were, she was most drawn to a simple white gown with a silver sheen rippling through it. It was made in the fashion of the Regency period with a beautiful high bustline and deep neckline edge with pink silk, and a romantically slender skirt. Beneath the bustline was another rose-pink ribbon that continued around the back to a large bow, and more trailing ribbons that rippled over the hips.

To Annie, the white gown seemed to come from another time altogether, romantic and evocative. She pictured herself with her tawny red hair piled high in the Regency style, with enticing little curls caressing her cheeks, and knew she had found her costume.

'Wouldn't you prefer something more dramatic, Annie?' Aunt Morag said doubtfully.

'No, I love this one, Aunt. Don't you want me to wear it?' she asked, as the lady seemed to hesitate.

'Och, it's no matter. I was just being fanciful, that's all, and since there's no reason to think anything of it –'

Annie could see her getting ever more flustered and put her hand on her aunt's arm.

'Hadn't you better tell me what's wrong?'

Morag shrugged. 'It's just that Miranda always wore white, that's all, and you did seem to be as drawn to the gown as to the tragic story, my dear. But as I said, it's no matter. It's old history, and none of the other side will be present, nor would know of the lassie's preference anyway, I daresay.'

The other side being the Mackintys of course. Annie thought how odd it was that no matter how any of them tried to avoid it, sooner or later the Mackinty name cropped up.

'Miranda wouldn't have worn this style though,' she said practically. 'It wasn't fashionable until long after her time '

Married in 1745, died in 1746, she remembered. . .

'As you say, dear. So now let's choose your mask,' Aunt Morag said, obviously wishing she'd never brought up the subject.

There was an entire case of masks, from the dramatic to the frivolous. Annie chose one in rose-pink silk to match the ribbons on her gown, and decided she would also wear a few rose-buds of similar colour in her hair in the pretty Regency manner. She hoped that the splashes of colour in her attire would end Aunt Morag's faint apprehension on Miranda's account.

It was all so silly to worry so much over old hurts. One of the things Annie remembered her father saying was that it was a waste of today to spend too much time in mourning yesterday. For all his tale-spinning ways, he had always been a practical man, and Annie prided herself on being like him in that respect.

'You must try on the gown and we'll see if it needs altering,' Aunt Morag was saying now. 'There's an excellent seamstress in the village who will see to it if necessary.'

'And what about you?' Annie said. 'What will you wear?'

'I think a court dress,' she pointed out a splendid affair in rich purple with deep flounces at the hem, and a white ruff around the neck. 'It's one I've worn at a previous ball, but that's no matter either. It's quite regal, don't you think?'

It was indeed, and absolutely right for the lady of the house, Annie told her.

Rob came home from Edinburgh the night before the ball, bringing house-guests with him. There were three young men and two young ladies, the most attractive one by the name of Helen Fraser. She was so popular that Annie was never quite certain which of the men Helen was supposed to be with. Once the ball was in full swing, she danced with them all in turn, and then with most of the older men present, including Rob's father, who she declared was possibly the lightest on his feet of any man present.

'I think that young lady is a charmer,' Annie grinned up at Rob through the eyelets of her pink mask as he whirled her about the dance-floor in an exhausting reel. 'Who else but a canny Scots lass could wheedle your father into dancing when he'd said so firmly that nobody was going to get him onto the dance-floor, and then flatter him so outrageously!'

Rob laughed, his own eyes twinkling behind the rakish mask he wore to match his French Revolutionist's costume.

'Helen's a canny lass all right. Do you like her, Annie?'

'Nobody could help liking her,' she said, and then she was struck by something in Rob's voice. But before she could decide just what it was, she was threaded along the line of dancers to the next man, and she felt her fingers gripped tight.

She looked up to smile politely into her new partner's eyes, and felt her heart stop. Some of the guests were barely disguised at all, either by their costumes or their masks. Some chose to be clearly recognisable in this fashionable affair. Others delighted in appearing as incognito as possible to tease their dancing partners and hopefully to claim a prize at the final unmasking.

The man in whose arms Annie was held so tightly now had no need of any disguise as far as she was concerned.

After a moment's total disbelief, she recognised him instantly, despite the jaunty kerchief he wore over his hair to hide its colouring, the elaborately large mask with the painted eye-patch, and the false moustache. Below it he wore a pirate's garb, the loose shirt sleeves and scarlet cummerbund encircling the waist of the black trousers. It was familiar enough disguise to Annie from the old Wanted Man posters kept mostly as museum pieces around the Devon coasts. And well in keeping with the audacious appearance at her aunt's costume ball of this particular uninvited guest.

'Are you mad?' she said in a cracked voice, as the grip tightened around her and she was swung into a whirl of feverish dancing. The Scottish reels were energetic enough to catch the breath, but it was more than the dancing that was making Annie's heart thud in her chest as she looked into the gypsy dark eyes of Stewart Mackinty. He totally ignored her question.

'Are you aware that you're the most sensational woman here?' he whispered close to her ear. 'All these others in their peacock colours can't hold a candle to you in your virginal white. You've a canny way of showing your breeding, Annie Blair.'

The next minute she was released and weaving hand by hand down the line of dancers to a portly gentleman made even larger as Henry the Eighth. She answered his puffing small talk without ever hearing a word he said. All she could think of was that Stewart was here in the middle of her aunt's costume ball, and if her uncle ever realised it, there'd be a terrible scene. . .

Three partners later she was back in his arms again.

'Did I tell you how beautiful you are?' he said, before she could speak. 'How clever of you to dress with such stunning simplicity and avoid the remotest competition –'

'Will you stop it and get out of here?' she said almost desperately.

'Why on earth would I do that, when I'm having such a good time? I couldn't miss this chance of seeing you, Annie. I'm a wee bit surprised and disappointed that you didn't expect me here though. What do you think of my disguise?'

She didn't answer for a moment, finding the situation too bizarre to know quite what to say. Of course she should have expected him. Hadn't she sensed that he was listening to Fiona Moray's over-loud conversation about the Blairfinnan ball in the tea-rooms at Earnlie. . . ?

It was the last set of the reel now, and he would be her final partner. And quite suddenly she relaxed, accepting that his presence was more piquant and exhilarating to her than anything else here tonight. She glanced around. Nobody else appeared to have noticed anything unusual about the pirate. There were plenty of strangers at the house, including Rob's friends. There were people she'd been introduced to at the recent card evening that she hadn't even recognised tonight in their disguises until they'd confided their names, so why should anyone recognise the dashingly disguised Stewart Mackinty?

'You know you're taking a terrible chance,' she murmured, a hint of laughter in her voice. 'I could denounce you here and now if I wanted to, and you'd be hounded out of Blairfinnan.'

'It's worth any chance to hold you in my arms like this,' he said. 'And if you were going to give me away, you'd have done it by now. I knew you wouldn't. You're not averse to adventure, are you, Annie? You relish the risk of it as much as I do.'

She felt a shiver of annoyance, coupled with something else. He knew her almost better than she knew herself. This situation, however much it went against her uncle's wishes, was daring and exciting, and appealed to everything in her.

'Are you so sure of me?' she taunted him, tilting her face up to his.

'I'm sure of *us*, Annie Blair,' he said softly, as the music came to an end, and reluctantly he had to let her go.

She stood still for a moment, and then felt the touch of someone's hand on her arm. She turned quickly, to see Mary Queen of Scots looking at her with wide eyes through her frilled mask.

Trina Moray's voice was eager and curious. 'Won't you introduce me to your partner, Annie?'

Annie felt the laughter bubbling up inside her. So even Trina didn't recognise Stewart. It was all a harmless game, and she was starting to enjoy it now, becoming more amused than angry at the deception Stewart was playing on her family.

'I don't know him, any more than you do,' she said lightly, knowing she was burning her boats, and quite unconcerned. 'I think he may be one of Rob's friends, and you know the form, Trina. If someone doesn't volunteer to tell you his identity, you mustn't guess it and spoil the surprise at the unmasking.'

It was a genuine and convenient way out. But in any case, when they turned around to look for the pirate, he was gone.

'Never mind,' Annie said, hiding her own feeling of disappointment. 'I'm sure you can manage to wheedle a dance with him later. Let's go and have something to eat instead.'

The musicians were taking a welcome break. The evening was warm, and the dancing made it warmer. Added to that, the heavy costumes some of the guests wore was making it decidedly uncomfortable for some.

'You're so sensible to have chosen that pretty dress, Annie. I wish I'd thought to choose a thin costume instead of this hideous thing.'

'You look absolutely wonderful and you know it, so stop angling for compliments,' Annie said, more at ease with this nice girl than with any other she had known before.

'Perhaps,' Trina grinned. 'Geddes Cameron seems to think so anyway. Will you excuse me for a moment?'

Annie smiled as she saw the young Cameron lad moving towards Trina. They made a handsome couple, she thought, Trina in her Mary Queen of Scots outfit, and Geddes in his Admiral's uniform. She turned away from the obvious adoration in his eyes as he approached Trina. The music had stopped for the time being, and everyone was partaking of the food, or moving towards the open windows for a breath of fresh air.

'Can I capture you for a few minutes?' Stewart's voice said close to her. 'You know it's a pirate's right to claim his prize, Annie.'

'It is not!' she said, laughingly playing his game. 'You should know it's a lady's duty to fight for her honour to the death!' She caught her breath between her teeth, wishing she hadn't used those particular words. Miranda hadn't died defending her honour but she had died because of her involvement with a Mackinty all the same. And who was getting fanciful now!

'I only want to talk to you,' he said, suddenly serious. 'Will you come outside with me?'

Out of the corner of her eye she saw her uncle looking their way, a small frown between his eyes. If he once suspected who her companion was, the ball would be in ruins. And Aunt Morag would be humiliated.

'All right. It's getting very hot in here,' she said. 'And we're also in danger of attracting too much attention.

My uncle wouldn't take kindly to being made a fool of, Stewart.'

To her surprise, he gave a small bitter laugh.

'Your uncle and my father are two stubborn old fools. They keep this ridiculous feud alive when they could be good friends. Neighbours shouldn't be at loggerheads.'

'You don't subscribe to it then?' she asked. 'What of you and Rob? Would you be willing to be his friend?'

'Why not? We played together as children often enough, until the elders got to hear of it and stopped it. There have been times when I've missed Rob.' He shrugged. 'But a Mackinty has too much pride to make the first move.'

'You see?' Annie said. She stood walking in exasperation, hardly realising they had already come a fair way through the fragrant gardens into the seclusion of the shrubberies.

'What do I see?' he said.

'Both of you – both sides, I mean. Neither wanting to admit to the other that it's all so ridiculous, so the thing continues. It's probably always been the same.'

She realised he was laughing at her indignation.

'I see that I have a champion, Annie –'

'You do not! I'm not speaking for you, but for the situation,' she said, floundering now. 'I simply don't understand how you can all bear to be so unsociable towards one another, when individually you're all such garrulous people!'

'And you're something of a philosopher, aren't you?' he said softly.

Before she could decide if it was a compliment or not, he drew her into his arms. He didn't force her, and she had every opportunity to resist. But he was her family's enemy, not hers. He was also the most exciting man she had ever met, and there was a great yellow moon above, and the mountains all around were silver-edged

70

and majestic, and their own little fights seemed so puny in comparison. And why should she resist, when it was the last thing in the world she wanted to do. . . ?

She felt his arms fold around her more demandingly, and with a little sigh she leaned into him, aware of the strength in his body, and the way she seemed to be almost powerless against it. She *wanted* to be here, in his arms, pressed close to his chest and feeling his heartbeats blend into hers. She *wanted* his mouth on hers the way it was now, and to know that arrogant as he was, he was as affected by her as she was by him.

She sensed it with a new kind of knowledge that was an added stimulus to her feelings for this man. However devious his reasons for courting her – if courting her he was – he was undoubtedly stirred by her.

'So. What are we going to do about us, Annie Blair?' he said softly against her mouth when the kiss finally ended.

'Nothing,' she said after what seemed an endless moment of indecision, when the longing to throw caution to the winds and let herself be taken anywhere he would take her, was almost overwhelming. But common sense was rushing back at her now, coupled with the sounds of chatter and laughter as other people drifted out of the close confines of Blairfinnan during the lull from the dancing, into the seductive fragrance of the evening.

'Nothing?' Stewart's voice was hard-edged now. His hands moved softly up and down the length of her bare arms. Annie shivered, though the action had nothing to do with the coolness of the air, and everything to do with the man.

'Whatever my feelings, I'm under an obligation here,' she spoke in a low voice that trembled, despite her efforts to stop it. 'I've no money of my own, and my uncle took me in –'

'Nonsense,' Stewart said briskly. 'Your uncle was under obligation to bring you home. When your father died he could do nothing else but welcome you back where you belong.'

'All the same, I owe him my loyalty, and you know as well as I do that even by speaking to you like this, I'm going against his wishes.'

Moments ago they had been so close. Now they had broken apart, physically and mentally, but Annie was conscious of her growing distress as she recognised the truth. She could so easily fall in love with Stewart Mackinty – if she hadn't done so already. And by her own family's code, it was a forbidden love.

'I thought you were made of stronger stuff, Annie. I'm disappointed in you.'

'Please don't be!' she was stung into an angry reply now. 'You must know we can never be anything to one another –'

'I know nothing of the sort. What I know is that we could be everything to one another, and you know it too.'

She heard approaching footsteps, and turned blindly to rush away from him. He echoed too much all the thoughts inside her own head, and it was madness to let herself be swayed by the moonlight and the scent of roses and honeysuckle and the gaunt beauty of the highland night. Madness, to think her uncle would ever sanction a union between Annie Stalwart Blair and Stewart Mackinty. . .

She ran straight into someone's arms, and heard a laughing male voice ask her if there was a fire. She looked up into the handsome face of one of Rob's Edinburgh friends. She remembered his Russian Hussar's outfit more than his name, and thought back frantically to when Rob had introduced them.

'Lorn! I didn't see you coming –'

'I should say you didn't, my wee Regency beauty,' he said with exaggerated gallantry. 'But what are you doing out here all alone?'

Annie glanced behind her. There was no sign of Stewart, and she didn't know whether to be relieved or not. He was obviously unrecognisable in his pirate's garb, and anyway, Lorn Thomson probably wouldn't know him.

'I needed a breath of air. It got very hot inside, didn't it?' she said quickly.

'It did indeed. May I escort you for a stroll?' he asked.

'Do you mind if I decline, Lorn? I've had enough walking for the present, and I believe the charades will be starting soon. My aunt will be wondering what's happened to me if I don't appear soon,' she said with a smile. Besides, the last thing she wanted was to walk around the gardens with this young man, charming though he might be. The mood for walking in the moonlight had deserted her. . .

'Then charades it is,' he said gallantly, proffering his arm. He was charming and uncomplicated, and it was a pity she couldn't fall for his brand of charm, Annie thought ruefully. But she knew she never could. For one reason, he was too bland and lightweight a man. For another, she was already half-enamoured of someone else. . .

Aunt Morag was already organising the charades amid much laughing confusion when they returned to the Great Hall. Annie was directed into Rob's team, and told that they were to mime the opening scene of Macbeth. She listened to her instructions, hardly noticing what she was meant to be doing, while all the time her eyes searched the room in vain for a figure who was no longer there.

73

She told herself crossly that she was letting Stewart Mackinty get under her skin, and the sooner she got him out the better. But it wasn't so easy when she saw how attentive Geddes Camerson was being towards her friend Trina Moray, and how that young lady wasn't doing anything to dissuade him. It gave Annie an odd feeling of isolation, such as she hadn't felt since first coming to Blairfinnan.

She shook off the feeling with annoyance. She should be glad for Trina, not jealous . . . not that she was jealous on Geddes Cameron's account, of course, just for the closeness that seemed to be growing between them, and the kind which was obviously going to elude her if she were to abide by her uncle's rules.

'Why so glum, my wee cousin? Do you not want to be one of the witches? I'll allow that I never saw a prettier witch, but you're all we've got, lassie!' Rob looked sharply into her eyes, clouded now behind her mask. She forced herself to smile.

'I'm not glum at all,' she said. 'Just practising for the part. You don't want a witch to look too cheerful, do you?'

It was a feeble excuse, but it seemed to satisfy Rob and the others. If the truth were told, she didn't want to play-act in the game of charades. She didn't want to be here at all. For no reason at all, she was suddenly plunged into a fit of depression, and it was no hardship to mime the actions of the three witches stirring the cauldron and glowering into it with her two companions.

They were guessed all too easily, and then it was another team's turn. Annie retreated thankfully to the back of the room, watching it all as if it was a cameo scene, and she was no longer part of it. It was how she felt. She was still the outsider, still the poor relation, and even though she knew her aunt would be truly horrified

74

to know what she was thinking, at that moment she just couldn't help it.

She was glad when midnight came, and the unmasking revealed the identities of the guests. Most of them had been recognised by then, but the most successful disguises still won prizes. Annie was not among them, but she couldn't help thinking that if Stewart had still been here, he must surely have won. His was the best disguise of all – and the one to whom Uncle Dougal would have been least likely to award a prize.

He had obviously decided to leave before there was any chance of him being discovered. And Annie missed him to a ridiculous degree. As if to rid herself of the way her thoughts kept returning to the man, she allowed herself to be whisked around the dance-floor time and again by Lorn Thomson.

At the end of the exhausting evening, when everyone but the house-guests had finally gone home, and they were all enjoying a last drink of cocoa, Lorn asked her tentatively if she was coming to Edinburgh at all.

'I certainly hope so. My aunt has suggested we go there on a visit,' Annie told him, longing to go upstairs and kick off her shoes, but knowing good manners decreed that the family should wait for guests to retire before they did.

'When you do, I hope I may have the pleasure of escorting you to the theatre, Miss Blair,' he said, and only then did she really notice the colour in his cheeks, and the simple adoration in his pale blue eyes.

'Perhaps,' she said, managing to keep any inflexion out of her voice, warm or otherwise. 'But I shall have to rely on my aunt's plans, of course. I'm sure you understand.'

He said immediately that he did, accepting her words as Stewart Mackinty would never have accepted them. She brushed the thought aside, because it was kind of

Lorn to offer, but knowing all too well that she didn't want his company. She didn't want to encourage him in the slightest degree.

She stifled a yawn, and to her enormous relief she saw that the girls in Rob's group were beginning to droop as well now. One of them murmured that she could hardly keep her eyes open, and soon afterwards it seemed as if everyone was making for their bedrooms at the same time.

When there was just herself and her aunt and uncle left downstairs, Annie kissed them both good-night with genuine affection.

'Thank-you both for a wonderful evening,' she said. 'I really have enjoyed myself.'

'Have you, dear?' Aunt Morag said doubtfully. 'I thought at one time you looked a wee bit lost. And I never saw your dashing pirate partner after the first part of the evening. Did you ask his name?'

Annie laughed as naturally as she could, considering the way her heart was beating so fast.

'Oh Aunt Morag, you know we weren't meant to ask the names of our partners! It would spoil the surprise at the unmasking. I'm afraid he had to leave early, and he asked me to make his apologies. It was remiss of me not to have done so.' She babbled out the invented excuses, furious at being made a party to Stewart's intrusion.

'Aye well, I daresay someone will know who he was. At any rate you made a very handsome couple,' Morag said agreeably, at which Annie thankfully made her escape before her aunt could start wondering about her scarlet face.

Chapter 5

The visitors from Edinburgh left after two more days.
Annie was glad to see them go. Not because she didn't
like them, but because it was becoming increasingly
obvious that Lorn Thomson had taken a definite fancy
to her. Rob had noticed it, and teased her when they
were briefly alone in the library on that last morning.

'It looks as if Lorn will be giving the Mackinty
a run for his money, cousin,' he began, startling
her.

'What on earth do you mean?' she stammered,
wondering if he could possibly have guessed at the
pirate's identity.

'I mean that if Lorn has his way, he'll be coming
courting, and that will upset yon Stewart, if he still has
a mind to come sniffing at your heels.'

'Sometimes, Rob,' she said crossly, 'you have the
most objectionable way of putting things.'

'It's the lawyer in me,' he replied, not in the least
put out. 'It has the effect of putting people off their

guard, and making them say things they didn't mean to say.'

'Well, I've got nothing to hide, so there's no need to try your lawyer's tactics on me,' she said, tetchy at knowing she did indeed have something to hide. Rob laughed.

'Och, I know that lassie, but you have a fine way of bridling when you're put out about something. And you didn't exactly dance the night away with me at the ball, did you? I thought we were to put our wee pretence into action, but it was the mysterious pirate who got your attentions in the first half of the evening, and Lorn who got most of the second.'

'I assumed the pirate was one of your friends,' Annie said artlessly. 'But in any case, there were so many people there, and all in their disguises, that it hardly mattered you and I weren't seen to be together overmuch, did it?'

'Not at all,' Rob said. 'I'm not criticising. But the pirate was no friend of mine, and I daresay he came with some of the Earnlie guests. But what of you and Lorn?'

'What of us? I assure you there's nothing to tell,' she said, glad that his interest was diverted away from the pirate.

'He's not a bad lad, if a bit on the slight side,' Rob went on. 'You could do worse –'

'And I'll thank you not to match-make for me, Rob!' she exclaimed, beginning to laugh now. 'You're as bad as your parents! You don't take too kindly to being managed yourself, so I'll thank you to let me manage my own affairs. And while we're on the subject, what about that document you were going to draw up for us? I haven't see it yet!'

With a flourish, he produced two identical scrolled documents from an inside pocket and handed them to her. Annie read them quickly. They stated exactly what they had decided upon. That they had no romantic interest in one another other than that of affectionate cousins. Rob picked up a pen from the desk, dipped it in the ink-well and handed it to her.

'This is precisely why I've sought you out before my friends and I leave for Edinburgh. Will you sign both copies beneath my signature, please?'

'Willingly, but don't we need witnesses as well?' she asked. He shook his head.

'There's no need. You and I are the only parties concerned, and I hardly think either of us is about to profess undying love for the other, are we?'

'No,' Annie grinned. 'However much that may hurt your masculine pride, Rob, I definitely think not.'

He gave her a cousinly kiss on the cheek to seal the agreement, and then handed one of the documents to her.

'Keep it in a safe place, Annie. I doubt that it will ever be needed, but if it gives you peace of mind it serves its purpose. And now we'd better face the family as if we're reluctant to say goodbye to one another, don't you think?'

They walked out of the library with linked arms, to where the rest of his friends were talking on the steps of Blairfinnan with her aunt and uncle. Annie saw the look that passed between Rob's parents and guessed they would be assuming the couple had just made a lingering and private farewell.

If they only knew, Annie thought, finding the situation not only piquant but suddenly charged with humour. Impulsively she clung more tightly to Rob's arm, told him how much she had enjoyed seeing him again and that she would miss him.

'Hurry back, Rob,' she said huskily, hardly able to contain her bubbling laughter at his sly wink. He bent to kiss her cheek again, and she could feel his laughter too.

'I will,' he promised. 'And I hope you and Mother will make that trip to Edinburgh just as soon as you like.'

They stood and waved the party off until the dust had settled from the carriage wheels. Annie wondered idly which of the young ladies at the ball had been Rob's particular fancy – or if any of them had been. He seemed to pay them all equal attention, and she couldn't have guessed. Aunt Morag turned to Annie as they went back into the house.

'I'm always a little sad when Rob goes away,' she said. 'And you will be too, I daresay, Annie. You certainly seemed to enjoy each other's company.'

'Oh, I think we understand one another very well, Aunt,' she said serenely.

'I knew you would,' Aunt Morag said happily, and Annie felt a brief pang of guilt, knowing the lady's fond hopes were doomed to disappointment.

But you couldn't help feelings, and if what she and Rob felt for one another was no more than a warm friendship, there was no changing it.

'I think I'll go for a walk, Aunt,' she said now, not wanting any more questions about her and Rob to come her way.

'Of course, love. You'll need some time on your own to think over things.'

It wasn't that at all. She just wanted to get away from that happy round face of her aunt's, guessing that Morag Stalwart Blair's vivid imagination was already revolving around bridal-gowns and honeymoons. . .

Her uncle had already disappeared in the direction of the stables, and Annie went that way also, having decided against going towards the loch. She hardly expected Stewart to be around every time she went there. But just in case he was, she wasn't yet ready to face the him again, after the way she'd shown her feelings so readily at the ball. Her face flamed whenever she thought about it. She had gone so willingly, if not wantonly, into his arms, and had so longed to remain there. . .

She heard the sound of angry voices as she rounded the corner of the stables, and stood still in embarrassment. Her uncle was arguing very forcibly with his head groom, and Annie wished desperately she could avoid being a witness to it.

'You'll take that back, man!' her uncle was shouting. 'You must be soft in the head if you believe what you're telling me. The rogue wouldn't dare –'

'Ask her then, Sir!' the groom said loudly as soon as he saw Annie. 'She was dancing with him half the night, and when they went out into the garden I followed them.'

'And who gave you the right to follow my niece?' Dougal snapped. 'Did I appoint you her guardian?'

She felt sick, knowing at once what all this was about. It was the practice at Blairfinnan to invite any of their estate workers to watch the revellers at the ball, and to have their own modest feast on the balcony that overlooked the Great Hall. The groom, Siddons, had evidently done more than that.

'I'm telling you, Sir, the Mackinty lad was dressed as a pirate, and the young lassie went into the garden wi' him. Aye, and there was a wee bit more than walking that went on between them an' all –'

'That's enough, Siddons. I'll deal with this myself,' Dougal roared. 'Now then, Annie, you'll have heard what this fool has to say. What have you to say to the charges?'

She bristled at once.

'*Charges*, Uncle? Am I on trial?'

81

He scowled, his brows drawing together in a black line. 'Now then, girl, don't play with words. Was it yon Mackinty lad dressed as a pirate at the ball? The truth now!'

'I've already told Aunt Morag the man didn't tell me his name,' she said heatedly.

'But perhaps he didn't need to,' her uncle said, astute enough to recognise an evasion. 'You're already acquainted enough with the ne'er-do-well, I believe.'

'Why must you call him that? He's done nothing to deserve it –' she stopped, biting her lip.

'Are you going to tell me the truth or not? Was it Stewart Mackinty dressed as a pirate and coming uninvited into my home?' he bellowed.

Annie swallowed, knowing she had no choice but to brazen it out.

'All right, then I did realise it was Stewart Mackinty, but he didn't stay very long, and if I'd denounced him there and then it would have spoiled everything for Aunt Morag, wouldn't it? I kept quiet about it for her sake, Uncle –'

'Don't forget the kissing,' Siddons put in, seeing he was being vindicated and adding his last ounce of treachery. 'I seen 'em kissing, Sir.'

'Is that true, Annie?' Dougal said, icily calm now. 'You allowed the man to kiss you, when you had already indicated to Rob that you were becoming fond of him?'

She stared at him speechlessly. She had indicated nothing of the sort, and anything between herself and Rob was all in his parents' imagination. And then she remembered their loving good-bye less than half an hour ago, and the way they had been seen to be in one another's company to the exclusion of other people. And she saw how she had been put into this awkward position through no fault of her own.

'I didn't kiss him. He kissed me,' she said sullenly.

'You didn't resist much though, did you, Miss?' Siddons said artfully. Dougal rounded on him at once.

'That's quite enough from you, man. This is between my niece and myself.' As the man melted away, he glowered at Annie. 'I don't have to tell you how disappointed I am in you, Annie.'

'No, you don't,' she said, before he could say any more. 'And I don't have to listen to you censuring me because I choose my own friends, Uncle. I *won't* listen to it.'

She stormed away from him towards the stables, hearing him give an explicit oath that made her gasp, and then she heard him stride away in the direction of the house. She felt badly shocked. She hadn't had much to do with the groom, but now she marched into the dim stable where he was brushing down a sleek grey horse.

'I'll thank you to mind your own business, Siddons,' she snapped.

'I've worked here a good many years, Miss, and what goes on between the Mackintys and any man here is my business,' he said, a glint in his eyes.

'Well, I'm not a man, and in future I'll thank you not to spy on me! Is that horse ready for riding?'

The glint became sharper. 'That he's not, Miss, but if you've a mind to take a ride, you can take Filigree. It will only take me a moment to get him saddled up.'

Annie looked at him suspiciously, and then nodded curtly. She was only a passable rider, but in her present mood that was the least of her considerations. She refused the groom's helping hand to mount the black horse and used the mounting block. She wasn't dressed for riding, but she didn't care about that either. All she wanted was to get as far away from these people as possible, and with that in mind she kicked her heels into Filigree's flanks, gripped the reins and urged him forward.

He didn't need much urging. As soon as he moved, Annie knew she had a powerful horse beneath her. If this was Siddons' idea of a joke, she didn't altogether appreciate it, but she'd soon show the oaf whether or not she was capable of handling a horse! She pressed her knees tight into the animal's sides and felt the wind take her hair and stream it away from her head.

Despite her lack of real expertise, she had always felt an exhilaration in riding, and right now it was what she needed to get the thoughts of these arrogant and dogmatic people out of her mind.

Did they never compromise? she thought furiously as she leaned low over Filigree's back. Her uncle with his short-sightedness when it came to anything to do with the Mackintys. And Stewart's family, presumably just as adamant at keeping the feud alive, and seeing in her the way to triumph over her relatives. She was heartily sick of the lot of them.

She tried to keep that thought uppermost in her mind as she rode to the far end of the loch, well away from where she'd first seen Stewart. She preferred to be well away from civilisation altogether, since everyone she had met so far seemed to try pulling her in different directions.

Though not quite all, she conceded. The refreshing friendship of Trina Moray, and her cousin Rob's assertion that he didn't wish to marry her any more than she wished to marry him, were the only bright spots in this new life. That, and the glorious panorama of the Highlands themselves.

After riding for half an hour, Annie reined in the snorting horse, realising she had been galloping him hard. She had no idea where she was now, but the quiet was almost absolute. The scents of heather and bracken were sweet and sensual in her nostrils, and the sun was warm on her face. She lifted up her cheeks to it for a few blissful moments, closing her eyes as if she offered a benediction.

She felt herself suddenly jerked backwards as something moving in the bracken startled Filigree. He whinnied loudly and reared up in fright, and before she could stop herself Annie had slid off his back and landed heavily and awkwardly in an ungainly heap on the ground.

'Filigree, come back! Come back here, you stupid horse!'

But no matter how much she yelled at him, he simply bolted, kicking out his back legs and tossing his mane furiously.

Annie sat up slowly, wondering if she would be bruised all over by tomorrow. She was winded, but seemingly nothing more. She made to stand up carefully, and then fell back with a gasp as pain seared through her ankle. She looked down at it, to see it discolouring and swelling rapidly. It was impossible to stand on it, let alone walk.

Tears of pain and frustration filled her eyes. She was the Lord knew where, with nobody except the wretched Siddons knowing she'd gone off on the horse, but she knew well enough that the animal was racing off in the opposite direction to Blairfinnan.

'Help! she cried out in panic. 'Hello, anybody! Is anybody about?'

But there was only the echo of her own voice, thrown back the encircling mountains, to mcck her. She began to feel weak with fear, and her imagination was rushing away with her. Supposing nobody ever found her?

The nights were warm enough, but she'd had a shock, and she was aware of how quickly pneumonia could set in after such a shock, even to a young healthy person like herself. People could die of pneumonia if they were left unattended, and with an ankle that was either broken or sprained, she was totally helpless. The scattered thoughts went hysterically round and round in her head.

She told herself not to be so foolish. Once it was discovered that she was missing, people would come looking for her. Siddons would tell them she had gone riding . . . she remembered the spiteful look on his face, and prayed that it would be so.

Eventually, she tried to kneel up on one knee, keeping the leg with the injured ankle splayed out to one side. She bit her lip as the slightest jarring sent stabs of excruciating pain shooting through her, and she was almost enveloped by waves of faintness. She fought them back desperately. She daren't faint. If she did, she had a grim fantasy that she would be swallowed up in the waving grass and bracken for ever . . . it was no longer a fragrant cushion, but her enemy. . .

She had closed her eyes against the pain, but she opened them quickly as she heard a faint sound. Filigree! He'd come back for her . . . but her hopes were dashed at once as she realised there was no sign of the frightened animal. And then she saw what she had heard. Perched on an outcrop of rock was a small figure, staring at her unblinkingly. It might have been a pixie sitting there so still, her imagination taunting her again, had she not recognised the figure.

'Kirsty!' she stuttered. 'Kirsty, can you help me?'

It was obvious to her now that she must have somehow ridden onto Mackinty land. The head of the loch narrowed, and she had ridden right around it without giving any thought to where the two properties joined, since there were no fences or obvious divisions.

She gave a tremulous smile of encouragement to Kirsty. The child continued to stare blankly back at her, and Annie felt her heart sink. The first wild hope died. How could this small child help her? But she could bring help – if only Annie could make her understand what was needed.

'Kirsty.' She put her fingers to her lips again, as she had done in the tea-room at Earnlie, willing the child to follow the movement and read her lips, even if she wasn't sure what the sounds meant. She didn't even know if she was going the right thing. She merely did it from instinct.

'Kirsty, will you come here, please?'

She beckoned the child gently, sensing that if she made any urgent movements, Kirsty would take fright and run. The girl slid down from the rock and stood still for a moment.

Annie pointed to her rapidly swelling ankle. It was purple and ugly now, and it smarted abominably.

'I'm hurt,' she said loudly. 'Can you fetch somebody? Go and fetch your Uncle Stewart, Kirsty.'

She knew at once there was no point in asking for anyone else. The child would never go to Blairfinnan, and anyway, she had already deduced that if Kirsty was here, then Stewart must be somewhere in the vicinity. He would surely never let this mite wander about by herself!

The girl edged forward, looking down at Annie's ankle with curious eyes.

'Please Kirsty,' Annie almost sobbed now. 'Go and find your Uncle Stewart. *Stewart*!'

Slowly Kirsty mouthed the name without making any sound. And then she repeated it in a small flat voice.

'Stew-art.'

'That's right. *Stewart*! Go and find him for me.' She gesticulated wildly as she spoke now, praying the child would understand what she wanted.

After an endless moment, Kirsty turned and ran, her small figure lost among the bracken almost at once. Annie lay back, the effort of it all leaving her totally exhausted. She had no idea whether or not her urgency had been transmitted to Kirsty, but she could do nothing else but lie and wait, and hope.

She must have drifted into a delirious sleep, and the next thing she knew she seemed to be floating somewhere in space. For a horrified second, she wondered if she was dead, because it was such an odd, weightless feeling. There was a dull ache at the back of her head. She hadn't been aware of it before, but she presumed she must have banged her head as well as her ankle when she fell from the horse. . .

Recollection came rushing back. Despite the floating sensation, she knew she wasn't dead. She couldn't be, because the pain was still there, dull in her head, severe in her ankle. She seemed to be held in bands of iron. She opened her eyes a fraction, and looked straight into Stewart Mackinty's eyes.

'So you've come back to us, have you?' he said, his voice gruff. 'For a minute or two, I had my doubts about it.'

She was aware of the thud of his heartbeats now, as if they beat inside her own chest. Two sets of heartbeats, beating almost as one heart . . . Still disorientated, still fanciful, she thought how extraordinary that was. And then came the abrupt realisation that she was being carried in his arms, and that the small girl was running along beside them.

'Kirsty –' she said faintly, her mouth as dry as dust.

'Aye, Kirsty,' Stewart confirmed. 'The wee bairn came running to find me, scared out of her wits, and dragged me to where you were. What in God's name were you doing on Mackinty land anyway?'

At the words, which she saw as being censorious, a surge of indignation almost overcame the pain. Annie struggled to sit up in his arms, and failed. They held her close in that rigid embrace, and he told her shortly to keep still or she'd be wrenching her ankle all over again. She glanced down, to where it was hanging loosely and painfully, and she longed for it to be strapped up and rested. . .

'I was riding,' she whispered, finding it a great effort to talk at all. 'My horse bolted and I fell. I'm sorry to cause you such inconven—'

'Och, stop blathering, woman, and just be glad this wee bairn had the sense to come to me. It's probably a miracle that she took your meaning, and I'm still wondering how you managed to persuade her to do as you wanted?'

'I just asked her, of course,' Annie said.

Was he stupid, that he couldn't see that Kirsty could be taught with patience and care? But probably not. It seemed that the Mackintys were short on patience, however much they cared for the child. She admitted that impatience seemed to be a failing in both highland families, and wondered if it was a national trait.

She tried to speak less tremulously, hating to be caught at such a disadvantage. 'Look, Stewart, I know I asked Kirsty to fetch you, since I couldn't think what else to do, but I'd be perfectly all right if you would just put me down now and send for a carriage to take me home. I'm very grateful to you, but I feel foolish like this, and it's much too far for you to carry me to Blairfinnan.'

'I'm not carrying you to Blairfinnan,' he retorted. 'I'm taking you to Craggan.'

Her heart leapt. She was being taken straight to the enemy camp. Not just taken, but carried there, helpless . . . she swallowed, as the unbidden thoughts swept into her mind. Stupid, illogical thoughts, but simply impossible to obliterate.

'I can't think your father will be very happy to see me arrive! Won't he object strongly?' she said, since it was the only coherent thing she could think of to say at that moment.

'He will not. Why should he, when he's had quite a hankering to see again this paragon of virtue the Blairs have among them now? He knows your background, of course, and I've told him about meeting you, and so has Kirsty, in her own way.'

Exasperated at the way everyone seemed to know everyone else's business here, she looked up into his face. It was very close to hers. Too close. She thought fleetingly that he only had to lean towards her to kiss her, and she couldn't do anything to stop it. But it seemed he had no such intention in mind and she didn't know whether to be glad or sorry.

'Stew-art.'

Kirsty's small voice made him stop a moment. He turned to wait for her to catch up.

'I forget her little legs,' he said, and there was a perceptible softening in his voice. He was definitely vulnerable where the child was concerned, Annie thought. At least his love for her was genuine. She must hold on to that thought. There was some good in him.

'How far from your house are we, anyway? I assure you I had no idea I was even on your land. You do believe that, don't you? I wouldn't knowingly have trespassed –' Annie said, suddenly embarrassed at being found there at all.

He laughed shortly. 'Oh aye, I'm sure of that, lassie. But we're not far from Craggan at all. If you'd ridden over the ridge, you'd have seen it. Look ahead of you now.'

She looked, and to her amazement they were within a few hundred yards of a large house now, similiar in style and architecture to Blairfinnan, but with none of the sculptured gardens of which her aunt was so fond. It was a house that from the outside lacked a woman's touch, Annie thought at once.

'So you weren't actually spying out the land, Annie Blair?' Stewart taunted her now.

'I was not!' she said indignantly. 'I was merely riding, as I told you, and had no idea how far I had gone, nor how near to the head of the loch Craggan was. How could I know, when all this is strange country to me?'

'All right, I believe you,' he grinned as her protest became vehement. 'I was merely making conversation in the hope that it would keep your mind off your injury a wee while. And I daresay you didn't want to indulge in any reminiscences about the masked ball.'

She felt her face flush. It had been so cold before she guessed it must have been deathly pale after the accident. No, right now she preferred not to remember the pleasure of dancing in his arms, and walking with him in the moonlight, and being held more amorously in his arms and surrendering so willingly to his kisses. . .

'Is that why you kept talking? To keep my mind off the pain?'

'Of course. Why should I not? Do you think me completely heartless and insensitive?'

He gave a half-smile. She hadn't noticed before how white and even his teeth were. She realised that by now she could have traced the shape of his mouth blindfold, but there was always something new to discover about him. Like the texture of his skin, so tanned and healthy and alive, and the dark depths of those brooding gypsy eyes. . .

'If you continue to look at me like that, I shall have no option but to put you down on the ground and let you hobble to Craggan by yourself,' he said abruptly.

'Like what?' she said, provoking him.

'I think you know, Annie Blair.'

She wasn't sure exactly what he meant. What she did know, because of their close proximity, was that his heart was racing now, where before it had registered a steady rhythmic beat. Before she could analyse just why this was, he had turned to the small girl running at his side.

'Kirsty, go and fetch Granpa,' he said loudly. '*Granpa.*'

She scuttled off to do his bidding, and before they reached the front steps of the steps the man she recognised as Stewart's father appeared outside, accompanied by a stout woman Annie rightly assumed was the housekeeper, and a startled maid.

'What's happened?' Callum Mackinty said.

'She's been thrown from her horse. You'll remember Annie Blair, Father, and from the looks of her she needs medical attention. One of the stable lads had best go for the doctor.'

Callum didn't waste words on further inquiry. He spoke to the gaping maid at once. 'Go and see to it, lassie. Tell him to hurry and bring back the doctor right away, and be sure and say he's to come to Craggan to attend to Miss Blair.'

Annie remembered being told that one of the maids here was the sister of a maid at Blairfinnan. It wouldn't be long before the tale would spread like wildfire that Stewart Mackinty had come striding up to Craggan with Annie Blair in his arms. . .

'How badly are you hurt, lassie?' Callum Mackinty said kindly to her now. His genuine concern made the tears stab at her eyes again.

'It's only my ankle. I hope it's only sprained, but it's very painful,' she said, weakenig anew now that she was safe.

If safe was a word she could apply to being in the Mackinty stronghold! But that was the least of her considerations. At that moment Craggan was a haven.

They were inside the house now, and it was far more luxurious that the wild exterior had suggested. That would be the housekeeper's influence, no doubt, Annie thought dryly. There were bowls of flowers on tables, a faint aroma of beeswax on the polished oak furniture, carpet squares on the floors, and the usual mixture of tapestries and family portraits on the walls that seemed to be normal here. There was no neglect in the house, however much they neglected the child im emotional terms. And Annie didn't know yet how far that was so. When she could separate her mind from the pain for a moment, she realised that now that she was here, she had a golden opportunity to find out.

Stewart laid her down carefully on a narrow couch in the drawing-room and she gave an involuntary gasp of pain as her foot touched the firmness of the couch. The housekeeper bustled forward, tutting at the inflamed and badly swollen ankle.

'I'll be fetching you one of my powders directly to dull the pain, dearie,' she said. 'Doctor will no doubt bind up the ankle tightly, but meanwhile I'll put a vinegar compress on it and my old remedy will soon let you sleep. You'll not be wanting to be moved for a while yet, and I think you'd be far better off in a bed upstairs.'

'Oh, but I can't stay here!' Annie said in alarm. 'My uncle will be worried about me and wanting me back at Blairfinnan as soon as possible –'

'Don't worry your head about Dougal Blair. I'll send word to him,' Callum said shortly. 'This is an emergency, and if he's got any sense at all in that stubborn old head of his he'll no be taking umbrage at our hospitality.'

She was immediately embarrassed on her uncle's account at the generous words.

'I didn't mean it to sound like that,' she mumbled, avoiding everyone's eyes, knowing they were all well aware that it was just what she had meant.

'Mrs Innes is right,' Stewart said. 'You'll be far more comfortable upstairs, Annie. No arguments now.'

She was in no position to argue. She could only do their bidding. And as she felt herself lifted in Stewart's arms once more, she put her own arms around his neck, and resisted the urge to put her head on his shoulder as he carried her up the curving staircase to a bedroom, with the others following and fussing.

'Can I send a note to my uncle to tell him what's happened?' she asked, embarrassed at the enforced intimacy of herself and Stewart, and even more so at the little entourage witnessing it.

He smiled knowingly. 'So that he'll believe you really have been injured, and that the wicked Mackintys haven't taken you captive for their own ends?'

'Something like that,' she murmured. She saw no point in denying it, since it was exactly what she had been thinking.

It would do nobody any good for her uncle to come storming over here, demanding to see for himself that she really had been hurt, and that there was no treachery going on. She was beginning to wonder who was the strongest upholder of the old feud, and she suspected that the odds came down heavily against her uncle.

Besides, if treachery there had been, it was surely in the action of Siddons, who had allowed her to ride a horse that was too strong and spirited for her, she thought grimly. She would have words to say about that when she returned home. For now, she was ready enough to be laid gently on top of a comfortable bed with a white quilted coverlet, and to await the ministrations of Mrs Innes and the doctor from Earnlie.

'I'll bring you writing materials,' Stewart promised, before he left her to the housekeeper's fussing. 'And if it pleases you, I'll ride over to Blairfinnan myself to deliver it.'

She looked up at him. She was the one who was in pain, yet as far as she could tell, his dark eyes were as dilated as hers must be. It must have been a shock to him to find her injured on his land, and to have no choice but to bring her here. No doubt he'd been dubious over his own father's reaction.

'Would you do that?' she said through dry lips, knowing at once what it would cost him to go to Blairfinnan again. These families, who seemed so autocratically determined to keep themselves so distant. . .

'Of course I'll do it,' he said tersely. 'You wouldn't have it said that a Mackinty was afraid to go where he minded?'

Of course not. She should have known. It was as much a daredevil infiltration into enemy territory as a wish to let her uncle know she was safe. The initial fury of Dougal Stalwart Blair at the sight of the Mackinty going right up to his sacred portals would be dashed immediately when he knew the reason for the mission, and he would be under no small obligation to those on the far side of the loch.

Suddenly she was weary of the whole affair, and turned her head sideways into the pillow, so that she wouldn't have to look at him, or Kirsty, or his father, or Mrs Innes, all hovering anxiously around her bedside. She wished she was away from here, choosing her own destiny, back in the gentleness of Devon or anywhere else on earth, rather than thrust into the midst of these hot-headed people.

Chapter 6

Annie awoke in darkness, aware that this wasn't her room at Blairfinnan, but for a moment unable to co-ordinate her thoughts at all. The minute she tried to turn over in the bed, memory came surging back with a sharp stab of pain from the rigidity of her bandaged ankle.

She was at Craggan. The doctor had been and gone, the powder Mrs Innes had given her had done its work and she had obviously slept for hours. She realised she was still wearing her day clothes, but someone had loosened the fastenings and covered her lightly with a thin coverlet so as not to put undue pressure on her ankle. She was in the enemy camp, but for all that she remembered she had been shown only kindness.

Self-pity enveloped her for a second, and she felt the wash of tears in her eyes. She swallowed, and blinked them away. She was going to do nobody any good to lie here and weep over her misfortune. Especially herself, when she barely felt able to get out of bed to reach for a handkerchief – and wouldn't know where to find it if she even ventured out of bed at all. It was far safer to stay exactly where she was and try to go back to sleep.

But the effects of all the ministrations were wearing off, and the throb of pain in her ankle was getting noticeably worse. She eased herself into a more comfortable position, hearing the bed creak as she did so, and hoping she wouldn't waken the household. It was unlikely, she thought, remembering the thickness of the walls. Even if she cried out in pain, no-one would hear her.

The thought made her feel more alone and isolated than ever. Though she managed to see through the dimness that her door had been left ajar, presumably in case she cried out and needed help during the night. . .

And then she almost stopped breathing as she became aware of another sound inside the room. A low, rythmic sound, almost like the rumbling of carriage wheels on a dusty road. . .

At her gasp of fright, she heard a voice come out of a dark corner in the far side of the room.

'Bless me if I didn't wake myself up with my snoring, dearie, and you too!' she heard Mrs Innes say apologetically.

Now that her eyes were becoming more accustomed to the darkness, Annie could make out the large shape of the housekeeper in a tumble of blankets on a couch. Her astonishment at seeing her there overcame her fright.

'Have you been sleeping there all night, Mrs Innes?'

'That I have, in case you awoke and needed anything,' the woman said, padding across to her at once, all voluminous cambric nightgown and corkscrew rag curlers. 'Is the ankle paining you, lassie? You called out once or twice in your sleep, but you never woke properly, so I didn't disturb you. I'll away and fetch you another powder and a warm drink now.'

'Oh no! I don't want to put you to any trouble. I've put everyone to such trouble here already –'

'Och, it's no trouble. It's a pleasure to be having an intelligent young woman in the house to wait on, after those flibberty ninnys in the kitchen. I could be doing with a hot drink myself, so if it makes you feel easier, we'll take it together. Would you be liking a wee drop of Craggan's Best in your, Miss?'

She lit the bedside candle and looked down at Annie thoughtfully as she spoke, and then she gave a small smile at the lack of response.

'Aye well, mebbe not, but you'll no object if I lace my cocoa with a dram to keep out the cold, will you, Miss?'

'Of course not, if I knew what Craggan's Best was,' Annie muttered, though she was beginning to realise that the woman was giving the words some importance.

Besides which, she didn't know if it was her imagination playing tricks, or if there were other sounds in the passage outside the room. The sleeping draught was still making her head feel muzzy, and her nerves were still jumping, but she prayed the whole household wasn't going to be disturbed, or she would feel doubly guilty at her unintentional intrusion here.

By then Mrs Innes had lit another candle and was preparing to go downstairs. She paused at the open door to answer Annie's question with a hint of surprise in her voice.

'Why, the name of the Mackinty whisky, lassie. Surely you knew of the distillery just south of Earnlie that bears the name, and of the distinction of Craggan's Best?'

'No,' Annie said. 'Should I have heard of it?'

Mrs Innes laughed. 'Well, I suppose there's no reason why you should, considering, though it wouldn't have been like that some years back. It's unlikely your uncle would have mentioned it now, of course, since the

98

name's been taboo in his household. 'Twas an unlikely partnership from the start.'

'What partnership?' Annie was fully awake now, and tired of these riddles she didn't understand. She managed with some difficulty to manoeuver herself into a sitting position and looked at Mrs Innes impatiently.

She knew she was keeping the woman from bringing the powder and cocoa, and she certainly had need of the first now. But this was more interesting than cocoa . . . even as she thought it, she saw a shadow outside the door, and then Stewart appeared behind Mrs Innes, a dark dressing-robe covering him from head to foot, his hair tousled. His voice was indolent as if he had recently woken from sleep.

'If you really want to hear the story, I'll tell it while Mrs Innes goes to the kitchen. I'll have a dram in my cocoa too, thank-you, Mrs Innes,' he said, at which the woman hurried off, embarrassed at being seen in such disarray, and obviously not quite sure whether she was being censured at telling their guest enough to interest her in Mackinty business.

Annie pulled the bedding more closely around herself, careful not to disturb her ankle more than necessary. Even though she was perfectly properly dressed, she knew the impropriety of being in a bedroom alone with a man, especially a man like Stewart Mackinty. Though she had to admit such improprieties seemed of less importance here in the wilds of the Highlands than in a country Devon town. She saw the slight smile on his face at her swift movement.

'You needn't fear for your honour this night, Annie Blair,' he said dryly. 'Nor any other night, come to that. I'll take it willingly, or not at all.'

She gasped with indignation. 'And you'll wait a very long time for that, I promise you!'

'We'll see. Now then, you wanted to know something about Craggan's Best, I understand?'

'Not particularly. At least – I don't want you to think I was prying,' she said edgily, but knowing all the same that she was intensely interested in everything about these two warring families. Since his concerned hers so much, she told herself she had every right to know their history as well. And the more she knew, the more exasperated she became.

'Oh yes you were, however beautifully you do it,' he said easily, 'but it's no matter, since both our ancestors were involved,' he added, confirming her suspicions.

She stared. 'You don't mean the Blairs were mixed up in this distillery as well? Was there ever anything in which the two families weren't intertwined?'

'Not much, though I'm not so sure I like your inference that the distillery is a somewhat shady business. It's an honest, legitimate company. You're not about to tell me you're a temperance worker, are you?' At her vehement shake of the head he grinned with relief. 'Well then. Yes, our families began the distillery together. Do you wonder now why I'm so confident you and I are destined to be together, Annie Blair? You can fight most things, but you can't fight fate.'

She seethed at his arrogance, and the way he always managed to turn any conversation to this advantage. If only she had two strong legs she would get out of this bed this minute and march right out of here! But somehow his words took away the embarrassment of having him sitting on an armchair at the side of her bed. It no longer seemed incongruous to be having this conversation in her bedroom in the middle of the night, because for the moment she was seeing Stewart Mackinty as no more than her adversary, and not the most attractive man she had ever set eyes on. . .

'I've always thought fate was something to be manipulated,' she said, as haughty as he. 'There are always choices to be made, however bad the circumstances.'

'Mebbe,' Stewart said. 'But you still chose to come to Scotland, out of all the other choices you could have made. Doesn't that tell you something?'

She drew up her knees to clasp her arms around them. The action automatically stretched her foot, and she immediately put her legs down again as the pain wrenched through her ankle, and made her extra sharp.

'I don't want to discuss why I came here,' she snapped. 'Are you going to tell me about this whisky business or not?'

'Why not? I doubt that anyone yonder would have told you that your grandfather and mine started what was then known as the Earnlie distillery, against other family opposition, naturally. That goes without saying, Annie. But the two men were great friends, and I daresay would have remained so, until one and then another family member became involved. That's when the arguments began about changing the name, since it was decided that a personal name would be more advantageous –'

'Let me guess,' Annie put in. 'One side wanted it called Blair Whisky, and the other wanted it called Mackinty. Am I right?'

He nodded. 'In the end they gambled over the choice of name, and naturally the Mackinty won.'

Annie bit her tongue and refused to be drawn into any comment on this additional bit of arrogance.

'It all stirred up fresh bitterness among the families, and ruined the friendship of the two men most concerned. The Blairs sold up their interest in the distillery altogether, but the Mackintys renamed the distillery Craggan's Best, rather than using either family name.'

Annie certainly hadn't come across any reference to this in her superficial searches through the family records. She guessed at once that all mention of it had been deleted from visual memory. And certainly no spirit of that name was in evidence in the house, she recalled, nor had been mentioned by any guests. It was all somehow sad, and so *pointless*. . .

She shook her head slowly. 'It seems to me that a lot of good friendships over the years have been lost for ever because of this old family rivalry.'

'Isn't that just what I've been trying to tell you?' she heard the seductiveness in Stewart's voice now, and knew she'd given him just the lead he needed.

'Oh well,' she said, not falling into the trap, and apparently speaking quite objectively. 'I can quite see that with my arrival, you and your father thought you could score over your old rivals. But it's very unlikely. I shall choose my own future, and I assure you I don't lack for admirers, even in this Godforsaken place! My cousin Rob is very warmly disposed towards me, and so is his friend Lorn from Edinburgh –'

She gave a small cry. One minute Stewart was sitting some distance from her. The next, he had moved swiftly to her side, and was ostensibly straightening her pillows to make her more comfortable. But as they both heard Mrs Innes making her laborious way back upstairs with a tray, he whispered in her ear.

'It won't work, my lassie. You were always meant to be mine, and there's no man alive who will dare to say otherwise.'

By the time Mrs Innes came into the room he had moved across to the door and was taking the tray out of her hands. It held three cups of cocoa and a small jug, out of which Stewart poured a fair dram of golden liquid into two of the cups.

'Are you sure you'll not take a wee drop?' he asked. 'It will do no harm and will help dull the pain and make you sleep. You have my word it's no drug to render you helpless.'

He spoke mockingly, his meaning for her alone, but she declined at once. She hated the bitter taste of any spirit, and from the liberal amount Stewart poured into Mrs Innes' cup, she doubted that the housekeeper would be sensible to much more until morning.

It didn't matter. She didn't need nurse-maiding, and preferred to be alone with her own thoughts. Besides which, she guessed that whisky may well react adversely with the comforting herbal powder Mrs Innes was pouring into her night glass of water. That had been a godsend earlier on, making her drowsy within a very short time, and thankfully dulling the pain.

'I think I shall sleep now,' she said very soon after she had drained the sleeping draught and the cocoa, and looking pointedly at Stewart. 'I promise I shan't disturb anyone else until morning.'

And please don't make some fatuous *double entendre* about being disturbed by me at any time of day, she thought silently. To her relief, he did not. She watched him go, hearing him say good-night to her for the second time. She was already sleepy, the powder doing its work almost immediately.

It was also making her unaccountably maudlin, as she drifted into sleep, wishing that things could be different. Wishing there had never been this feud between their two families, and they could have met under different circumstances, in another time, another place. Wishing she could trust his feelings for her. Wishing they could be the same as hers. Wishing he could love her . . . wishing for the moon. . .

103

She was treated as a mixture of honoured guest and invalid. She was embarrassed by the first, and forced to accept the second, since it was clear she wouldn't be able to put her foot to the ground for at least a week. It was a bad sprain, and the doctor said it was lucky she'd been found before nightfall, or she might indeed have succumbed to pneumonia, strong and healthy though she was.

'I have to thank Kirsty for that,' she told him huskily the following afternoon, when he came to visit her again. She decided to seek his advice. 'Doctor, do you think it would do any good to try and coax Kirsty to talk more clearly and teach her her letters?'

'Of course it would do good, lassie! If there was someone to undertake the task, it could work miracles for the bairn. She's far from stupid, but I fear that apart from Stewart and his father, there's no-one here who does more than shout at her to make her understand, which only frightens the child.'

'I've noticed that. I could try to encourage her while I'm here. It would give me a purpose and made me feel less beholden to the Mackintys.' She blushed as she said it, but there was no need. Everybody knew of the situation between these volatile neighbours.

She went on quickly. 'Kirsty responded to me when I was hurt, and I'd be happy to have her come up here and talk to her. It's so frustrating to just lie here if I could be useful.'

'I'll suggest it to Callum,' the doctor said. 'He's aye been protective with Kirsty, and I'm sure he'll welcome the idea. In my opinion half the bairn's problems arise from the fact that she's no young female stimulus around her as well as no tutor. You'll be fulfilling all that admirably, Miss Blair.'

When he'd left the room, Annie lay back on her pillows. Callum would be pleased. Stewart would be pleased. Of Kirsty, she wasn't sure, but she hoped so.

Her uncle Dougal . . . she ran her tongue around her lips. Uncle Dougal would be incensed, so the less he knew of it the better. She had written the note to tell him what had happened, and Stewart had delivered it as promised. But when she'd asked him about her uncle's reaction, he had definitely been evasive. How Dougal must be hating this situation, she thought, with swift sympathy for his feelings, however she opposed them, but there was simply nothing he could about it but accept it.

She closed her eyes. It was still unreal to her that she was here at Craggan. She should be at Blairfinnan, listening to her uncle's irascible voice as he stamped about the place. Yes, she admitted, he was undoubtedly the main instigator in keeping the old feud alive. . .

For a second she wondered if she was dreaming. Uncle Dougal's voice seemed to be reverberating in her head, the echo of Aunt Morag's behind it . . . and Stewart, remonstrating angrily. . .

She sat bolt upright in bed as the three of them burst unceremoniously into her room. Aunt Morag rushed over to the bed, clearly ill at ease at being here, but relief washing over her at the sight of her niece, especially since Annie was lying on top of the coverlet now, and even the heavy bandage barely disguised the dark bruising on her ankle.

'How are you feeling, my lamb?' she exclaimed at once. 'It was a terrible unfortunate thing to happen –'

'What the devil were you doing on Mackinty land, lass?' Uncle Dougal brushed aside the platitudes and stood over her like a Colossus. 'Have you no sense of direction?'

She felt a spurt of anger at his insensitivity.

105

'And have you no thought for the fact that I'm still a stranger here, and have no idea where one plot of land ends and another begins?'

'Well said,' Stewart said. Annie glanced at him. He leaned against the wall with arms loosely folded, clearly enjoying the impossible sight of Dougal Stalwart Blair here at Craggan, when the man obviously wished himself anywhere else in the world.

'I can't think why you bothered to come here, Uncle, since it clearly offends you so much!' she went on, ignoring Stewart's comment.

Dougal snorted. 'I came to assure myself it was true, despite the writing in your own hand. For all I knew, the lad might have forced you into writing it and kept you here under false pretences.'

She gasped, seeing the flashing anger in Stewart's face now. 'You're quite mad, the lot of you,' she stated. 'Nobody forced me into anything, and nobody's *going* to,' she added meaningly. 'Do you doubt the evidence of your own eyes?'

She pointed to her ankle with a hand that suddenly trembled. She felt so weak, so unlike herself, and the injury was enough to contend with, without these unrelenting people.

'Dougal, you can see the lassie's hurt –' Morag began.

'Aye, I see it,' he began gruffly. 'And I'll own that it looks painful enough. But she'll be far better off in her own bed in her own home, than here.'

'I'm sorry, but the doctor says I'm not to be moved, Uncle,' Annie said, angry at the way everyone seemed to know what was best for her, and intent on taking away her independence. 'I'm not to put my foot to the ground for a week, except for the necessity of my personal needs, and Mrs Innes attends me for those.'

106

Her face flushed even more at having to say such things, but finding them necessary in the face of her uncle's obstinacy.

'Mrs Innes is a good woman, Annie. She'll look after you as well as anybody,' Morag said, clearly trying to take the heat out of the conversation.

'Look, man, it's obvious to anyone that your niece will have to stay here for the time being,' Stewart said shortly, at which Dougal rounded on him.

'Oh aye, and it will suit your purpose very nicely, won't it? To have a Blair lassie beneath your roof again is something your family's been hoping for in many a year –'

'For pity's sake, do you think I engineered Annie's accident?' Stewart snapped.

'I wouldn't put it past you,' Dougal bellowed back. 'Your sort is sly enough for anything. And while we're at it, I'll thank you never to set foot in my house again, though the garb of a scoundrally pirate obviously fits you and yours very well –'

Morag gasped, and Annie realised it was obvious that Dougal hadn't passed on Siddon's treacherous remarks to her.

'You don't mean the man in the pirate disguise was –'

'Aye, that's just what I do mean,' Dougal said grimly. 'You see now to what depths the Mackintys will go to take their revenge in any way they can?'

'I think you forget whose roof you're under right now, Sir,' Stewart said coldly. 'And I'd ask you not to insult my family.'

'And what have your family ever done but be a constant thorn in the flesh of mine!' Dougal said, with all the scorn he could muster.

'The same could be said for us,' Stewart retaliated. 'But I've no wish to stand here and waste words with you. When you've done your visiting, you'll know the way out. Good-day to you, Ma'am. You have my sympathy,' he said to Morag, his meaning clear as he strode out of the room.

Dougal glowered after him. 'And that's the man who thinks he has the wherewithal to tame a Blair lassie,' he snorted. 'You'll do well to ignore any overtures he might make to you, Annie, do you hear?'

'I hear,' she said, weary to the bone of his dictatorial manner, and thinking it more than likely that everyone in the whole house could hear.

It was a relief when they left for Blairfinnan, after extracting her promise that she'd return home just as soon as the doctor told her she was able. It struck her that Callum Mackinty hadn't accompanied his son when her visitors arrived. She had already deduced that he was far less interested in the old feud than her uncle, and that Dougal Blair had a lot to answer for.

Soon after her aunt and uncle had left Craggan, Stewart came back to her room with Kirsty, limpet-like, at his side.

'There's someone here who wants to say hello to you,' he said, his voice perceptibly softer than before.

Annie smiled and stretched out a hand to the child, who merely buried her face into Stewart's side all the more.

'Well, for someone who wants to say hello, there's a very quiet person in my room,' she said clearly. 'Perhaps it's a bird who can only whistle.'

Kirsty's head moved a fraction, and one eye came into view.

'Look out there,' Annie said, pointing to the window, where a flock of birds was twittering in the swaying branches of the tall pines outside.

'Do you see them?' she asked, and Kirsty nodded, moving away from Stewart to run to the window and tap on the glass. The birds swooped into the sky at once, except for one lone survivor who pecked at the glass hoping for something to eat, and Kirsty began to laugh.

'It's a bird,' Annie said. 'Can you say that?'

'I've never heard her say it,' Stewart said, but Annie ignored him for the moment, all her attention on the child.

She tapped her finger and thumb together to imitate the bird's pecking as she repeated the word, and she saw Kirsty's fingers twitch in response.

'Bird,' she mouthed. And then she said it louder, as she cautiously pecked with her fingers against the glass.

'Bird! Bird!'

Annie laughed, certain now that this was a child who could be taught. She had no training, but instinct told her how to begin to teach her. She realised that Stewart had gone silent at Kirsty's pleasure in her own small achievement.

He scooped the child up in his arms and kissed the top of her head. And Annie felt a ridiculous pang of jealousy at the sight of it. She saw how carefully he put her down again and smoothed the tangled dark hair, and she was jealous of his touch. She heard how his voice gentled as he spoke to Kirsty, and knew to her horror how badly she wanted to hear that caressing tone for herself.

She was completely mad, she told herself. In was unseemly and downright humiliating to be jealous of a man's affection for a child! Especially a man whom her uncle had expressly forbidden her to know, let alone love.

But it was too late for that. She already loved him. However wrong, however hopeless, she loved him. And she would have to be doubly on her guard whenever he looked at her, or touched her, or held her, because she would never know whether the feelings he professed for her were genuinely for herself, or for that ingrained Mackinty need to triumph over their rivals.

'I think we'd like Annie to stay with us for ever, wouldn't we, sweetheart?' he asked Kirsty now in a teasing voice.

'No, Stewart, please don't suggest it,' Annie said sharply. 'Children take things at face value, and you know it's impossible –'

'Why is it? Because of some old feud that we both know belongs to another age?'

'Try telling that to my uncle – and your father too, I suspect.'

'My father always did think your uncle the most stubborn man alive. It's a trait that runs in your family.'

'And you're including me in that, I suppose?'

She became aware that Kirsty was looking from one to the other uncertainly, and she forced a smile to her face.

'Shall we write some letters, Kirsty?' she said now.

With her finger she indented the letter K on her pillow and pointed to Kirsty as she did so. 'K is for Kirsty,' she said.

The child looked blank for a moment and then leaned forward to scratch her finger in the same indentations. Annie looked quickly at Stewart.

'Will you fetch us some writing materials? I think we could make some progress with this, if you've no objection.'

'None at all, if it will keep you here a while longer,' he said. 'I told you the bairn has taken to you.' He looked at Kirsty. 'You stay with Annie now, and I'll be back in a wee while.'

She nodded, and climbed onto the bed. She had a direct, unblinking stare, and her eyes were Stewart's dark gypsy eyes. Annie felt a brief pity for the handicap she suffered, and even more so for living in this house with its plethora of shouting servants whose loud voices probably only frightened the child, and the over-indulgent Mackintys who did everything for her, so that she didn't have to bother. . .

'Oh Kirsty, I bet there's a lot you could say already if only you had the courage,' she said softly now. She saw the child's brow pucker, and realised she had spoken too quietly. And yet Annie was sure she had almost understood. She was watching her lips, and reading the words. Annie felt a huge excitement, knowing her instincts had been right all along.

'Where's Stewart?' she said now.

'Gone,' Kirsty said, in her flat slow tones.

'We're going to write some letters,' Annie said, indicating the action. 'K for Kirsty.'

'K – for – Kir-sty,' the child repeated.

'That's right, you clever girl!' Annie said, completely forgetting her injury as she gave the child a hug. The next second she shrieked with pain as Kirsty landed on her ankle with all her weight, and then scrambled off like a scared rabbit to go rushing out of the room and down the stairs.

Five minutes later Stewart came back alone.

'What happened? I can't get any sense out of Kirsty, and she's gone sobbing to Mrs Innes.'

Annie was as upset by the way the child had gone scuttling away as by the searing pain in her ankle.

'It was all my fault! I leaned forward to praise her and she landed on my ankle. I couldn't help crying out, and it scared her half to death. I'm afraid it may have undone all the good I've done so far,' she said in genuine distress.

'And do you think you've done any good?'

She glared at him indignantly. 'Yes, I do! Just by giving her my time, I think I've done her some good. How often do the people here stop and listen properly to Kirsty and try to help her with her words? I doubt that you give her much time if you have to be at your old distillery during the week.'

She didn't care if she was offending him, nor his father, who had come heavily into the room to enquire after her health, and was pausing thoughtfully to listen.

'So you've learned about my distilling the demon drink, have you? And does it offend your sensibilities?'

'Why should it?' Annie said, thankful that the first searing pain in her ankle was easing a little now. 'My father was not above taking a dram, as you call it, and I never saw it do him any harm. My uncle neither,' she added, 'though I'd never heard the name Craggan's Best mentioned at Blairfinnan.'

'Nor will you, lassie,' Callum Mackinty said keenly. 'It's a sore point with Dougal that the distillery flourished without the assets of yon Blairs. He could be in with us now, if he chose, but there's no changing the ways of a stubborn man.'

'I really don't want to discuss my uncle, or to feel I have to defend him,' Annie said, feeling suddenly disloyal in this company.

'Nor you should,' Callum said comfortably. 'The man's capable of fighting his own wars without sending a wee lassie into battle.'

It wasn't what Annie had meant at all, but she kept her gaze steadfastly on the coverlet and refused to be goaded into any more arguments.

'Anyway, it's not what I came to see you about,' Callum said. 'I've heard from my son that you've a way with the bairn, and that she's taken to you. I know you've been educated – your fine way of speaking tells me that. So if you'd a mind to it, perhaps you'd care to take a bit of schooling with her, Miss Blair, for a regular tutor's fee, of course.'

It was so exactly what Annie had been toying with herself ever since she had learned of Kirsty's handicap, that she wondered if he could be a mind-reader! And coming from Callum Mackinty, the idea was just as impossible as coming from herself.

'You know my uncle would never agree to it,' she said. 'And I owe him my first loyalty and respect –'

'Do you not have a mind of your own then, Annie Blair?' Stewart said softly. 'I'm disappointed in you!'

She felt her face flush.

'Of course I do, and I choose to exercise it by not upsetting my uncle any more than I must. I'll willingly devote all the time I'm incapacitated here to being with Kirsty, but after that, I'm afraid it cannot be. I'm sorry, Mr Mackinty,' she said to Callum. 'The idea had occurred to me as well, but that was before I'd given it sufficient thought.'

'Well, if that's your final word –' he said regretfully.

She nodded vigorously. 'It is. It has to be.'

Into her mind came the thought that he too would be well aware of the way the lives of the Blairs and Mackintys had been intertwined over the years. And all too aware of the Mackinty boast that one day, however long it took, one of them would yet tame a Blair lassie . . . she looked into his bluff, genial face, so less bombastic than her uncle's, and still couldn't help wondering guiltily just how much deviousness was hidden behind those bland features.

She wished for the umpteenth time that she'd never heard of the boast. Even if she was eventually charmed out of all common sense by Stewart Mackinty and swept into his arms . . . just as long as she believed that the love he professed for her was real and not

113

for some kind of vengeance all tied up in an ancient feud.

She turned her face away from the two men. There had never been any mention of love, she reminded herself sharply. Love hadn't been a word that Stewart used when he came dancing into her life at the costume ball and took her walking in the fragrance of the moonlit night to woo her and weaken her resistance . . . there were plenty of other names for it, but it wasn't love. . .

'Do you want me to send Kirsty back to you?' he was saying now, and she realised his father had left them alone again. 'I daresay she'll have got over her fright by now, and I'll explain to her what happened.'

'No, don't send her. Let her come when she's ready,' Annie said, her voice husky. 'It's not right to try and force anyone to do what they don't want to do, not even a child.'

And especially not a woman already half in love, so that the thought of a man wanting her for no more than revengeful reasons was enough to make her break down and weep. Or it would have been if she'd been the weeping kind. . .

Chapter 7

During the rest of that week at Craggan, Annie discovered that Kirsty liked to draw pictures, and that she was extraordinarily good at it. Annie saw at once this was the way into Kirsty's reluctant mind. They drew pictures together. They drew flowers and trees and shoes and dogs, and the child blossomed under Annie's tuition to the extent that she was soon shrieking out the word for each object she drew before Annie herself could say it. It had become a game, and one that was phenomenally successful. The doctor himself remarked on it when he called to see Annie, and reiterated the Mackinty men's own suggestion that Annie should tutor the child.

'Miss Blair, can I really not persuade you to come here on a regular basis with Kirsty?' Callum said, when she was pronounced well enough to go home. 'It would be such a service to the barin and to my family.'

'You know as well as I do it's your family that's the problem, Mr Mackinty,' Annie said frankly. 'I'm very grateful to you for your kindness while I've been here, but I hope you'll believe that I've repaid it in helping Kirsty – and also that anyone here could continue what I've begun! I'm not a teacher, after all.'

'But for all that you have a way with her, and she's comfortable with you, lassie. Still, if you must go, then there's no arguing with it. I respect your reasons, even if I don't altogether hold with them.'

He bade her good-bye as Stewart and Kirsty came into the drawing-room where she awaited the arrival of the Blair carriage to take her home. The child ran to Annie at once, climbing on her lap, but mindful of the ankle now. Annie gave a rueful laugh.

'It's ironic, isn't it?' she said to Stewart, knowing he would have overheard his father. 'I came to Scotland with no idea that this feud existed, and all this time I've been saying how pointless it all is. Now it's your father who's respecting my decision to go home to Blairfinnan, and I'm the one who's keeping the gap between us all just as wide.'

'Haven't I been telling you just that? I'd forget our differences in a minute, but you're the one who's determined to disbelieve anything I say.'

She shrugged. 'Only because I know what I know! And I don't want to go into that any more today,' she added as she saw the frown between his eyes deepen. 'Especially when little ears aren't as slow to pick up things as was once thought!'

'Is it me that has little ears?' Kirsty said, her speech more fluent in a week than any of them would have had believed possible. Annie laughed and gave the child a quick hug.

'You have, my love, and very pretty ears too.'

'Aye, she's as bonnie as her teacher,' Stewart said dryly, 'and just as stubborn when she doesn't want to

116

admit to hearing things. The teacher listens, but she doesn't hear.'

Annie looked at him. She didn't want to get into an argument on this last morning, nor to see Kirsty's face droop as the sound of carriage wheels was heard outside the open windows. She spoke to Kirsty now.

'You're going to practise your letters with your Granpa, like you promised, aren't you, Kirsty? And Stewart will draw some pictures with you.'

For a moment she thought she was going to get away with that, but the next second Kirsty's face had puckered, and her arms were flung tight around Annie's neck.

'Don't go! Stay with Kirsty! Stay, stay, *stay*!'

'Well, she's certainly learned that word all right,' Stewart said. 'So how do you intend to handle this, Miss Teacher? It seems you've done your job too well after all.'

He folded his arms with satisfaction, and Annie realised she'd fallen into something of a trap, however unwittingly. She gently unwound the child's arms from her neck, looked into the tear-blotched face and made up her mind. It would be too cruel to undo all the good she had done this past week.

'Kirsty, I have to go home now because my family will be missing me,' she said. 'But I promise I'll come and see you another day, and we'll do some more letters and pictures –'

'What '*nother* day?' Kirsty said sullenly. 'Tomorrow?'

'I can't. I'll still have to rest my ankle for a while,' she said quickly, imagining her uncle's reaction if she said she was coming straight back to Craggan the next day. As Kirsty began to wail again, Annie gave her a small shake and spoke firmly.

'Now listen, Kirsty, I said I'd come back and that's a promise. But you have to promise me something as well. I want you to practise writing your name for me. I'll come back in a week's time and spend the afternoon with you. Do you understand?'

The child nodded slowly, clinging to Stewart again as the housekeeper came into the room to say the carriage from Blairfinnan was here to take the young lady home.

'Thank-you, Mrs Innes. And thank-you for all your kindness too,' Annie said warmly.

'Och, 'twas no hardship to be pleasant to a young lassie like yourself! I only wish you didn't have to leave us – for the bairn's sake as well as the rest of us. 'Tis a more cheerful place with a woman in it,' she added darkly.

Stewart spoke briskly. 'Well then, Mrs Innes, if you'll take Kirsty up to the nursery after those words of wisdom, I'll see Miss Blair into the carriage.'

'I can manage perfectly well –'

'No you cannot. You heard what the doctor said. That ankle will be weak for a good while to come, so you'll do as you're told and lean on me.'

Annie gritted her teeth as she was obliged to obey, guessing how he must be savouring this. A badly sprained ankle wasn't healed in a week, and she admitted she would have to go carefully for some time yet. There would be no more dancing in the foreseeable future . . . even as she thought it, a swift vision of herself being twirled around the floor in Stewart Mackinty's arms flashed into her mind, more sweetly nostalgic than she expected, and enough to make her catch her breath with the memory. His grip on her arm tightened at the small sound.

'Are you in much pain?' he asked, as he took her through the door of Craggan into the softly-scented air.

'Not too much. It was just the strangeness of walking again,' she said, hoping he would believe her, even

118

though he knew very well she had been walking tentatively around her bedroom for the past few days now, wanting to get back to normal.

She saw her uncle's small open visiting carriage waiting near the house, and she felt her face go hot with annoyance as she saw the man standing awkwardly beside it.

'Oh no, not him! Why couldn't my uncle have come himself?' she exclaimed, seeing Siddons' embarrassed face.

'Is there some problem with the man?' Stewart said at once, catching the anger in her words.

'You could say so! He was the one who told my uncle it was you disguised as the pirate at the costume ball, and forced me into admitting that I knew. He also took much relish in telling him. *And* he gave me Filigree to ride, when he must have known very well the horse was too boisterous for me. He's the last person I want to take me home!'

'Then he's not taking you. I am.' Stewart retorted.

When they reached the carriage, Siddons began mumbling apologies. Whatever had been said to him since Annie had been at Craggan, it was obvious he'd been completely crushed by it. For Annie, it didn't change anything. But for this man, she would have had two good legs to walk on now, instead of the gnawing ache in her ankle that still troubled her abominably at times.

'Miss Blair will not be requiring your services,' Stewart said coldly. 'I shall take her home in the carriage myself, and you can make your own way, man. It's a fair walk, but I daresay you're up to it. You have no lameness in either leg, I take it?'

Siddons reddened furiously. 'Mr Blair gave me full instructions, Sir. I'm to take the young lady home at a slow pace so as not to jar her ankle –'

'And I prefer Mr Mackinty to escort me,' Annie said swiftly. 'You needn't fear what my uncle will say to you. I shall take full responsibility, but I will not ride with you.'

He turned to her, his voice anxious and defensive. 'I meant no harm, Miss, and certainly not to you. I'm loyal to my employer, and I only did my duty as I saw it.'

He strode off, clearly trying hard to keep his dignity intact, and Annie might have felt almost sorry for him, but for the memory of his vicious remarks, and the way he'd allowed her to ride Filigree.

'Don't waste your pity on him,' Stewart said, seeing the softening in her eyes. 'Though it's true what he says. He'll undoubtedly be thinking he did right by your uncle. His sort can be as hard and implacable as the mountains, but he'll probably be your willing slave from now on.'

'I don't want any man to be my slave,' she said, suddenly sick of them all. 'I just want to go home and forget any of this ever happened.'

Stewart helped her into the carriage. His face was very close to hers and he looked into her eyes so intently she found it impossible to look away.

'Just so long as you don't forget me, Annie. But I defy you to even try. The past binds us too closely, and the future is one that we're destined to share, and that's *my* promise.'

He climbed into the seat beside her and took up the reins, clicking the horses into gentle movement as Annie chose not to answer. When the journey had begun she found she was biting her lip, as even the smallest motion jarred her more than she had expected. She said very little on the slow ride back to Blairfinnan, finally ignoring Stewart's attempts at conversation, though more because of the pain than for any other reason.

'Did Mrs Innes give you some of her powders to take home with you?' he said at last, seeing her white face as they neared the Blair house and demanding to know what was wrong.

'Yes,' she said, finding it hard to talk at all now except in monosyllables. 'I'll take one as soon as I'm home.'

'I'll suggest to your uncle that the doctor comes to see you again very soon. You're not over the worst of it yet.'

Her eyes filled with weak tears as she leaned against the velvet backrest of the carriage.

'No. Leave it to him. Please. Don't cause a fuss.'

She spoke laboriously. She realised the horses had stopped and she opened her eyes slowly. The world swam in front of her through a mist of tears, and then Stewart's face blotted out the sun and she felt the gentleness of his mouth on hers. Without any forced passion, there was still all the tenderness she could ever yearn for in that kiss. He spoke softly against her tremulous lips.

'Oh, Annie Blair, don't you know I'd cause a fuss in heaven if it would prove to you that my intentions are honourable, despite all you've been told to the contrary about me and mine?'

She felt her heartbeats quicken. She'd give the earth to believe him, but how could she? Out of the corner of her eye she could see her Aunt Morag bustling out from the house, and her dark-faced uncle wasn't far behind. She gave a small sigh and pushed Stewart away from her in the carriage. But of course it was too late, and they would have already seen them apparently embracing.

'Just wait for the fuss now, when they see you've brought me home instead of Siddons,' she managed to say, wondering vaguely why the carriage still seemed to be swaying even though the horses had stopped.

Dimly, she became aware of a sensation she had known before. Of strong arms holding her in a way she had felt before. Of heartbeats she knew, matching her own . . . and in the midst of it all her uncle's roaring voice demanding to know what was happening. . .

'I'm taking your niece into the house, that's what's happening,' she heard Stewart's voice snap. She felt the sound vibrate against her chest and realised instantly that he was carrying her. He strode across the Blairfinnan threshold and into the cool interior of the house.

The last time he'd been here it was under false pretences, and only Annie had known the identity of the dashing pirate. His appearance now was no less welcome. . .

'My niece will be perfectly well attended to now, Sir, and I thank you for your trouble,' Dougal continued.

Annie felt the arms around her tighten momentarily, and sensed that it was more with tension than possessiveness.

'Do we not have names any more?' he said in a mocking voice to Dougal. 'I know that your niece is Annie Blair, and you hardly need telling that I'm Stewart Mackinty. Do neighbours really need to be so formal, Dougal?'

'You're no neighbour of mine,' Dougal growled. 'Only in the physical sense that I can no more avoid you than I can avoid breathing, more's the pity. Not unless your family were to consider selling up and moving away, of course, in which case I'd help with the removal –'

'And you'd see hell freeze before that happened,' Stewart said pleasantly.

Annie had had enough.

'Will you both stop it! You're like children, the pair of you! Stewart, please put me down. I'm quite capable of walking to a sofa, and I think it's best if you go now. And if my uncle's ungracious enough with his thanks for your hospitality, then I am not. I do thank you and your father, and most sincerely.'

'We all thank you, Mr – Stewart –' Aunt Morag put in nervously. 'And if you'd care to take a dram with us before you go –'

'That he will not!' Dougal roared out. 'Have you taken leave of your senses, woman? No Mackinty drinks under my roof.'

Stewart gave a slight smile, but his voice was razor-edged. 'It will hurt your pride to realise I've already done so at your ball, Dougal, but in any case I'm not keen to repeat the experience. You keep a poor cellar these days.'

Annie could see the dark veins standing out on her uncle's neck, and wondered just how long this baiting could go on before he exploded altogether. She gave up trying to intervene now, realising that Morag had done the same. There was no stopping two pig-headed men with their dander up.

'A poor cellar indeed! The most excellent being that which stocks Craggan's Best, I suppose!'

'Naturally. And Annie's grandfather and mine were in perfect agreement on that score, if you weren't such a stubborn old cuss to acknowledge it.'

Annie saw Morag's lips twitch. Her aunt was actually enjoying this – and so was she! It had somehow ceased to be an embarrassing scene and had turned into a battle of wits and gall. The opponents were too frank with one another for any subleties to come into play, and her own head and Aunt Morag's turned from one to another of the men as if they watched a fascinating game of ball-play.

Into the back of her mind came the interesing little snippet that for these people, a good verbal fight was every bit as stimulating as a good drink of whisky . . . they thrived on it. The feud wasn't so much a vicious thing as a means of keeping competition alive in a wild part of the world where nothing else much happened. Or so it seemed to Annie at that moment.

'You'll come to my cellar and take a dram of the finest whisky Edinburgh has to offer, man, and then deny that the city brew doesn't have the edge on your backwoods methods.'

'The city now, is it?' Stewart said scornfully. 'You sing a different tune now that your fine son is away being a lawyer, I see. You'll be filling the house with culture next.'

'There's already more culture in this house than was ever seen at Craggan,' Dougal snapped. 'My niece is an educated young woman and my son's a lawyer. A well-matched pair, I'd say, wouldn't you, Mackinty?'

The inference was obvious, and Annie caught her breath as Stewart said nothing for a moment. His eyes glittered blackly in his strong-jawed face, and then he laughed.

'And you don't think I'm a match for your Robert when it comes to the marrying stakes? A Mackinty man has always carried off a Blair lassie, in case you've overlooked the fact, but I don't recall a Blair man finding favour with one of mine!'

Annie gasped anew, her own eyes sparkling with blue fire. This conversation was getting dangerously personal now, and she bitterly resented the suggestion that Stewart and Rob might be in competition for her favours. It seemed that for one family to score over the other was the ultimate in achievement, no matter whose feelings were hurt in the process. And she would seem to be the prize fought over by Rob and Stewart.

Except for the bit of paper that absolved herself and Rob from any romantic attachments, she remembered

124

instantly. At that moment she thought of it as a talisman, a secret to be savoured, and the one sane piece of evidence that she and Rob at least refused to be manipulated by the past, in a world that had still gone made with rivalry and dissent.

'There's time yet,' Dougal said smoothly. 'You've a wee lassie growing up at Craggan, and there's plenty more distant Blair kin –'

'Will you stop this!' Annie suddenly found her voice and yelled at the pair of them, appalled at the way the talk was going now. 'I'm no prize pig to be bartered over, and I won't hear you talk about Kirsty like that, Uncle. She's just a child, and I refuse to let her be drawn into your devious ways!'

'*You* refuse, do you?' he rounded on her now. 'And who are you to come here, knowing nothing of our ways, and presume to tell what I can and cannot do!'

'I'm a Stalwart Blair! And I was given to understand that our middle name meant something special. It stands for honour and decency, and so far I've seen precious little of that here. I'm sorry if it offends you –'

'You're damn right it offends me, girl! Is this what I paid good money for, to educate you into rebelling against everything our family stands for?'

He stopped abruptly at the sound of Stewart's laughter.

'I'm glad you find this amusing, Sir,' Dougal said sarcastically. 'I wasn't aware that we were a peep-show for the Mackintys, and I'd ask you to leave so that we may continue our business in private.'

'We've nothing more to discuss –' Annie said at once.

'And I thought I was being offered a dram, or has that offer been withdrawn now that your self-righteousness has come to the fore?'

'No man accuses me of offering and then with-drawing,' Dougal snapped. 'You'll come with me to the cellar and take of Edinburgh's finest. And then I'll be shot of you.'

Annie could have sworn that Stewart winked at her as he followed Dougal's bristling shape, but she kept her face poker-straight until the men had gone from the room, and then she let out her breath in an explosive sound.

'Is it always like this?' she said to Aunt Morag. 'I can't believe that a few innocent words can suddenly erupt into a full-scale battle!'

Morag gave a wry smile. 'It seems there's no place for half-measures between our two families, my dear. There have been those who loved passionately, or whose friendship was as close as brothers', and the rest, who fought like wildcats.'

And in which category was she destined to be, Annie wondered? If Stewart had his way, it would be the first. If she continued to repulse him, it would undoubtedly be the last. As Aunt Morag said, there could be no half-measures. The thought made her shiver.

'Are you cold, love? The journey must have been uncomfortable for you,' Aunt Morag said sympathetically.

Annie had forgotten all about her ankle until that minute, but now she realised the throbbing was still there, as unrelenting as a pulse-beat.

'It wasn't the best I've ever taken,' she said. 'Mrs Innes gave me some powders that help dull the pain. Perhaps I should take one.'

Morag rang a bell and a young servant appeared almost at once. So quickly, in fact, that Annie would have wagered she had been listening agog to the argument between the two men. Probably to repeat in the kitchen, and then relayed to the Mackinty house with much relish and exaggeration.

She hardly cared. Right now there was a strong inclination to leave this rugged country behind and go home to Devon, where life had been simpler . . . she was struck by her thoughts, because before coming here she had expected this to be the simple life, miles from anywhere, and she had grieved for the loss of her busy life among her farming friends . . . but now, she knew that life here was anything but simple, due in no small way to the temperaments of the occupants of these two neighbouring estates.

But tempting though the idea of returning south was to her just then, she knew in her heart she would never go. There were too many pulls here now. In the short time she'd been at Blairfinnan she'd become very fond of her aunt and could put up with her uncle's irascibility. She hardly knew Rob well, but she thought of him as an ally more than a friend, and one she felt she could count on if it ever became necessary.

As for her surroundings . . . she had fallen totally in love with the wild beauty of the Highlands, the pure clean air and the feeling of space and majesty. It was her heritage and it was in her blood. Despite the traumas of family feuding there was peace to be found here. There was friendship too. There was Catriona Moray, whom Aunt Morag said was coming to visit her as soon as she returned to Blairfinnan. There was the delicate little Kirsty, whom Annie still yearned to help. And there was Stewart Mackinty.

'We'll take a hot drink too, since it's always good for shock, Annie, despite the warmth of the day,' Morag was saying now, jerking her thoughts back to the comfortable room in which they sat. 'I made some oat cakes this morning, too, knowing you were coming home. I daresay the fare at Craggan was adequate, but you'll be ready for some of our own good baking.'

'Oh Aunt,' Annie began to laugh at this artless way of comparing the two houses. 'Tell me something honestly. Don't you ever wish this nonsense could end and we could all be friends?'

Morag didn't answer for a moment, and when she did she was a mite cooler than usual.

'Firstly, Annie, I'm never less than honest, and secondly I'd be grateful if you wouldn't refer to something your uncle takes very seriously as nonsense. He's a volatile man, as you know very well by now, but he means well, and his loyalty to his family is absolute, no matter how strange you find his methods.'

And she had to be content with that, not realising until later that Morag had neatly avoided saying whether or not she wished the feud could end and they could all be friends.

They had been drinking hot chocolate and eating more of the delicious oat-cakes than was good for them, when they heard the raucous singing. At first it seemed to come from beneath their feet, and then it moved upwards and closer and finally emerged in the gardens beyond the long open windows of the drawing-room. Annie had been half-dozing from the effects of her pain-killing powder, but suddenly she was wide awake. Her stiffened ankle prevented her from leaping to her feet, but she hobbled towards the window as fast as she could in the wake of Aunt Morag.

'Will you just look at this?' her aunt said in exasperation. 'I could have predicted it, Annie! There's no logic in men, for all that they think they're so superior to the rest of us.'

Annie looked to where her uncle had his arm loosely around Stewart Mackinty's shoulders. In his free hand he held a pewter drinking cup, and was raising it aloft as he bellowed out a traditional song. She couldn't understand the words at all, until Morag remarked pithily that it was Gaelic, and it was pathetic that the only time he remembered the old words was when he was rip-roaring drunk.

'Are they both drunk?' Annie said in astonishment, wondering how they could have got in this state in such a relatively short time.

'Probably not,' Morag said shrewdly. 'Your uncle has a low threshold when it comes to holding his drink, though he'll never admit it, since it offends his Scottish nature. But I had the whisky well-watered down for him on the night of the ball, so he wouldn't disgrace us all.'

Annie looked at her with new admiration, this seemingly fluffy-headed woman who knew her husband all too well, making allowances for him and steering him in sensible directions without hurting his male pride. But the other one . . . Stewart Mackinty . . . did he also know of Dougal Blair's 'failing', if failing was the word for it?

Annie had a deep dark suspicion as Stewart steadied her uncle with a firm hand and never a tremble in any part of him, compared with the older man.

The song came to an end, and Dougal clapped Stewart on the back in a gesture of cameraderie.

'You've a fine carrying voice on you, lad, and I'd fight any man who says different,' he slurred loudly.

'Mebbe it's been developed by shouting insults at my neighbours,' Stewart grinned, which Annie thought was definitely chancing his luck. To her amazement her uncle chuckled. He swayed dangerously on his feet, keeping them planted well apart now to keep him upright.

'Oh aye, but there's insults and insults,' Dougal said, tapping the side of his nose meaningly. Though what meaning he was trying to imply, Annie couldn't imagine.

'He'll have a head on him in the morning, the old fool,' Morag muttered by her side. 'I wish the lad would go home now and leave him to us. He'll be wanting to sleep this off.'

'Shouldn't you ask Stewart to help him upstairs? I'd be little help to you, Aunt Morag –'

'The servants can do it. They're used to it,' she said shortly, which told Annie far more than her actual words.

Stewart turned round to the women, and Annie knew at once she'd been right. He wasn't inebriated at all, and she wondered what little game he'd been playing. Between them all, it seemed nothing was done for innocent reasons, she thought in annoyance. Everything had a purpose. . .

'I'll leave your man to you, Ma'am,' he said to Morag. 'But I'll be back in a week's time for Annie. It's all arranged.'

Annie felt her heart jump and then race on. Was he mad? It was enough to set her uncle off into one of his ranting rages again. To her utter shock she saw him slap Stewart on the back once more.

'That's right. The poor wee lassie will benefit from Annie's tutoring. Annie's a good girl, and she'll be glad to do her best for the bairn.'

Annie felt her mouth drop open. How on earth Stewart had changed her uncle into this paragon of sweetness she couldn't imagine. She felt Morag's hand on her arm.

'Leave it, lass. If it's what you want, then you've got your wish. He'll remember it when he's slept this off, and he'll abide by his word, however much he hates it when he's sober.'

Stewart's wink was unmistakable now, but Annie refused to smile or respond. Instead, she turned and walked back into the house with her head held high, as a manservant and several maids appeared to help their master indoors and up to his room.

Her cheeks were burning as she sank down again on the drawing-room sofa, knowing she had got her wish to tutor Kirsty, at least for that one afternoon next week, but despising the way it had come about.

Later that day she was aroused from her dozing to see Trina Moray looking down at her.

'Thank goodness. You looked so pale I thought you were really ill,' the girl said at once. 'You poor lamb! It must have been hateful for you – except for being taken into the Mackinty lair, of course. I'd have had no objection to that myself. So tell me how you are, Annie. And then tell me about Craggan.'

Annie struggled to sit up, feeling dishevelled and less than her best. She was fond of Trina, but right now her bubbling enthusiasm left her breathless.

'How do you think it was?' she said crossly. 'They're normal people not monsters.'

At Trina's astonished face, she spread her hands contritely.

'I'm sorry, I didn't mean to snap. It's been an awkward time for me lately, but I shouldn't take it out on you. And I really am so very pleased to see you, Trina.'

'That's all right then, though I began to wonder if I should go out and come in again,' she said generously. 'I'm glad to hear you say the Mackintys aren't monsters, anyway. I guessed you'd be too strong-minded to be coloured by your uncle's opinions, Annie.'

'Does everyone know our business around here?' she enquired without too much malice.

'Oh aye. What else do we simple souls have to fill our days with?' Trina said airily.

'You could have told me about the distillery then. Craggan's Best or whatever it's called.'

'Why on earth should I do that?'

Annie shrugged. From the way her head was going round, she began to feel as if she was the one who'd been drinking. And she was still lethargic from the effects of the sedative powder.

'No reason at all,' she said. 'Have you seen my uncle since you arrived?'

'No, but I've heard him,' Trina grinned. 'Is that why you asked about Craggan's Best? He'll not have been drinking any Mackinty spirits, whatever else he's been at!'

'Not exactly, but he's been down in the cellar drinking with Stewart, if you can believe it,' Annie said. 'The two of them as daft as monkeys, and each as devious as the other, though I've an idea Stewart was only play-acting –'

'The way he played at being a pirate at your aunt's costume ball? Oh yes, the story's all around Earnlie by now, Annie, so no wonder you wouldn't give the game away on the night. And weren't you the lucky one after all?'

'Why?' Annie said, pink-cheeked.

'Come on now, didn't I tell you every red-blooded lassie for miles around would give her eye-teeth to dance in Stewart Mackinty's arms? Still more, to be taken walking in the gardens and kissed in the moonlight!'

Annie gasped. That damnable Siddons and his gossiping tongue! She realised Trina was looking at her enviously and kept her temper in check. It wasn't this girl's fault that the story had got around so fast.

'Would you like some lemonade?' she asked Trina. 'It's such a warm afternoon, and if you'll just ring the bell, one of the maids will bring us some.'

'All right. And the subject of Stewart Mackinty is out of bounds, is that it?' she smiled mischievously. 'I promise I won't say another thing about it if you'll just tell me if it was worth it, Annie. It was very clever to fall off your horse like that just so you could be taken to Craggan. I don't suppose you bargained for a sprained ankle as well, but it gave you a lovely long time in the man's company didn't it? I do envy you!'

Annie was speechless for a few minutes. She looked into Trina's eager face, waiting for any snippet of gossip she could get about the Craggan men. She didn't know whether to feel angry or tired of the whole lot of them, and then she saw the funny side of it and doubled up laughing. Trina looked blank, unsure quite what the joke was all about, but finally thankful her friend seemed to have recovered her equilibrium at last, she obligingly joined in.

Chapter 8

Annie's heart had been behaving erratically all morning. For a while she had even wondered if there was something seriously wrong with her, or if it was quite normal for a young woman to get so het-up just because a man was calling for her to spend the afternoon at his home.

'You're an idiot, Annie Blair,' she declared finally to her reflection in her dressing-table mirror. But she gave up trying to make herself look as truly tutorial as possible. She tugged at the unruly curls that persisted in slipping out of their pins, knowing she couldn't resemble a strait-laced school-marm however much she tried, and recklessly pinched her cheeks to make them rosier.

'Did you say something, Miss?' came the voice of the maid hovering about in the room behind her.

'I was just talking to myself, Maisie. Don't you ever do that?'

'Och aye, but myself never has a sensible answer to give me,' the girl said bluntly.

Annie grinned. 'Well, never does *my*self, come to that.'

Maisie was in the mood to be argumentative.

'But you've got naught to worry about, Miss. You don't have freckles that make a face look as if it's covered in a dark cloud as soon as it's summer. And you don't have miserable wispy hair that won't stay tidily inside a cap no matter what. You have lovely red hair and so much of it it canna help but look wonderful whatever you do. And neither can it help but make me envious, no matter how evil the minister considers envy to be.'

She gulped for breath and rushed on. 'And your eyes are that clear blue that men are so fond of, while mine are so pale I sometimes doubt the good Lord remembered to put any colour in them at all. And your uncle has a real fondness for you, for all his rude ways, and I know we're all going to be in for a roasting when you've gone off today –'

'For pity's sake, Maisie, will you stop! And if you're so worried about your freckles, which are nothing like as bad as you say, then rub some lemon juice into them.' By now Annie was laughing aloud at this unusual outpouring until she saw the expression in the girl's eyes.

'There's something else bothering you, isn't there, Maisie? You'd better tell me, since I've no idea what you're really so hot and bothered about. I shall only be away for the afternoon, so my uncle will hardly have time to roast anybody!'

'That's not what I've been told,' Maisie muttered.

Annie stared. 'What do you mean? What's not what you've been told? Tell me right now!'

The girl suddenly looked frightened. 'I'm not supposed to say, Miss. But my sister swears 'tis true all the same.'

Annie felt impatient with her. Maisie could be infuriating at times, dropping hints about things her sister had overheard at Craggan, and never finishing the tale. But this time, Annie intended getting it all out of her, if only to relieve the disturbing way her heart raced whenever she thought of seeing Stewart Mackinty again. Today's visit was all on Kirsty's account, she reminded herself, but that thought did little to assuage the way her heart leaped, even at the mention of his name.

'Well then, I'm told you're to be going over to Craggan every day to teach the bairn.'

'Oh, did you indeed? I assure you nothing of the sort has been arranged –'

Maisie's words tumbled over themselves in her agitation. 'Nettie says it has. She says the young Mackinty was boasting to his father that when he got your uncle roaring drunk on the whisky he persuaded him into it. And 'tis well known that your uncle never goes back on a promise, for all his – 'tis well known he never goes back on a promise,' she finished lamely.

Annie felt her mouth drop open. Her thoughts winged back at once to that day when Stewart had brought her home and he'd as good as goaded Dougal into taking him into the cellar to take a dram. She remembered the singing when they both appeared again, and the inebriated state her uncle was in. And she remembered too, that moment when Stewart had winked at her, and she had thought it odd that he seemed hardly the worse for drink in the way her uncle was.

So it had all been a scheme, she raged. If Stewart couldn't persuade her honestly to go to Craggan regularly, then he'd do it deviously. It was a word she'd previously used in relation to her uncle, but now she saw how adequately it applied to Stewart Mackinty as well.

She pursed her lips together and tilted her chin. She

136

straightened the bodice of her thin summer gown and fastened the little sprigged cotton cape around her neck. Finally she rammed a flowered bonnet over her curls and turned to Maisie again with flashing eyes.

'I assure you, Maisie, that no-one dictates where I'll go or whom I'll see,' she snapped. 'I certainly do not intend to go to Craggan every day, so you can just take that doleful look off your face.'

'And you won't say I told you, Miss? Nettie would have my hide if she thought I was stirring up any trouble.' She began to sniffle into her apron. 'It's just that things have been a wee bit more peaceful since you came, Miss, and especially since word got about that you're going to marry Master Rob. 'Twould be a shame to upset the apple-cart –'

Annie spun round angrily. 'It seems to me this entire country is one gigantic gossip-place! And I'd be glad if you'd please stop discussing your betters, Maisie!'

'Yes Miss,' the girl said contritely as Annie swept out of the room and down the stairs.

It was a good thing she couldn't read her mind at that moment, Annie was thinking. She was ashamed of herself for speaking to a servant in that way, when but for circumstances, she herself might have been in the very same position as Maisie. Uncle Dougal had saved her from that, and she should be grateful to him, but it was sometimes hard to hold on to the gratitude when he infuriated her in so many other ways. But if the story that she and Rob were eventually to be married was being bandied about, Dougal was in for a bigger shock than he bargained for.

Both her aunt and uncle were away from the house that afternoon. Morag was visiting in Earnlie, and Dougal was answering a torrent of complaints from tenants on the Blairfinnan estate as to roofs needing repairs, and that the occupants were beginning to see more stars through the slates than could be seen in the sky.

'Damn stupid exaggeration,' he'd snorted when he left the house earlier. But since the cottages were full of estate workers who would be obliged to stay off work if they fell ill, he had no choice but to see what was needed and attend to it.

So there was no-one else in the family to witness the arrival of Stewart Mackinty but Annie herself. And she simply gaped when she looked beyong the man to see no waiting carriage.

'You're surely not expecting me to walk all the way to Craggan? My ankle's not strong enough for that yet!' she exclaimed at once, feeling the June sun beating down on her head, and remembering the distance she had ridden around the head of the loch and inadvertently onto Mackinty land.

'I am not,' he grinned. 'Your groom is providing a trap to take us to the lochside where I first saw you. Don't fret, I'm handling the horse myself.'

She blushed, remembering that first time she had set eyes on this man, and remembering her instant impression of him. Monarch of the glen . . . laird of all he surveyed . . . all the traditional phrases flashed into her mind, and made her sharper than she intended.

'I thought we were going to Craggan. Isn't Kirsty expecting me?'

'Oh aye. But I thought we'd go by water this time. And I'm not in the process of abducting you, lassie. I keep my word, just as your uncle keeps his.'

It was the second time that day her uncle's integrity had been vouchsafed. First from Maisie, now Stewart. She saw Siddons bring the trap round to the front of the house now, and heard him tell Stewart he'd send a lad down to the loch to fetch it back shortly. It was an odd way of going on, Annie thought, but as Siddons avoided her eyes, she guessed he was more than ready to comply with Stewart's wishes, which he assumed were also hers.

'What's this Maisie tells me about you and my uncle agreeing to my going to Craggan every day?' she said without wasting time as they began the ride down to the loch. 'And about you getting him drunk?'

Stewart laughed. 'It's no fault of mine if Dougal Blair can't hold his drink,' he said easily. 'And if I caught him in a rare mood of expansion and pressed my case for my bairn missing a woman's fair touch, and he agreed with it, who am I to complain?'

'You mean you planned it all,' she stated.

'I made certain suggestions, and the man fell in with them. Come on now, Annie, do you deny it's what we both want?'

She wasn't sure if his words were meant to be ambiguous or not. If she took them at face value, then yes, this was what they both wanted, and so did his father, and presumably Kirsty too. The benefits were weighted heavily on the Mackintys' side.

'Is Kirsty happy about seeing me again?' she asked.

Stewart gave a mock sigh. 'She's talked of nothing else. As far as she's concerned, the sun shines out of your eyes, my lassie.'

She looked at him uneasily, unsure if such adoration was a good thing or not. 'But she knows I'm only here for this afternoon, doesn't she? You do promise to bring me back to Blairfinnan later?'

'How suspicious you are. Yes, I'll bring you back through the glen later, and Kirsty will accept that as long as she knows you'll be back tomorrow.'

Annie glared at him. She played with just this idea, but now that it had all been arranged by such underhand methods, and without even consulting her, she was resentful of his interference.

'I will if it pleases me,' she said, and then cried out as his large hand fastened over her wrist.

'You can't disappoint the child,' he said roughly. 'She's been told you're coming every day, and she's set her heart on it. Even your uncle will think it a slight against his word if you refuse to come now.'

'My Lord, you think of everything, don't you?' she said bitterly. 'And I suppose all this subterfuge on Kirsty's behalf is in aid of that stupid vow for a Mackinty to tame a Blair lassie?'

Stewart laughed. They were nearing the edge of the loch now, where the small rowing-boat was tied up in the still water.

'Sweetheart, I expected more of you than that! Don't you know that taming a Blair lassie means something far more than encouraging her to be a teacher to a child! It means that a Mackinty man will have a Blair lassie in his bed. And that's just where I mean to have you.'

She gasped at the rich seduction of his voice, but she heard the words as nothing short of insulting. To her heightened nerves, she felt she was being treated as little more than one of the street women who frequented the Devon waterfronts.

'You'll see hell freeze before that happens,' she said in a choked voice, using one of her uncle's favourite expressions and hardly noticing it.

She had stepped down from the trap now, waiting for him to fasten the horse's reins to the block. She moved away from him and stumbled slightly, the movement reminding her that her ankle was still tender. Stewart's arm was around her instantly, and he took advantage of the moment to draw her into his arms.

'Why must you fight me so much?' he said softly. 'Why can't you accept the inevitable?'

She swallowed, because if he only knew it she had accepted part of it long ago. She was fully determined

140

to resist the overtures that obviously meant nothing to him, but she was honest enough to know she could never deny her own feelings. She loved him . . . maddening and infuriating and insensitive man that he was!

'Stew-art. Ann-ie.'

The impatient little voice drifted across the clear water, and they both saw the small figure on the far side of the loch, waving wildly to them both.

Annie waved back and moved neatly out of Stewart's embrace.

'Hadn't we better go across before Kirsty decides to swim over to us?' she said pointedly.

'She'll not try that,' he said. 'She's afraid of the water and she can't swim.'

'Perhaps you should teach her, then,' Annie said, trying to cover her nervousness and accepting his steadying hand as she clambered into what seemed to her a flimsy and frighteningly unstable boat.

'Why don't you?' he countered, his gaze wandering lazily over her shape as he rowed effortlessly away from the Blairfinnan bank towards the far side. 'It would be interesting to see you in a bathing-dress.'

Annie flushed, feeling an almost urgent need to cover her body with her hands from those interested dark eyes, but knowing it would only draw more attention to it if she did.

'I can't swim either,' she said primly. 'My father didn't consider it a necessity, and we only occasionally paddled in the sea at home. There were bathing machines on the beach for those who were daring enough to undress so publicly, but we never ventured into such things.'

A wave of nostalgia more powerful than she had expected, swept through her at that moment. The scent of the sea was in her nostrils, the feel of the warm sand between her toes, the sound of her mother's laughing voice filling her ears as Annie and her father poked about for shrimps in the rock pools, the plaintive screech of seagulls high on the cliffs. . .

'Come back, Annie. Wherever you've gone, it does not good to wallow in remembering.'

'Would you have me forget?' she said, stung into replying sharply as she felt the shine of tears in her eyes, and wondering if he was mind-reading or just especially intuitive at that moment. Memories flooded into her mind, water-colour soft and muted by time, but none the less emotive for all that.

On days like this whole farming families would go to the nearby beach together. There were often communal picnic baskets filled with good farm produce, Devon ale for the men and lemonade for the women, and afterwards games for the children, tag and touch and I-spy while the grown-ups lazed and chatted and mused how good it was to be alive. . .

And now her parents were both dead, and she was here in the Highlands of Scotland, the land of her ancestors, but still not truly home . . . she was lovingly welcomed into this new family, but there were still times when she felt very alone. . .

She heard the splash of an oar in the loch, and a small spray of water cooled her face. And then Stewart was hauling both oars inside and pulling expertly on a rope from his landing-stage and securely tying up the boat before they made the short stroll up to Craggan.

The afternoon was more relaxed than Annie had expected. Once they arrived at the house, she was relieved that Stewart went off on business of his own and left her alone in the nursery with Kirsty. The child and the tutor looked at one another awkwardly for a few minutes, and then Annie picked up one of her simple picture and word books and held out her hand.

'We should be in the garden,' she said clearly, making as many gestures as necessary. 'Shall we take the book outside and do our lesson there?'

Kirsty nodded, and made to run out of the room at once, but Annie made her wait.

'No, Kirsty. You must always answer my question. When I say shall we go into the garden, you say "yes please Annie".'

She held her breath, wondering how the child would accept this idea. She had already sensed that whenever Kirsty wanted anything it was simply done for her, without her ever having to say yes or no or even to ask the endless questions with which most young children bombarded adults. Kirsty was cosseted and pampered and loved, but it didn't always do to anticipate her every need, and Annie had already deduced that this was half the problem of her unresponsiveness.

For a few seconds the child seemed poised like a little bird ready to fly, and Annie got no reply. And then she experimented with the words.

'Yes please Ann-ie.'

'That's right!' Annie smiled in delight and clapped her hands, and Kirsty clapped back.

'That's right,' repeated Kirsty, and clapped again.

From then on, Annie felt she was making real progress. Kirsty discovered that it was fun to mimic, and get this smiling response from the pretty lady with the nice voice, and whatever words Annie said, she repeated parrot-fashion. It might not be orthodox teaching, but to Annie it was more successful than she could have ever hoped for.

By the time Stewart came to find them, they were both absorbed in looking at the picture-book and Kirsty could identify the words for top and hoop and had made simple drawings of them. They were flushed with success and with the warmth of the sun, and Annie looked up with a start as a shadow fell across the book, and found Stewart looking at her with an odd expression in his eyes.

As Kirsty saw him too, the book was dropped to the grass and she ran to him, all thought of lessons forgotten. But not entirely. . .

'Ann-ie's my friend,' she said carefully. 'We looked at pic-tures and I made words. Ann-ie says Kir-sty's a good girl.'

Stewart picked her up in his arms and swung her around to her squeals of delight. He looked over the child's shoulder at Annie, his eyes sparkling with amusement now.

'Are you some kind of miracle worker, Annie Blair, to get her to talk so freely and entertainingly!'

'Not at all! I'm just happy to do what I can – though I don't quite see what's so funny –'

'Do you not?' he said, on the brink of laughter now. 'Did you not hear the way the bairn's talking? She obviously adores you and is anxious to please you, and she's copying you so well she's speaking in a foreign accent!'

'*Foreign*?' Annie echoed.

'Aye. *English*, lassie. Did you not realise it? She's managed to pick up your own rounded vowel sounds, and she even called herself a good girl, instead of a good lass.'

Of course Annie hadn't realised it. Why should she? She had spoken to Kirsty the way she always spoke, and the replies had been so gratifying it had never occured to her to question whether Kirsty's halting words had sounded Scottish or rich rolling Devonshire! She was just thankful that such progress had been made this afternoon, and she certainly hadn't expected this national pride to rear its head and dash her pleasure.

'I'm sorry if it bothers you –' she began stiffly.

'Och, for pity's sake, can't you see I'm only teasing you, Annie?' he said, laughing out loud now. 'It doesn't matter a hoot, it just tickled me, that's all.'

He suddenly yelped as Kirsty ran her fingers up and down his bare arm, the thick hairs glinting in the sunlight.

'Kirsty tick-les Stewart,' she said clearly and loudly, with hardly a pause between the syllables.

Annie saw him catch his breath and kiss her soft cheek, and she knew in an instant how much this must mean to him. Kirsty was definitely his Achilles' heel, she thought in some confusion, because the small act of tenderness was oddly moving to her as well.

'I have to take Annie home now,' he said to Kirsty. 'But you know she'll be coming back tomorrow, don't you?'

For a moment the child just stared at him, and Annie prayed she wasn't going to withdraw into that silent world of hers again. She looked at Annie, who nodded encouragingly and then she smiled.

'Yes, Stewart,' she said. 'To-morr-ow.'

'You know how grateful I am to you, don't you?' he said later, as they rode side by side in the Mackinty trap taking her back to Blairfinnan. 'You're exactly what Kirsty needed, and I should have realised it long ago.'

'Well, I'm no expert, but I think she feels more comfortable with a young person who can give her more time, than being just with servants or even you and your father, no matter how much you love her. Someone outside can often be more objective,' she said briskly, with every intention of keeping this discussion impersonal.

'Don't be modest about your achievement, Annie. I said you're just what Kirsty needed, and she's not the only one –'

'You could always have married, and your wife could have given her as much care and attention as she needed,' Annie said quickly. 'Why haven't you?'

She remembered Trina Moray's comments about Stewart Mackinty. He'd be a catch for any young woman, and there must be plenty ready to walk up the aisle of Earnlie kirk beside him.

'You disappoint me if you think I'm a man who would marry for less than love, Annie.' he said mockingly. 'Even for the sake of providing a step-mother to a bairn who isn't my own.'

'But you'd have no compunction about taking a young woman to bed who wasn't your wife?' she flashed at him, and then felt her face burn with colour. She couldn't think why she'd said it. She'd never spoken so freely to a man in her life before, and to speak so to this man of all men. . .

'And just what put that delectable idea into your head, I wonder?' Stewart said, with obvious enjoyment at her embarrassment.

'You did!' she snapped.

'When did I do so?'

Annie took a deep breath. 'When you continued telling me about this absurd intention of a Mackinty taming a Blair lassie. You said it meant taking her to bed —'

Dear Lord, but she was making it ten times worse now, and his amusement was tangible. As he let go of the horse's reins and let the animal plod onwards at its own slow pace, his arms were suddenly encircling her.

'Oh, Annie Blair, so I did. But I never implied it was said in any spirit other than honourable, did I?'

She looked at him suspiciously, his face no more than a breath away from hers once again, so close she knew he had every intention of making the most of the moment and kissing her. And she was finding it difficult to resist

146

leaning forward to welcome that kiss, even to making it unavoidable. . .

'You're not trying to tell me you want to marry me!' she said thickly. 'That would really set all the cats among the pigeons, wouldn't it?'

'And would it be so impossible to consider if I were to suggest it?'

For one sweet wild moment she let the dreams fill her head, and knew instantly that she wanted this above everything. To be Stewart Mackinty's wife . . . even as the beautiful words entered her mind it was as if the cold clear water of a tumbling Scottish waterfall was dashed in her face.

'You know it would!' she pushed away from him, angry and upset at being taunted, and thankful that he could have no idea of the extent of her feelings for him. He must never know . . . she gathered up her dignity and turned her face away from him. 'I'm not ready to marry anyone yet, and when I am, I would certainly look to my cousin Rob before I looked at a Mackinty!'

'Why won't you look at me now?' He caught at her chin and twisted her face to meet his. 'Is it because you're afraid of what I'll see there, Annie? Can you tell me that if you ever agreed to wed Rob Blair, it would be anything more than a feeble marriage based on fondness? You're not the woman to settle for that, my lassie.'

'And you know so much about me, do you?' she said, recognising the truth in everything he said, and furious at the way he seemed able to read her thoughts.

'I knew you from the moment I set eyes on you, and you felt the same. I'd stake my life on it. The same kind of powerful attraction existed between our ancestors, Miranda and James, and it's something you'd be foolish to deny. You don't believe in re-incarnation, by any chance?'

She flinched. 'Stop it,' she whispered. 'Whatever it is you're implying, I don't want to hear it. I'm not Miranda –'

'You might have been, on the night of your aunt's costume ball. Was it just chance, or was it instinct that decided you on the white gown?'

She felt a chill run through her despite the heat of the day. She didn't want to listen to this, filling her mind with something she didn't understand and had no wish to pursue. Any mention of things beyond the normal unnerved her.

'Can we just go home, please? And if you persist in this kind of talk I shan't go to Craggan again.'

'You mean you would disappoint Kirsty?'

She looked at him steadily, her eyes as unblinking as his.

'If I had to,' she said deliberately. 'I went there today through my own choice, but if necessary I would insist that she comes to me instead. You won't blackmail me into doing what you want, Stewart, so don't even try.'

He released her at once and picked up the reins again. She had won a small victory, but it didn't feel like it. He didn't speak to her again, and she was oddly nervous for the rest of the silent journey. By the time they reached Blairfinnan, she was almost impatient to be out of his company. Love him or hate him, she thought miserably, she could never ignore him . . . as she made to step out of the carriage he was there before her, his arms around her waist to lift her down.

'You'll not wed Rob Blair while I have breath in my body to stop it, Annie,' he said, so softly she might almost have imagined it.

For the life of her she couldn't drag up one single withering reply at that moment. She merely twisted away from him and walked up to the front door of

Blairfinnan, aware that the ache in her ankle was still there and she was starting to limp again. It was one more thing to depress her.

It was Friday when she made the first afternoon visit to Craggan, so she had all the weekend to decide what to do about Kirsty. She was highly tempted to suggest the child came here, but it was hardly likely Stewart would agree to it. He would want her there, at Craggan. . .

But first she was able to spend a leisurely Saturday in her aunt's company, without the added pressure of thinking about Stewart Mackinty. At least, not consciously. Dougal's black moods, a direct reaction from his drinking bout with Stewart, was reminder enough of the man.

'Just keep out of his way as much as possible, my dear,' Aunt Morag advised. 'I've learned it's the best way, and he'll have to be minding his manners when we go to kirk on Sunday.'

Such a prospect was not to be, for on Sunday morning Dougal awoke with such a fierce attack of gout he swore his foot was on fire, and he wasn't putting it to the ground for God nor man. . .

'You'll please stop your blaspheming, man!' Morag chided him, loud enough for Annie to hear the rumpus from her own room. 'You'd do far better to stay here and think on your disgraceful behaviour recently, than to sit piously inside the kirk with all the wickedness of a sinner inside you.'

'What's that meant to mean, woman? You talk in riddles these days –' he roared out.

'You know full well what I mean,' she said, as serene now as he was bellowing. 'You and the Mackinty drinking together, and letting him persuade you to let Annie go there to teach the bairn! You let him

149

get the better of you, and now we're all suffering for it, and don't think I don't know it, you old goat!'

'Aye well, she'll not be going there again,' Dougal shouted. 'I'm putting my foot down –'

'You do, and you'll be in double the pain you are now,' Morag whipped back. 'You'll leave Annie to decide for herself. It's time this old feud was ended –'

'If you were a natural-born Blair, you'd have more sense than to say it, woman –'

But she was no longer listening to him. She walked into Annie's bedroom, where the girl was putting on her bonnet with hands that shook slightly. Morag saw at once that she must have heard every word.

'Take no notice, Annie. You're to please yourself what you do about the Mackinty lass, and he'll get over it.'

'I think I must, Aunt Morag,' Annie said slowly, 'otherwise I shall begin to feel I don't have a will of my own any more.'

She turned to walk downstairs with her aunt, more unsettled than ever. She had never been pulled so many ways before. Life in Devon had been so easy, so carefree . . . now everyone wanted her, but only for reasons of their own. Nobody, it seemed, wanted her for herself. She knew in that instant it was what was wrong. But there was one person who wanted her for herself, she remembered, and that was Kirsty. A small feeling of warmth crept into her heart at the thought.

Once the service at Earnlie kirk was over and the congregation spilled out into the sunlight again, the child ran across to her quite naturally to say hello while the Mackinty men stood waiting.

'Will you come back soon, Ann-ie?' Kirsty said, proud of her words.

'I said so, didn't I, darling?' she answered. She felt awkward and almost evasive, but she hardly knew what

150

she should do any more. Stewart's father moved nearer and spoke approvingly.

'You're a remarkable young woman, Miss Blair, and I thank you for it. Any time you want to be rid of your troublesome relative, there's a home for you at Craggan where I know Kirsty would welcome you.'

'Now then, Callum Mackinty,' Aunt Morag said severely, 'you know Dougal would never agree to that!'

'I wasn't asking Dougal,' he said. 'But I'll leave the lass to think it over. Craggan's there whenever she needs it.'

And Stewart didn't even comment, Annie realised.

She and Aunt Morag climbed into the trap, and she felt an odd sense of unreality, as if she was no longer on an even keel with herself. There was still that overriding sense of being swept along where others wanted her to go, in spite of all she tried to do to the contrary.

'I've been hearing about this distillery place that once belonged to my grandfather and Stewart Mackinty's,' she said jerkily. 'Is it around here somewhere?'

Aunt Morag looked at her. 'It's not far. Do you want to see it? It's just a large group of buildings, Annie.'

'But it's part of our history, isn't it? I should at least know what a distillery looks like!' she said. 'Don't worry, I'm not suggesting going inside and sampling the produce!'

She didn't mean to imply that one drinker in the family was enough, but once she'd said it she hoped desperately it hadn't sounded that way.

They left the village of Earnlie behind and were crossing another verdant glen now. The mountains on either side of them seemed to crowd in a little, and a rushing waterfall glinted like diamonds in the summer sunshine. Apart from that, and the noise of their horse's hoofs, there was utter silence all around them.

'There!' Aunt Morag said eventually. 'That's what's known now as Craggan's Best. There's the barley store and the peat kiln, the malt storage and mash house and so on, but I know very little about what goes on there apart from the names, my dear, so there's no use asking me more.'

There were half a dozen large buildings all connected to one another, some low and long, others with chimneys. It was all quiet today, as befitted the sabbath, but Annie assumed it would buzz with activity through the week. It was a quite splendid barrack of brick and stone, only slightly marred by several jagged cracks that had been cemented together down some of the walls.

'What happened there?' Annie said curiously, pointing.

'Och, that was the result of the earthquake in 1839. Some of the houses in the village had their walls cracked a wee bit too, but Craggan's Best took it the worst. I mind that your uncle was quite gloating about it at the time, saying it was probably a judgement on the Mackintys,' she said dryly.

Annie wasn't interested in hearing about her uncle's pleasure in his enemy's problems. She was only just realising that the earthquake story, that she'd half thought no more than a fairy tale, was all true after all.

This area did lie on something called the Highland Boundary fault, and here was the frightening evidence of it, staring her in the face. These seemingly solid structures had been slashed across as if by a giant sword, and all in a single moment when the earth shook and erupted. She shivered as her imagination took hold, thankful she hadn't been here to experience it at the time, and praying such an occurrance wouldn't happen again in her lifetime. Lighting didn't strike twice, did it? Hopefully, earthquakes didn't either.

Chapter 9

Dougal's attack of gout got worse before it got better, and the whole household couldn't fail to be aware of it. Morag was well used to these fractious times when no-one dared say a word out of place to the man, and even Doctor Glenn, taking a look at Annie's ankle as well while he was at the house, remarked with dry humour that he had few patients as *im*patient as this one!

'I wonder you're not tempted to take up the Mackintys' offer of house and board to tutor the bairn,' he commented. ''Twas always a more peaceful house than this one!'

'What's that you're saying, man?' Dougal's roaring voice came from the top landing where he hobbled now with the aid of a walking stick before making his painful way downstairs. 'Are you suggesting my niece lives under the Mackintys' roof? 'Twas bad enough when she was obliged to stay there while her ankle healed, but any further contact will be over my dead body!'

Annie's temper exploded. Kin or not, beholden to him or not, he was pig-headed and stubborn and she'd had enough of him.

'You can hardly say that, Uncle, when between you and Stewart Mackinty and your drinking bout, you agreed to my going there daily to help Kirsty!'

'And now I forbid it!' Dougal bellowed.

She leapt to her feet from the sofa where the doctor had finished tending her ankle and pronouncing it well enough.

'You can't forbid me to see whom I like,' she said, her eyes blazing. 'I told you that when I came here. I'm not your puppet to dance on your string, Uncle, and I must be free to live my own life –'

'Aye, you've a wayward streak in you, just like your father! Well, if that's your attitude, lassie, then you can live it elsewhere and be damned to you –'

Morag gasped as he coughed and spluttered in his fury, clumping down the stairs and into the room more like a harridan than the dignified landowner of Blairfinnan.

'Dougal, think what you're saying! Blairfainnan is Annie's home, and she has every right to be here –'

'Not if she refuses to obey my rules,' he said dogmatically. 'I'm still the laird here, and I still have the last word on who I invite here.'

'*Invite*?' Annie said, her voice unnaturally shrill and upset. 'I wasn't aware that I was exactly invited. It seemed more like a royal command to me, and with the sly intention of pushing your son and myself together. I was the poor relation who was apparently acceptable enough for Rob to marry because of the family connection, but not good enough to be allowed sufficient rein to be her own person.'

'Oh aye. I see your learning has served you well, Miss. Learning that I paid for, I'd remind you, and now I'm having it thrown back at me, am I? And whatever that high-falutin' expression means, you'll do as I say while you're under my roof, do you hear?'

He sat down heavily on a hard chair now, the leg with the heavily bandaged foot sprawled out in front of him. Annie was briefly sorry for the pain he obviously suffered, but less than sorry for the stand she was obliged to make now.

'Then there's only one alternative for me, isn't there?' she said, visibly shaking, but refusing to let this fierce old man break her. 'I shall pack my things and leave at once.'

'No Annie! Please, my dear, don't be foolish –' Morag cried out in distress. Annie turned to her and gave a quick shake of the head.

'Aunt Morag, I'm sorry, but it's impossible for me to stay and cause so much ill-feeling,' she said, her voice muffled and her throat tight with tears. 'I'm sorry –'

She turned away before she humiliated herself and showed how much she cared about this decision. In the short time she had been in the Highlands, she had grown to love Blairfinnan and the sense of ancestry she felt here. She had absorbed its atmosphere, breathed its history, consciously and unconsciously gloried in walking the paths her father had walked, reading the books he had read, tracing the relentless yet sometimes poignant feud the Stalwart Blairs shared with the Mackintys. Insidously, almost without her realising it, Blairfinnan had become home, and she was deliberately turning her back on it.

She heard Doctor Glenn's voice calling after her.

'I'll be happy to wait for you, Miss Blair, and take you wherever you wish to go.'

'So you're a traitor as well now then?' Dougal's voice followed his.

'Not at all man, just realistic, and I'm taking no part in

this feudal nonsense between neighbours. I'm thinking
more to your niece's comfort –'

The voices receded as Annie reached her own room,
went inside and slammed the door shut. She leaned
against it, her head against the wood, her eyes tight
shut. How had this all happened so quickly, and with
so little provocation?

She had always expected her uncle to be volatile – long
ago her father had warned her of that trait in his family,
and the constant arguments between them all had been
one of the things that had driven him south – but she had
never expected to be virtually thrown out of the house
because she had a mind of her own and wasn't afraid to
use it!

Her throat thickened again as her eyes slowly opened
and she looked around the room that was now essen-
tially her own. If she was never to see it again, it was
her own doing. She only had to say the word and all of
this would be wiped out but for the memory. For all his
temper, there was a rarely-seen soft spot inside Dougal
Blair, and it was only a woman who could wheedle her
way around him, as she'd seen Morag do.

But this time he had gone too far. And Annie
considered she was made of sterner stuff than her
Aunt Morag! Besides, she had done nothing wrong as
far as she could see. The distress, and the rapid beating
of her heart were gradually lessening, and resentment
was taking over again. She couldn't let him win. She
must leave Blairfinnan.

She began ramming clothes into her travelling bags,
uncaring of their state, knowing they would be a hotch-
potch of creases by the time she reached. . .

Her hands stopped their work. She had no idea
where she would go. She thought wildly, trying to get
her thoughts in order now. There was Trina Moray
somewhere in Earnlie, who would presumably give

her hospitality for as long as she needed it, but Trina's mother was an old gossip, and the story would soon be around the village that Dougal Blair had thrown his niece out, and she would have to see those curious faces every time she left the house. And her every discussion in the Moray household would undoubtedly be ferried back to Aunt Morag.

There was Rob in Edinburgh . . . she dismissed that idea as soon as she thought it, since fleeing to Rob would make Dougal think she was playing right into his hands and his nuptial plans for the two of them. So that left only one place. . .

A brief knock on her door made her start, and seconds later Morag came into the room, her face flushed and upset, more so when she saw what Annie was doing.

'Oh my dear, please reconsider. You know he doesn't mean half what he says, and he'll be distraught to-morrow. He's so very fond of you, Annie –'

'He has an odd way of showing it then!' she said, choked.

Morag smiled wryly. 'Aye, he has an odd way of going about most things, but he's genuine in his love for this house and this family, and you must believe that, if you believe nothing else.'

'I do believe it. If it wasn't for his obsession, I suspect the feud with the Mackintys would have been over years ago. He's the one keeping it alive, isn't he, Aunt Morag? The others would be willing to let it go. I'm right, aren't I?'

She nodded sadly. 'I fear so. But what you're doing now will do no good, Annie. It'll not help the cause.'

'The cause! That's a poor name for it, Aunt. I would have thought the people here were sensible enough to forget lost causes after what happened a hundred years ago. Don't you see, it's no good to dwell in the past?'

'Aye, I see it, but Dougal does not. And I have a duty to be loyal to my man, Annie.'

She stood awkwardly, a round, dignified little figure, her fluffy head all at odds with her worry, clearly torn who ways. Annie ran to her and put her arms around her.

'It won't be for ever, Aunt Morag. Nothing ever is, and I'll only be a short distance away.'

'You're going to him then?'

Annie swallowed. 'I'm going to be a tutor for Kirsty, which is what I promised – and you can't deny that my uncle virtually promised the same.'

'He was coerced into it –'

'I think when it comes to coercion the Blairs and Mackintys run a close contest,' Annie said.

Morag said nothing for a moment and then she spoke abruptly. 'I'll send Maisie to help you pack, Annie. And it goes without saying that my love goes with you.'

Maisie was round-eyed and talkative when she came to the bedroom, but Annie simply refused to answer any of her questions, or give her an inkling as to where she was going. It hardly mattered, of course. Once Maisie's sister Nettie caught sight of her at Craggan, the whole story would be passed from household to household, and it would be all over Earnlie in a matter of days anyway.

Once she was ready she walked stiffly downstairs, followed by Maisie, struggling with the bags. If she had expected to be greeted with more verbal abuse, or even a gruff good-bye, she was wrong. The only person waiting for her was Doctor Glenn.

'I advised my patient to rest,' he said, before she could speak. 'And you and I will take a pleasant ride together, my dear. The day's a perfect one, and it's a pity to waste it indoors. Have you seen the blossom on the trees this year?'

He was being very kind, covering the moments of saying good-bye to this house, and ushering her into his calling trap as graciously as if she was an honoured personage. The lump in Annie's throat wouldn't go away, but as the wheels of the vehicle began to turn, she refused to look back. It was something her father had never done. One of his favourite sayings was that you could never go back and expect to find everything the same, so perhaps it was best never to try. He'd turned his back on his past and Blairfinnan and it had been Annie's lot to come here instead. At that precise moment, she wished she never had.

Doctor Glenn's calm voice came into her consciousness.

I take it we're going to Craggan, my dear? There are people there who will welcome you, and the bairn will be overjoyed at your decision.'

'Yes. There seems nowhere else for me.'

She felt weary beyond belief after the strain of the past hour. She had the extraordinary sensation that she had been running a very long way for a very long time, and now her final destination awaited her. Whether she wanted it or not, it was inevitable that she went there. To Craggan. And to Stewart Mackinty. The brief thought that she could still change her mind and find lodgings in Earnlie, or aywhere else in the world, simply died. Somehow it all came back to Craggan.

And anyway, Kirsty needed her. She clung to that fact, and wouldn't let herself think about whether Stewart Mackinty needed her or not. Or why.

Mrs Innes opened the door to her, and gaped in astonishment as she saw the doctor carrying the travelling bags.

'Why Miss, we didn't expect you until this afternoon.'

Annie looked back just as blankly for a minute, and then remembered she was due to come here for a couple of hours anyway.

'There's been a change of plan,' she said. 'Is Mr Mackinty at home?' She didn't differentiate between Stewart and his father, feeling suddenly embarrassed at arriving unannounced like this, and so obviously intending to stay!

'Neither of them is at home, and nor is the bairn. They've taken her off to Craggan's Best with them for the morning, as they sometimes do when she's fretful.'

Annie was more concerned with the child's spiritual welfare than her physical at that moment. She recognised her unintentional pun at the thought.

'They've not taken a child to a distillery?' she said indignantly. 'I would hardly think it's the proper place for her, Mrs Innes.'

She blushed, knowing she was censuring the actions of the Mackinty men, when she had no right to do so and it was none of her business what they did. Mrs Innes shrugged her ample shoulders, evidently thinking the same.

'Och, dearie, men have minds of their own, and since the bairn's in their charge, 'tis not for others to question them. But come you inside at once, and the good doctor too. You'll be taking a dram before you leave?' she enquired.

It was clearly Mrs Innes' way to offer a dram whenever the chance arose, ostensibly to promote the goodwill of the house and of Craggan's Best, and also to partake a drop herself. . .

'Thank-you, no,' Doctor Glenn said. 'It's a wee bit early in the day for me to be indulging. As you'll see, Miss Blair has come to stay, instead of just for the afternoon, and I'm sure I can leave it to your capable

160

her comfortable until the menfolk arrive back.'

'Of course you can, and pleased I am to see you, Miss,' the woman said, her eyes filled with interest now, and already seeing past the doctor's words.

'Thank-you, Doctor,' Annie said, holding out her hand to him. It trembled just a little now, and he squeezed it comfortingly.

'I'll be calling on you in a few days' time, lassie. I like to keep an eye on Kirsty, and I'll report on any other matter that will interest you.'

'Thank-you,' she smiled at his elaborate way of saying he'd go to Blairfinnan first and see how the climate was there before coming to Craggan. Just as if there was any need for this subterfuge where Mrs Innes was concerned. Annie knew she'd be telling her what had happened soon enough anyway. There was no point in doing anything else.

By the time the Mackinty carriage rattled up to the front door, Annie had spread out her toiletries, hair brushes and combs on the dressing-table, hung up most of her clothes in the wall closet, and let Nettie take the rest downstairs to be steamed and ironed. Mrs Innes had listened with sympathetic ears to the whole story of how she came to be here, and Annie guessed that by now every other servant in the house knew it too.

She no longer cared. All she cared about now was the sudden shriek from below as Kirsty was informed that she was here and in her old bedroom, the sound of her small feet hurtling up the stairs, and the sight of her starry dark eyes as she burst into the room and straight into Annie's arms.

'I knew you'd come!' the child said exuberantly, more coherent in her excitement that Annie had ever heard her.

'Well, of course I came. I promised, didn't I? And nobody ever breaks promises, darling.'

'Can we read this – this –' the word deserted her. 'Can we read la-ter on?'

'Of course we can. We can do anything you like. I shall be here all the time now, Kirsty.'

The child's gaze went to the dressing-table and registered the signs of habitation. She clapped her small hands, and despite the trauma of the day, Annie hugged her again, her heart warmed by this obvious delight. Somebody definitely wanted her, and it was so good to feel wanted.

Above Kirsty's head she saw that Stewart had come into the room, and her heart leapt at the sight of him. He said nothing, merely looked at her impassively, and the facetious words she intended to say faded away. She spread her hands helplessly.

'There was nowhere else for me to go. Can I stay?'

She dared him to smile in triumph at that moment, and to her relief he did not. He spoke gravely.

'Where else would you go but here? Of course you can stay. Welcome home, Annie Blair.'

She flinched. They were the same words her uncle had said to her when she'd first seen Blairfinnan. They didn't sound right on Stewart's lips. Not yet, maybe not ever. This was only a temporary measure, she told herself, and wouldn't think of it as anything else.

'You're sure your father won't object to having a house-guest for a week or two?' she asked deliberately.

'My father wouldn't object to having you live here permanently. How many times do I have to tell you? Did your education stop at recognising the feelings between a man and a woman, Annie?'

'Please don't talk that way,' she said quickly. 'This is not the time or place, and if you had any sensitivity at all, you'd realise that this hasn't been an easy time for me. This has been a very harrowing day.'

The words sounded far too trite to describe the real feelings inside her. She had truly hated the row with her uncle, and the decision to leave Blairfinnan that had been as good as forced on her. She couldn't go back . . . and now she realised she couldn't feel entirely comfortable at being here. Much as she mocked the idea of a family feud with these people, now that she could think objectively about it, she knew guiltily she should have shown more respect for her uncle and his beliefs, and sided with her own family. She owed them her loyalty.

Her temples throbbed with the weight of it all. None of it was her doing, but she was right in the middle of it. Being here was no real solution. This wasn't her rightful place, and so far she still hadn't found where that was. She was barely eighteen years old, and still in mourning for her parents. She was not ready yet to be strong and to take on these aggressive people. More than ever she missed the loving counselling of her mother and father. Without them she was somehow lost.

Dinner that evening was somewhat embarrassing as far as Annie was concerned. The two Mackinty men were obviously trying to put her at her ease and trying hard not to show any feudal pleasure in her being here. In fact, they were trying much too hard, covering every topic but the one closest to them all, and finally Annie turned to Stewart's father in some exasperation.

'Mr Mackinty, I appreciate that you would prefer not to mention my uncle's name at this table, but can we please get things out in the open? I don't hold with bad feeling between neighbours, and I regret very much that my uncle's disposition forced me to come here like this.

However much I'm glad to be of service to Kirsty, I do feel disloyal to my own family, and I want you to know that. I'm not here to score over them, and I'm sorry to know that my action will be upsetting my Aunt Morag.'

She was forced to stop as her mouth trembled and her tongue began to run away with her.

'And I'd not upset the lady for the world,' Callum said mildly. 'She was always a gentle soul, and never the one for such a man as yon Dougal. But all that's past and done with now, and a matter that doesn't concern you, lass. But you're right. None of us can avoid mention of the others, and I'm sure my son and myself were only trying to spare your feelings and bid you welcome.'

'I know,' she replied, only half wondering what his vague references to her aunt were supposed to mean. 'And I'm grateful.'

'We're the grateful ones, Annie,' Stewart said abruptly. 'You do us a great service in coming her for Kirsty's sake, and we'll not forget it. You may have been indoctrinated into thinking there's no good in the Mackintys, but you'll discover otherwise.'

'I know it already,' she murmured. How could she think differently, when the two men gave such obvious care to the child?

'Kirsty will be wanting you to say good-night to her,' Stewart said, as if he could read her mind. 'She likes a tale before she goes to sleep if you've a mind to it.'

'Of course! I'll go now if you'll both excuse me –'

'You've eaten barely enough to feed a sparrow,' Callum protested. 'Though we don't serve up the meagre portions they provide at Blairfinnan, I daresay.'

Annie laughed, the sparkle back in her eyes now as she recognised his banter. At least while they could joke about themselves there was less to worry about, she thought.

'Not at all. I just don't feel hungry tonight, but I'll do justice to your excellent fare tomorrow, I promise.'

She was glad to escape from the dining-room which suddenly seemed far too cosy for the three of them. It was a large baronial room, with heavy oak furniture and groups of candelabra on the panelled walls. It could have been austere but for the family portraits, but to Annie the real intimacy of the room came from the three occupants seated at one end of the long refectory table. For all the world it represented a little cameo scene of a man, his son and his son's wife. She couldn't rid herself of the thought, and it was for this reason that she was glad to leave the men to their cigars at the end of the meal and go up to the nursery.

'Please don't disturb yourselves, one of the maids will show me the way,' she said quickly as they both began to rise.

Nettie pointed it out to her, openly envious of the lovely Miss Blair. Annie didn't need telling that she'd be agog to tell her sister how well Annie was fitting into the Mackinty household, and to find out all the interesting details from the other end as soon as possible.

'You should have been asleep a long time ago,' she chided Kirst gently, though the Mackintys dined early enough that it was still hardly twilight . . . the *gloaming*, she reminded herself.

'I wai-ted for you,' the child said. She looked so small in the big bed, her playthings on the bed and in the room all around her; a rag doll with a painted china face; a wooden Harlequin-dressed jumping jack on a string; a Noah's Ark full of carved wooden animals; a rocking-horse; paper cut-outs, and a magnificent dolls' house.

'Where did you get all these lovely things?' Annie exclaimed. In the week she had been incapacitated with her ankle, she had been confined to bed and hadn't found her way to the nursery. But this was a child's paradise. It surpassed anything Annie herself had had in the way of toys, though if she had to weigh up the advantage of superb toys or two loving parents, there was obviously no comparison. . .

'Gran-pa gave me this.' Kirsty held the doll lovingly.

'She's beautiful,' Annie said. 'Does she have a name?'

'Dolly,' Kisty said, looking at her with raised eyebrows.

'Oh, yes, how silly of me,' Annie said hastily, thinking that of course the men wouldn't have had the imagination to think of naming a doll! 'Did Granpa give you all of them?'

All these beautiful wooden toys seemed to Annie to have been made by a craftsman's hand. . .

'And Stew-art,' Kirsty said. 'Stew-art made them.'

Annie stared at her. If it were true, her respect for the man grew enormously. But surely it couldn't be true. Each one was a gem of precision work, and must have taken infinite patience. And she had already decided that patience wasn't a trait of these hot-headed Highlanders.

'Are you sure? I expect he asked someone very clever to make them for you, my love –'

'No! Stew-art made the toys. He did, he did!' she said loudly.

'All right, I believe you,' Annie said, laughing, still not sure whether she did or not, but not wanting to upset Kirsty on this first night.

'You wouldn't doubt the lassie's words, would you, Miss Blair?' Stewart said from the door of the nursery.

She looked up quickly, seeing how Kirsty immediately reached out her arms to be hugged. A sliver of something unexpected and ridiculous shot through Annie then. It was impossible and humiliating to be jealous of a child! She dismissed the sensation at once, refusing to believe it had ever entered her mind.

'Did you really make all these toys?' she asked, covering the moment with a show of interest.

'That I did. I'll show you the next thing in progress if you've a wish to see it in my workroom.'

'What is it?' Kirsty almost leapt from the bed in her excitement.

'It's a surprise for your birthday, my wee one,' he laughed at her. 'You're not to know about it until then.'

And no matter how she pouted and pretended to sulk, he wouldn't tell her. He sat on the opposite side of the bed from Annie, and listened while she told Kirsty the promised tale of The Three Bears, simplifying it considerably, and this time she had the poignant sensation of two people sitting with their child as Kirsty's eyelids gradually drooped and she became flushed with sleep.

'I think I'll have an early night,' Annie murmured when she stood up carefully from the bed.

'Wouldn't you like to see her birthday gift? It's best for you to see it while she's safely asleep and not trying to see into my workshop and spoil her surprise.'

She hesitated, following him out of the nursery and closing the door quietly behind her. Was this wise? she wondered. She already knew how vulnerable she was where he was concerned, and how determined he was to win her over. But was *any* of this wise? she asked herself recklessly. She was already in the lion's den, and she had only herself to blame if she was bitten.

'All right, just for a moment then,' she said. 'When is her birthday anyway?'

'Next week. She'll be five years old then, and we're to have a special tea with a cake, and it'll be all the better with you here to share it.'

They walked down the curving staircase and at the bottom Annie turned to face him.

'I'm not here for ever, Stewart. You do realise that, don't you? I don't know how long this situation will go on, but please don't take it that you've won some kind of victory.'

'You're here, aren't you? And I didn't have to carry you off to bring you here.'

She couldn't deny it. Just as long as he understood that she was still her own woman, and not his. . .

'So where is this workshop of yours?' she asked, brisk and impersonal.

He gave a low laugh. 'Oh Annie Blair, do you know that your eyes give you away every time?' he said softly.

'What do you mean?'

'Your eyes are as blue as the sky on a summer's day, lassie, but whenever your emotions are affected their colour deepens considerably. Right now they glow like jewels –'

'I assure you my emotions are not in the least affected!'

'And that's where I have the advantage of you. Dark-eyed folk are more able to keep secrets from other people,' he went on coolly as if she hadn't spoken.

'Really? And what does that say for you, I wonder? I've always thought the most honest and straightforward people are those who don't need to have secrets in their lives,' she said, sarcastic now.

'That's naive thinking, Annie. Everyone has secrets. I'll wager that even your honest and upright Rob has secrets in his Edinburgh hideout.'

They had reached the drawing-room now. There was no sign of Callum, who had obviously gone to bed or followed some pursuit of his own. There were just the two of them, caught up in this bantering repartee, which Annie realised she was beginning to enjoy. But she couldn't let his reference to Rob go unheeded.

'If he does, it's only because his work involves it,' she retorted. 'A lawyer's bound to honour the secrets of his clients. Everyone knows that.'

'And what of his own secrets?'

'You've known Rob longer than I have. And you must know he's not the type to be secretive –'

She stopped abruptly, the hot colour flooding her face as she remembered the one secret she and her cousin Rob shared. It was almost as if Stewart Mackinty knew of the document they had each signed. Knew, or guessed . . . she looked at him suspiciously.

'I thought you were getting to know him very well,' he said lightly, opening the drawing-room doors to the garden and waiting for her to go outside ahead of him. 'That is, if marriage really is on the cards for the two of you?'

'Is there any reason why it shouldn't be?'

'I think you know that there is.'

His hand was beneath her elbow now, steering her through the gardens to a walled passageway at the side of the house. She didn't answer, wondering what she was doing in letting her take her outside like this. Wondering just where they were going, and if there really was a workshop at the end of it. Or was she being as foolishly naive in believing him as he had just said she was?

'Just where are you taking me?' she said tightly, as the walls seemed to close in on her for a moment in the tangled darkness of overgrown weeds.

Wild thoughts seemed to be filling her mind. She remembered the old gothic tales of the wicked villain leading the innocent maiden to his lair, there to be locked away in an isolated hideaway where only he had the key . . . she remembered the historical tales of this very landscape, told by her father, of the safe houses that had hidden Charles Stewart in secret rooms from the English oppressors who had hunted him down like a dog. . .

'We're nearly there,' Stewart said, and the mind-mist cleared somewhat as she saw the far end of the passageway. There was a wooden door of a small building at the side of the main house there. Though her nerves settled only a little . . . she could still be lured into some secret room and never heard of again. . .

'Are you all right, Annie? Is your ankle troubling you?' Stewart said as she faltered.

'I'm fine,' she said, angry at herself now. Hadn't she seen the evidence of a man's craftsmanship in the nursery at Craggan? Hadn't Kirsty herself said that Stewart had fashioned those exquisite toys for her? Annie realised she was becoming mistrustful of everyone and everything, and it was a miserable way to go through life.

She stood silently while Stewart unlocked the door and went inside first. She followed half-reluctantly and waited in the gloom while he lit a lamp. The pungent smell of oil swam in Annie's senses as she looked around the workshop and gaped.

'Well?' Stewart said. 'Is it what you expected?'

His voice was dry, and she knew at once that he'd realised why she'd been so hesitant. She moved closer to the workbench where a nearly-finished doll's cradle, beautifully carved and inscribed with Kirsty's name, was awaiting its final polish. She pushed it slightly and it swung gently to and fro, perfectly proportioned. Kirsty would love it. Ten years ago Annie herself would have loved it, if only she had known anyone able to fashion such a thing from raw pieces of wood.

'It's beautiful, Stewart,' she said sincerely. 'And Dolly wil fit into it perfectly.'

He began to laugh. 'I'm glad you accept the bairn's name for the doll and don't try to force her into some fancy English name for it –'

'I would never do that!' Annie said indignantly.

'Good. You'll not need telling that Kirsty needs stability in her life, Annie. And if the gods are with us, you'll be helping to provide it.'

She was about to retort that if this was some cheap ploy to persuade her to stay indefinitely at Craggan, it was just what she might have expected from him. But something in his manner stopped her.

Apart from his voice, which was too serious to be called mocking any more, there was something about the way he ran his hands over the smooth wood of the doll's cradle with its delicate and intricate carving at head and base. Something tender and almost far-seeing in the way he assessed his handiwork with a justly proud yet critical look.

For a moment Annie allowed her imagination to roam. This doll's cradle had been made with love, and was a piece of work that would be handed down for generations. Perhaps it would even be an heirloom that in time would be enjoyed by Kirsty's children and generations of other Mackintys.

'Seeing ghosts, Annie?' he said softly, seeing the way her eyes had softened. She felt the heat in her cheeks.

'Perhaps I am. Ghosts of the future,' she said, without explaining. And finding that she didn't need to, because Stewart merely nodded in agreement.

'It's time we went back to the house,' he said, with no attempt to make the most of these secluded moments. It was a relief . . . and yet, and yet . . . long into that first night in her old room at Craggan Annie remembered the way those sensitive fingers had caressed the wood of the doll's cradle. And dreamed that they were caressing her. . .

Chapter 10

The birthday was a complete success. The day was warm and bright enough for the tea to be taken out of doors, and Dolly was installed in the cradle with enormous ceremony. By then, Annie had been to Earnlie village and bought some small gifts for Kirsty herself. There were ribbons for her hair and some pieces of pretty fabric from the haberdashers which she sewed into a quilted coverlet and pillow for the cradle, and begged some pieces of old sheet from Mrs Innes to cut up and sew into a mattress-shaped bag.

'You can't have a cradle without bed linen for its occupant,' she told Stewart when he saw how diligent she had been. Yet until that moment she hadn't realised how unwittingly it also formed another link with him. The cradle without the bedding was incomplete. The bedding alone meant nothing. They needed one another, complemented one another. . .

'So this is the sewing you insisted you had retire early to attend to,' he commented.

'That's right, so you see why I didn't want to tell you about it until it was finished,' she said.

Though he must surely guess that it wasn't the only reason why she left the dining-room soon after dinner each evening. She continued to feel the intimacy in the household. Callum was used to retiring early, which left Annie and Stewart altogether too cosy for her peace of mind. She could indulge in her dreams, of course, pretending that they were a normal loving couple with their child upstairs asleep . . . but those were dangerous dreams, and ones that she dare not allow. The sewing had given her a perfect excuse to retire to her room, but now it was done. And Stewart knew it.

'So what will you be sewing next to keep you away from an evening stroll in the garden with me?' he said, as Kirsty prattled on with quite amazing speed to her Granpa at the new toys she'd been given that day.

'There are always things for a young lady to sew,' she said. 'Things for her wedding chest for instance.'

As soon as she said it she knew that was a mistake. His eyes narrowed against the brightness of the sun.

'Marry me and you'll not be needing any trappings,' he said, so softly she wondered if she'd really heard it. 'I daresay your cousin would be wanting his bride decked out in silks and velvets for a life in Edinburgh, but that's not for you. It's not necessary here, my lassie, and you're more suited to the country than to the city.'

'I'm not sure if that's meant to be a compliment or not,' she said suspiciously, remembering the rusticated and easy-going folk on the Devon farm where she'd grown up, the ruddy-faced men and apple-cheeked women, weathered by long hours outdoors in all the changing seasons.

'Everything I say to you is a compliment,' Stewart said. He was prevented from saying more by Kirsty flinging herself at him and telling him in a series of short

173

and erratic sentences to come and see Dolly sleeping in the new cradle, all tucked up in her new pink and blue coverlet.

'We 've stayed outside the circle too long,' Stewart said reluctantly, but smilingly allowing himself now to be dragged over to the plaid blanket where his father and Kirsty, Mrs Innes and the doctor who's called on this special day, were all slightly out of breath at being coerced into playing Kirsty's games.

As Annie and Stewart joined them, she caught a certain look between him and his father, and knew how insidiously she was being drawn into this family. Trina Moray had said as much.

When Trina had seen her at Earnlie kirk alongside Stewart in the Mackinty pew, with the Blairs on the other side of the aisle, she hadn't been able to believe her eyes. Dougal had kept his black frowning gaze firmly fixed ahead all through the service, while Morag had blown a surreptitious kiss to her niece as they entered and left. Apart from that there had been no communication between any of them afterwards.

When Annie was in Earnlie to purchase the material and ribbons for Kirsty's birthday, she had called on Trina and told her that had happened.

'You can visit me at Craggan any time you like,' she said, anxious to have this girl's approval of her action. 'The Mackintys make any guest welcome, and Stewart's father is so nice and friendly.'

'And what about the son?' Trina said. 'Is he nice and friendly too?'

'He's just – Stewart,' Annie said after a moment. 'You've known him longer than I have, so I hardly need to tell you –'

'But he's never paid court to me or any other lassie that I know of,' Trina went on. 'And you can hardly deny that he's pursuing you, Annie. He took a risk

174

going to your aunt's costume ball, and it wasn't for the sake of scoring over your uncle.'

'I wish you hadn't mentioned that old feud. Life is so peaceful at Craggan I can almost forget it,' Annie said slowly.

Almost . . . but not quite. But for the feud, none of the argument with her uncle would have started. But for the feud, perhaps she wouldn't have been welcomed quite so readily at Craggan. There was no way of knowing. It was easier to try and pretend it didn't exist at all. Only if she did that, she would fall into the Mackinty's determined trap of taming a Blair lassie . . . she ran her hand over her forehead and found it damp. The day was hot, and the Moray house was smaller and not so airy as either Craggan or Blairfinnan.

'Poor Annie,' Trina said, with a hint of sarcasm in her voice. 'It must be so troublesome to have a handsome young man lusting after you.'

'He is not *lusting* over me, and you'd do well not to let your mother or the minister hear you use such a word,' she said crossly, knowing that he probably *was*, and trying to ignore the undoubted little thrill the words gave her. Love or lust . . . in Stewart Mackinty's arms the one would merge into the other as far as Annie was concerned. . .

'Anyway, are you going to visit me at Craggan or not?' she repeated, thinking that this friendship was in danger of disintegrating if it wasn't sufficiently nurtured.

Trina gave her a quick hug, and the awkward little moment passed. 'Of course I am! I've never been inside Craggan, anyway, so it will be a good chance for me to brag about it afterwards! And that's not the only reason I shall call on you, goose, so don't get that huffy look on your face again.'

'I don't have a huffy look –'

'Oh yes you do! I wonder any man wants to get anywhere near you when you look so haughty, but you're so pretty I suppose the one outweighs the other,' she sighed generously.

Annie laughed, her eyes wicked. 'Then I must remember my *huffy* look when Stewart starts getting *lust*,' she said.

'And if you've got any sense, you'll forget it,' Trina said dryly.

She remembered that conversation now when Kirsty was tucked up in bed after the birthday tea, with the doll's cradle as close to her side as she could get it. The grown-ups were having a lighter dinner than usual that evening, having indulged in too many sticky cakes in the afternoon. All the same, it was a fine baked salmon that Mrs Innes presented at the dining-table, with fresh root vegetables from the kitchen garden, and a summer pudding to follow, glistening with red fruits and a creamy custard sauce.

'And tonight, Annie and I are going to take a stroll in the garden to walk off all this food,' Stewart said determinedly.

'Oh, I thought I might go to bed early,' she said. 'I'm quite tired, and my ankle's not really up to walking far yet –'

'That ankle of yours is fine,' he said bluntly. 'I'm thinking it's getting to be a useful excuse, Annie, and you heard what Doctor Glenn said. The more you exercise it now, the better. So I'll not take no for an answer.'

'You'd best agree to it, Annie, my dear,' Callum said with a smile. 'When Stewart gets a notion in his head, there's no turning him away from it.'

Hadn't she already discovered that for herself!

'Not too long a walk then. I told you Catriona Moray is coming to see me tomorrow, and I'll want to be alert enough to show her the house. That is, if you've no objection, Mr Mackinty?'

She turned to him in some dismay, suddenly realising how proprietorial she had sounded. This was not her house, but she had certainly been treating it as such while she had been here.

'Of course I've no objection, lassie. This is your home for as long as you wish, and your friends are welcome.'

'Thank-you.'

Even though she only had one friend of any consequence, when before coming here she had had so many. She missed them all, she thought sadly, and all the halcyon days she had left behind.

She missed Aunt Morag too, and she wondered if she dared ask Trina to ask her Aunt to come and see her. Or if Morag would ever consider such a thing. As the days went on Annie was truly hating the thought of being ostracised from her own family and the way in which she'd left Blairfinnan, even though at the time it had seemed the only thing to do.

Her grasshopper thoughts leapt ahead. She wondered if her uncle had told Rob what had happened. If only Rob wasn't so far away in Edinburgh. Surely if he was here, he'd see the sense in her removal, and wouldn't condemn her for it.

'Do you want to fetch a shawl, Annie? It's cooler now, and you might need something around your shoulders.'

She started, hearing Stewart's voice. For a few minutes, she'd been so wrapped up in her own world she'd forgotten she was about to take a walk in the moonlight with Stewart Mackinty. Without thinking sensibly, she knew the only thing she would want around her shoulders would be his arm . . . her voice was husky.

177

'I don't think I'll need a shawl,' she said. 'We won't be out long enough to be chilled.'

She certainly didn't intend to be. But she was also beginning to realise she couldn't constantly snub Stewart in front of his father. After the hospitality Callum had shown her, it would be like throwing his welcome back in his face.

They strolled at a leisurely pace through the gardens and down to the loch. She allowed Stewart to tuck her arm in his, simply because it made her footsteps feel more secure in the wild grasses of the glen. The summer night was still and beautiful with the purple-clad mountains etched in silver moonlight as she so often saw them now. Familiarity with her surroundings might have made her complacent about the beauty of it, but somehow Annie knew it never would. She breathed in the sweet scents of foliage and flowers that mingled with the pure clean air of the Higlands, and felt the peace of it all wrap around her like a warm and comforting blanket.

'Are you happy, Annie Blair?' Stewart said quietly

She hesitated, but she knew she couldn't be flippant if she tried. The night was too beautiful, the man at her side was too dear, and she was too honest

'At this moment I'm completely happy,' she said slowly. 'There are things in my life I regret, but since there's no changing them I'm putting them out of my mind for the present.'

'That's the first sensible thing you've said for a long while,' he commented.

'Is it?' she turned her face to his. 'But it doesn't mean I don't forget why I'm here, nor the unhappiness I've caused in my own family.'

'But you've been the cause of much happiness in mine,' he said, and before she could protest he had gathered her into his arms and his mouth was on hers, the kiss swiftly deepening into passion as he felt her response. For right now, here in the moonlight, with the man she loved wanting her, it was simply more than she could do to resist. Her arms held him close and she felt the beat of his heart against hers, and dear God forgive her, but she *wanted* him, rightly or wrongly. . .

'This mustn't happen,' she managed to say faintly a few minutes later, when his lips had moved a fraction away from hers.

'It was always meant to happen, my dearest one,' he said huskily. 'We both knew it the moment we set eyes on each other. Do you deny what you know is true?'

She swallowed, reason vying desperately with her own needs. What she knew was true was that hated boast of the Mackintys . . . what she could never forget was the fact that his need was undeniably physical, but not an emotional one . . . and she needed both from him. She needed his love as well as his lust. . .

'My uncle would never forgive me. Nor my aunt. For all her softness, she'd be loyel to him –' she said, her words stuttering as she tried to make the impossible choice between right and wrong.

Stewart's fingers had somehow reached the low-cut bodice of her gown. He caressed her throat, his palm moving gently downwards to the soft swell of her breasts, and wantonly she yearned for him to continue what he had begun.

She realised his fingers were suddenly still. She was holding her breath, wondering what he intended next, and if she had the strength or the will to resist wherever this night was leading her. . .

'You'll not know that your Aunt Morag once had a very different kind of loyalty, my lassie. Though I doubt you would ever have heard of it. They'd never have divulged it to you.'

The mood was instantly broken, and Annie brushed his fingers away from her bodice with a hand that shook. She stepped back slightly, looking up at this aggressively handsome man, his eyes darkly glittering in the light from the moon. Her heart turned over with love for him, but this was not the moment . . . and there was obviously something else here to know.

'Stop talking in riddles and tell me about this loyalty that doesn't apply to my uncle!' she demanded. 'I'm tired of all these secrets. First Miranda and James, and then our two grandfathers, and now you hint at something about my Aunt Morag! I know perfectly well that she wasn't born a Stalwart Blair, and only became so when she married my uncle, so what dark secret could she possibly have that concerns you and yours?'

She had folded her arms, and now he did the same. Seconds ago they had been almost lovers. Now they were opponents, she thought fleetingly, each with their implacable arms shielding their bodies from an aggressor as surely as if they did battle.

'You'd better come and see for yourself,' he said abruptly, releasing his arms and holding out a hand to her.

'See what? Why don't you just tell me?'

'Because you wouldn't believe me. You mistrust everything I say to you, so therefore I must show you the proof.'

Annie refused to take the proffered hand.

'I won't move from this spot until you tell me what this is all about. You'll show me the proof of what?'

The remnants of the gloaming were fading fast but she could still see the gleam in his eyes where they were lit by moonlight. And she could still see the expression on his face, guarded, defensive, determined. He spoke tersely.

'The proof that your Aunt Morag belonged to my father long before she ever wed your uncle.'

Annie gasped. Whatever she had expected to hear, it was never this!

'I don't believe you! You're mad to suggest it. And even if it were true – which it can't be – do you think Uncle Dougal wouldn't have crowed about marrying a woman who'd once belonged to his enemy? And just what does that imply, may I ask? My aunt's an honourable woman, and I won't listen to you demeaning her –'

'Will you calm down, lassie?' He grabbed her arms and tried to still her rising temper. 'Do you not remember how the voice carries across this water? Would you have any Blair eavesdroppers listening in on our discussion?'

'You'd hate that, wouldn't you? You'd be condemned then for the liar you are!'

She gasped again as he raised his hand as if he'd strike her. She flinched back a step, and he pulled her back in his arms at once.

'The Lord forgive me, but I almost did something I'd have regretted for the rest of my days just then,' he said, but she realised his voice was more angry than abject.

'I didn't think even a Mackinty would stoop to striking a woman,' she said in a muffled voice against his chest.

'Nor would he,' he said doggedly. 'But there are times when you sorely drive me near to it, woman. Now you'll come with me with no more arguing, and you'll mebbe understand a bit more of what binds us together.'

He strode too fast for her, and she made no attempt to keep up, pulling him back even as he pulled her towards to the house. It must be a ludicrous sight, she thought, her mind's eye seeing the ridiculous, even while she was so angry with him. The two of them were pulling against

181

each other the way two dogs fought over a bone, with neither willing to give way.

'Can we please do this in a more civilised manner?' she said at length, when she had given up pulling, but realised she couldn't possibly keep up with his long strides. 'I'll come with you to see this so-called proof of something that can't possibly be of any consequence in my life – if you'll only slow down and allow me to stop risking my ankle all over again.'

He stopped at once and she cannoned into him.

'Thank-you,' she said with quiet dignity, straightening her dishevelled hair with shaking hands and smoothing down the cool silk of the gown she'd worn on this special day. The birthday tea seemed a very long while ago now, and she had no idea where Stewart was taking her.

They went inside the house and along one of the passages where she knew his father had his library and Stewart his study where all the Craggan's Best accounts were gone over meticulously each week. She had already discovered during her time here that he was no idle landowner, but closely involved in all that went on at the distillery, and attended to the business side of it himself with the aid of an astute lawyer permanently attached to the firm. But this part of Craggan where he was taking her now, concerned men's business only, and this was strictly adhered to by the female occupants of the house.

Annie assumed he would be taking her into the library now, perhaps to show her some record or other that might prove a slight connection between Aunt Morag and his father. She simply couldn't believe it could be anything significant at all. But the Mackintys must have similar family records to the Blairs, she thought, with a flicker of interest. It would be interesting to see the other side of it through Mackinty eyes.

'Down here,' Stewart said.

She gaped now at the large studded door he was opening with an ornate key produced from behind a wall picture. He took a lamp from beside the picture frame and from is light Annie saw a flight of steps leading into blackness below the house.

'I'd rather not if you don't mind,' she said at once, her heart jumping with nerves. 'I don't like the look of it –'

'I'll be with you, and there's nothing to be afraid of. This is the Craggan vault, where all our records are kept and where I'll show you the proof I mentioned. I promise we'll be back in the drawing-room in less than an hour and drinking hot chocolate. Does that satisfy you?'

She looked at him, and then at the blackness below. She had hated the dark as a child, and she would never go into darkness voluntarily, even now.

'Not unless you let someone know where we're going,' she said. 'It's not that I don't trust you –' she saw him give a slight smile – 'it's just an irrational fear of darkness. Please, Stewart.'

'If I must,' he said without expression. 'You wait here while I give Mrs Innes the duplicate key. We can open the door here and the one below from the inside, but if we're not out of the vault in an hour she has permission to open it from the passage and come to find us. Is that agreed?'

'As long as I come with you now.'

Did he think she was stupid, to leave her standing here while he apparently gave the duplicate key to the housekeeper? She followed him to the servants' quarters silently, and heard him do exactly as he said.

'Are you satisfied now, my doubting lassie?' he asked.

She nodded, still very unsettled about going into the depths of Craggan, but not wanting to show it.

A short while later she was absorbed in looking at old family portraits that were stored away, and learning that one of Stewart's ancestors had been a highly prized woodcarver.

'I daresay it's where I get my talent from, if talent it is,' he commented.

'Oh yes, I can't deny you that,' Annie said.

'But you deny me everything else. And especially what I want most of all,' he said dryly.

She spoke sharply. 'I thought you were supposed to be showing me some proof that my aunt had once meant something to your father.' She stopped, not having put the thought into words before. '*Is* that what you meant?'

'That's exactly what I meant, Annie.'

'I don't believe it,' she said flatly. 'Someone would surely have said something to me.'

'Why would they? Your aunt is hardly going to stir up old memories when it's no business of yours. And your uncle's hardly going to admit that he won his bride by a wager and nothing more when her heart was already given to somebody else. And I doubt that Rob knows anything of it. The knowledge only came to me by accident when the reins of the family business were handed over to me, and I saw the evidence with my own eyes.'

'What evidence?' Annie said scornfully. 'I warn you, Stewart, if this is all some trick to get me down here, it shames you. As for a wager, I know for a fact that my uncle never gambles except for very low stakes at a card game –'

'Mebbe not now, but things were different thirty years ago. The two of them were big gamblers then.'

'The two of them?' Annie stared.

'Aye. Your uncle and my father. And when they gambled for the highest stakes, it was your uncle who won. But it was a long time before the wager brought him happiness, though the pair of them seem content enough now. It's a fact that he'll never look my father in the eye over it though, even now.'

'So you're saying that they both wanted to marry Aunt Morag, is that it? And she was willing to be the stake in a wager between the two of them? You don't know my Aunt Morag!'

'Neither do you – not the Morag she was then. According to my father, she was a frivolous lassie and thought it exciting to have two men wanting her, even though she was sure the one she really wanted would win. But all three agreed to abide by the rules, and well, you know the consequence.'

Annie stared at him, trying to equate the Aunt Morag she knew, comfortable and secure as mistress of Blairfinnan, if still a mite fluffy-headed, with a frivolous lassie willing to stake her future on the whim of two gambling men.

She shook her head firmly. 'I still don't believe it,' she said. And there was no-one else she could ask. Certainly not Morag herself. And no-one in the village. It wouldn't do. Besides, if anyone did remember it, it was thirty years ago . . . but she sensed that to the feudal minds of the two men concerned, it could still seem like only yesterday. . .

Stewart strode across the flagstone floor to where a large portrait on an easel was covered in a protective cloth. He pulled it away dramatically, and Annie stared at the loving couple seated on the circular bench beneath a tree that she recognised instantly in the garden of Craggan.

The girl sat on the bench with her hands demurely in her lap, while the handsome kilted man had one arm carelessly about her shoulders. There were no rings on the girl's fingers, but the intimate pose was instantly recognisable as that of an almost-betrothed couple . . . and the couple was just as easily recognisable.

'It's Aunt Morag and your father,' Annie whispered.

'Exactly. I don't know why he never got rid of the portrait. He married my mother soon afterwards, and they always seemed blissfully happy to me. I suspect that keeping the portrait is just a reminder, perhaps, of another Mackinty/Blair friendship that went sour.'

Annie's mouth was dry. The atmosphere in the vault was none too savoury, and she felt oddly light-headed. When they entered the vault, Stewart had pointed out the air vents in the ceiling, but the atmosphere was too cloying to be comfortable, and she felt suddenly stifled, and longed to be out of there.

'Can we go now? I've seen everything I want to see, and I can hardly doubt it now,' she said quickly.

'Of course,' he said at once. 'Mrs Innes will make us that hot chocolate as soon as we're upstairs –'

He was still speaking when he suddenly jolted against her. In normal circumstances she would have kept her balance, but she felt her weakened ankle give way again, and she was sent flying to the ground. She gave a loud cry, but the brief pain of that was nothing to the sudden terror in her heart as the lamp fell to the floor and she heard the glass smash. She heard Stewart's muttered oath as he stamped out the light, and then they were in total darkness.

'What's happening? Why did you do that?' she shrieked, clutching wildly all around her to try and get her bearings, and reaching nothing.

'Keep quite still,' she heard Stewart say. 'Don't move until I kick the glass from the lamp out of the way. I stamped it out to stop the risk of fire, or we could have suffocated.'

Her heart was beating so fast she was almost suffocating anyway. The feeling of claustrophobia was overwhelming and she was aware of the sound of her own sobbing as she felt Stewart's arms closing around her.

'It's all right, my darling. Walk carefully to the other side of the vault. The air vents will send down sufficient air to keep us breathing until somebody comes to let us out, and your eyes will get used to the gloom in a few minutes. See, there's a little light coming through the vents.'

She jerked her head upwards to see the pin-points of light from the grills above. It was pitifully little, and she still didn't know what had happened.

'Are we near the door?' she croaked, almost swooning with fright.

'I've tried it. It won't budge,' he said shortly.

'*What*? But how will we get out! We're trapped –' she said wildly.

'Not for long. They can push it in from the other side. It seems to be wedged tight here. I'm not sure what happened, but we've mebbe had a small earth tremor, and it's jammed the door from this side. All we can do is wait. At least someone knows we're here, so there's no need for alarm. It can't be a bad quake, because the ground beneath us still seems firm enough.'

Despite the terseness of his sentences, he was so calm, and she was so terrified. . .

'How can you be so unafraid when we're as good as buried alive?' she said, trembling uncontrollably.

He gave a short laugh, and held her tight in his arms.

'Because we'll be out of here in no time, you'll see. If it was an earthquake, it was only a mild one,' he reiterated, 'and nothing like the one some years ago.'

Annie shuddered. 'Don't they say there are after-quakes?' she said through dry lips. 'Aunt Morag told me so.'

And how would they be at Blairfinnan now, if what Stewart surmised was true? Her aunt would be hysterical, no matter how slight the quake, and needing her . . . so would Kirsty, she remembered. She tried to smother her own fear, trying not to let her imagination scatter her senses uncontrollably. But the very situation terrified her. The hated darkness, and the fear of what might yet happen . . . she would give the world to wake up and discover it had all been some terrible nightmare.

'You won't suffocate, Annie,' Stewart said over and over. 'Breathe normally and try not to panic, and remember I'm here with you. I'll not let anything happen to you.'

But there was unease in his voice, and she knew it. How could any man – even a powerful man like Stewart Mackinty – fight the elements of nature?

She hid her face in his chest, afraid she would start whimpering like a child at any minute, shaming herself, but finding the need for reassurance almost irresistible. She clung to him. She was barely able to take comfort from him, but she was desperately needing the touch of another hand, the beat of another heart close to hers to let her know she wasn't going through this ordeal alone. She was ashamed to know how quickly she had panicked, but she couldn't help it . . . and then she heard a different note in his voice.

'Annie, my lassie, since we're stuck here for a wee while, let's put a stop to all this fighting. You know as well as I do that it's well past time for us to begin the loving.'

He used quaint, old-fashioned phrases, yet to Annie they were oddly emotive. She must be dreaming, she thought, because his voice was no longer mocking, nor even overly seductive. It was . . . she tried hard to define it. He spoke the way a lover should speak, tender and passionate, conveying that same ache of

188

wanting that was inside herself whenever he was near her. Here in the darkness, she could hear every nuance in his voice, and it was telling her things she had never been aware of in the light.

'I can't think of anything but being afraid,' she mumbled. 'I'm afraid of dying, Stewart –'

She had never put it into words before, but she had experienced death too recently. First her mother, then her father. She knew the touch and the smell of death, and the fear was as irrational as it was real.

'Darling, nobody's going to die,' he said roughly. 'But if you fear it so much, would you choose to go to your Maker without ever knowing the sweet intimacies of a man and a woman?'

She felt his hand move slowly against her breast, and exquisite pleasure at his touch swept through her. Even in the midst of her fear, there was this. There was love – and even if love was only one-sided, there was the certain knowledge that Stewart wanted her. Everything about him told her so, from the way he breathed so raggedly, to the evidence of his own body, pressed so close to hers. She didn't even have to answer in words. She only had to surrender to what they both wanted so much. . .

She gave a soft sigh that was as near to acquiescence as she could manage, considering that her own heart was beating so fast. She lifted her face to his kiss and was inflamed by its passion. She felt his mouth leave hers and trail small kisses down her throat and to the softness of her breasts, and she couldn't stop it . . . she no longer had the will or the wish to stop it . . . she was Miranda all over again, bewitched by a Mackinty and succumbing so gladly and wantonly to her destiny. . .

'Stewart, you must know that I –' the words of love trembled on her lips, aching to be said. But they were never uttered.

189

Dimly, she heard the scrape of a key in a lock, and then the heavy vault door swung open, far too easily for it ever to have been jammed. And light flooded in to where Annie Blair was sittng on the flagstone floor in some disarray, in Stewart Mackinty's arms.

Annie's head jerked round at once, as all the implications poured into her brain as she saw Mrs Innes's astonished face.

'Why, whatever's happened? Did you break the lamp, Sir? I waited the hour as you said, and then came to open the door –'

'And is the ground quite steady beneath your feet, Mrs Innes?' Annie said angrily, as she scrambled to her feet, more humiliated and undignified than she had ever felt in her life before.

'Why yes, Miss. Why should it not be?' the woman said, mystified. She handed her lamp to Stewart and retreated quickly up the stairs, while Annie rounded on him at once.

'How could you?' she said in a choked voice. 'This was the meanest trick –'

'Aye, mebbe it was, but it was a trick that went astray,' he said, with no attempt at an apology. 'I never meant to knock you over, nor to send the lamp crashing. The suggestion of an earthquake was only a wee game to make you see how truly you belonged in my arms, Annie.'

'And of course the door was never jammed,' she said bitterly. 'What a fool you must think me. How many other games will you think up to try to seduce me, before you realise they're all doomed to failure?'

He caught at her arm, and felt the brittle tension in it. 'This was far more than a coarse seduction, lassie –'

'This was *nothing*,' she said, jerking her arm away from him. 'As far as I'm concerned the memory of what happened between us is wiped from my mind. I shall

190

just remember how devious you were, and how foolish I was ever to trust you.'

She turned away from him before he could see the brimming tears in her eyes, and moved towards the haven of the stairs. But her legs trembled, and her heart was filled with pain, for how could she ever forget how near she had come to belonging to him, body and soul? And how could she reconcile her anger to the aching, unfulfilled need inside her now?

Chapter 11

After two more weeks it was obvious to Annie that she could no longer be comfortable at Craggan. Ever since Stewart had staged what she called his mock earthquake, the tension between the two of them had become more tangible. She couldn't relax in his company and refused to be alone with him unless it was absolutely necessary. To her mortification, she knew her feelings towards him hadn't changed, and she wished desperately that they had. She was forced to accept the fact that she still loved him. His faults didn't lessen that love, they merely made him more vulnerable, more human, and not the paragon of strength he would appear to be.

'So have you decided what you're going to do?' Trina Moray said when she next came to call, still overawed by Craggan, but more familiar with it after several visits.

The two of them sat watching Kirsty at play with her toys on the lawn. Trina knew nothing of the real reason for Annie's restlessness, only the superficial one that she and Stewart were constantly at loggerheads, and that Annie was regretting her decision to go against her family's wishes.

'I just don't know yet -'

'You know you can always stay with us. Mother would be pleased to have you to stay, and you'd be like a sister to me. I've always had a fancy to have a sister, Annie.'

Annie's eyes misted over. The past days had been too uncomfortable for her to take too much kindness from anyone without becoming over-emotional.

'Thank-you for that. But I don't think Aunt Morag would forgive me if I did so, Trina.'

'Have you seen her at all, apart from at the kirk?'

Annie shook her head sadly. 'She'd never come here.'

And now she knew the reason why. She still thought it odd, and poignant too, that the young and impressionable Morag had been caught up in the Blair/Mackinty battle-field. How different her life might have been if she'd married Callum Mackinty. And if she had, Stewart wouldn't have existed . . . Annie's head ached with all the complicated relationships of these tangled families.

'Why don't you go back home?'

She started at Trina's voice, her mind a thousand miles away. Go back home? Trina obviously meant to Blairfinnan and not to Devon. But you could never go back . . . And yet, why not? Whose divine law had ever dictated such a thing? And who would gain or lose the most by her leaving here and going back to Blairfinnan? She knew that after the initial blustering her uncle would welcome her with open arms, sensing victory over the Mackintys. And Aunt Morag would be overjoyed . . . It wasn't what she wanted, but somehow she seemed destined to be the cause of new battles between them all, the catalyst to begin new antagonisms. . .

193

'Ann-ie, Dolly wants to go for a walk,' she heard Kirsty's flat little voice.

As she nodded to the child, she remembered there was another problem. But she couldn't let her entire life be ruled by some other woman's child, nor feel trapped by her needs into doing something alien to her.

'We'll all go for a walk down to the loch,' Annie said, scrambling to her feet from the soft grass and shaking the dust from her skirt. 'It will give us time to think.'

'Why do I suspect you've already done your thinking?' Trina said intuitively, and Annie gave a rueful laugh.

'Aye, mebbe I have,' she said in a fair imitation of Trina's own soft Scottish tones. And by the time they reached the cool still water of the loch, and across it, so near and yet so far, was Blairfinnan land, there was no longer any doubt in Annie's mind.

'But what of you and Geddes Cameron?' she said, remembering how close the two had been at the costume ball, and wanting to change this conversation.

Trina shrugged. 'Och, nothing came of it,' she said, which seemed to sum up both their lives at this moment.

Annie was prepared for Kirsty's wailings at her decision, but refused to be swayed by the sight of a small tearful face.

'I shan't be miles away. I've been here for weeks now, and my aunt and uncle are missing me. If you were away from your Granpa and Stewart for a long time, you'd want to see them again, wouldn't you?'

It was breakfasttime on the day after Trina's visit, and Callum and Stewart were at the dining-table. Kirsty looked at the two men. This was a surprise to them too, but if she expected Stewart to try and dissuade her, she was mistaken. Instead, he upheld her decision.

'Annie's right, pet. Her aunt and uncle will be feeling lonely without her. But she can visit you whenever she likes, and you'll see her at kirk on Sunday, and at the Games in August.'

Annie nodded quickly.

'Stewart's right. You'll hardly miss me, Kirsty!' She hoped the child wouldn't pick up on the word, since she'd made such a big fuss about her family missing her. But Kirsty was already thinking about something else.

'Will you watch me dance?' she said.

'Dance?' Annie asked.

'At the Games. The children always dance for their elders to the pipe band,' Callum put in. 'She'll want to perform for you, my dear, and I hope you'll join our party for that small part of the proceedings at least. 'Twould mean a lot to the bairn.'

'Of course I will,' Annie said swiftly, as her own treacherous tears threatened to come to the surface again. 'Now, if you'll excuse me, I'll put my things together. I know Kirsty's going out with you today, Mr Mackinty, so this would seem a good time –' she left the rest unsaid, but he nodded regretfully.

'Aye, though no time is a good time as far as I'm concerned. You're always welcome at my hearth, lassie.'

'Thank-you,' she muttered, leaving the remainder of her breakfast untouched. She couldn't think of eating anyway. All she wanted now as to get away, to be back safe at Blairfinnan . . . She could hardly bear to watch as Callum caught at Kirsty's hand and took her away from the dining-room with hearty talk of how they would spend their day together to distract the child's thoughts.

'I'll take you back,' Stewart said abruptly.

'There's no need. One of your lads can do it –'

'Don't be ridiculous. I shall see you're delivered safely off Craggan land, Annie. I never thought you the kind of a lassie to put safety so high in your thoughts. Do you intend to go through life never taking a risk?'

She flushed angrily at the implication that she was scared of her own shadow. 'I'd say I took a fair risk in coming to Scotland at all, and still more to living here. And I make my own decisions. I don't have them foisted on me.'

'Good. Remember that when your uncle starts trying to manipulate you into his order of things.'

'If that's an obscure reference to my intentions regarding my cousin Rob, then that's nobody's business but mine and his.'

'And mine,' he said darkly. 'But since you've made up your mind for the present, can we please move? I've business of my own this day, and hadn't intended spending part of it riding back and forth to Blairfinan.'

'I've already told you, there's no need -'

'And I've told you I'm taking you. So will you please stop blathering, woman, and do what you have to do?'

She wasn't sure whether he was just being argumentative or if his annoyance at her departure was making him extra aggressive. He would obviously see this as a score against him. The Blairs had won a victory against the Mackintys. He hadn't done what he intended and tamed her, or got her into his bed, by either fair means or foul . . . and her feelings were completely mixed about that. Wicked or not, there had been so many moments when all she yearned for was to be held in Stewart's arms, to forget all about convention and right or wrong, and let love carry them to the heights. . .

It was a silent ride to Blairfinnan. As yet, Annie had no idea of the reception she would get on her arrival, and she still thought it would have been far better for one of the Craggan stable-lads to bring her home. But there was no arguing with this implacable man beside her. As they finally neared the familiar house, she felt emotion thicken her throat, and she turned briefly to Stewart.

'You'll not let Kirsty slacken in her reading practice?' she said huskily. 'And her drawings – she's so good at them. You'll see to it, Stewart?'

'You've no need to remind me how to care for my own niece,' he said, in a voice so cold she wondered if she really had ever been held in his arms and kissed so passionately.

'I know that. But she's progressed so well, and I don't want her to fall back.'

He didn't answer and she looked away from his hard profile, unable to bear this hostility. Then she saw what he saw, the black-browed, stocky shape of her uncle striding out from the stables to face them, arms folded aggressively, eyes guarded.

'So what do we have here? Is this a unlikely social call or has my niece come to her senses at last?' he said, heavy with sarcasm.

'Uncle, I want to come back, if you'll have me,' Annie said quickly, before either man could begin a spate of insults that would lead nowhere.

She jumped down from the trap and ran to him. She couldn't tell whether or not his eyes softened imperceptibly at her anxious look. She wouldn't beg, and her chin was tilted high, but she couldn't stop the trembling of her mouth. He said nothing for a few moments, and then he gave a satisfied nod.

'And where else would you go when you've had your fill of the other side, lass? This is where you belong, and now you've had the good sense to see it, there'll be no repercussions.'

197

'I hope you mean that, Dougal Blair,' Stewart called out. 'Annie comes back out of loyalty to yourself, but I trust you'll not deny her the pleasure of joining me and mine at the Games. The bairn will be missing her.'

And what of you, Stewart Mackinty? Won't you be missing me too – just a little?

Annie swallowed, longing to ask the question she would never dare to put into words. Out of the corner of her eye she could see Maisie scuttling towards them and enquiring if the young lady's bags were to be taken into the house.

'That they are, miss, and you can put a warming-pan in Miss Annie's bed and tell your mistress to prepare a feast for tonight. And when we come into the house we'll have a hot toddy to celebrate her homecoming,' he added.

'Thank-you, but I'll not stay,' Stewart said pleasantly, just as though he'd been asked, but Annie knew that both men realised no invitation had been given, nor was likely to be.

She simply gave up on the pair of them and stalked towards the house after Maisie. From behind, her uncle's raucous words floated after her.

'It's as well the lass has regained her senses, man. We're to go to Edinburgh in a few days' time, and I was not anxious to go without her. 'Twill keep her out of mischief when she's under my eye, and she'll be anxious to see Rob again. The pair of them will soon be officially betrothed and that will be the end of any waywardness. She'll know which side of her bread is best buttered by now.'

Annie's footsteps faltered. She was sorely tempted to turn on her uncle and tell him in no uncertain terms that no such betrothal was likely to take place, now or ever. But she didn't do it. Let Stewart Mackinty think what he liked, and if he thought she was the type of woman to go from one man's arms to another, so be it. It wouldn't harm him at all to realise he wasn't the only eligible man in the world.

And then she stopped thinking of Stewart Mackinty altogether as she went inside the house and the comforting Blairfinnan walls closed around her. She was immediately clasped to Aunt Morag's ample bosom and welcomed by her cries of delight.

'My love, you've come home! How pleased I am to see you! And just in time to come with us to Edinburgh!'

'You really did intend to go there then? I heard Uncle Dougal mention it, but I thought he may have been teasing -'

'Oh aye, it's true enough! Your uncle thought it would stop me mithering on about you, Annie. We decided to go at the end of the week and surprise Rob. But now he'll be doubly surprised at seeing you, my lamb. He was sore put out to know you'd gone to stay at the Mackintys'.'

'Well, I'm not there any longer, and it will be good to see the city I've heard so much about,' she said, forcing some enthusiasm into her voice.

Annie was still hardly able to equate this comfortably round little woman with a *femme fatale* who'd once held two men's hearts in sway. But for her, there would have been no Stewart. If things had been different, there would have been no Rob. Annie decided there and then that neither Morag nor Rob must ever know that she was aware of the secret. It had already been shared by four people, she remembered, but she doubted very much that Rob himself knew anything of it.

But she slipped back into life at Blairfinnan with the ease of a well-fitting glove. To her surprise Dougal was less crowing than she had expected, and Morag confided the reason to her while they were sorting out the clothes they would need for their short stay in Edinburgh.

'He missed you badly, Annie. He's not a man for showing much emotion apart from anger, as you'll have noticed! But he's grown that fond of you, and he couldn't bear to think it was his fault that you'd taken the huff and gone off to Craggan of all places. You'd probably not know that 'twas partly his blathering that sent your father away, and he could see history repeating himself. Och, he admitted he was rare glad to see you back, especially when I reminded him forcibly of a few facts,' she added meaningly.

Annie wondered just how far Morag's reminders had gone, and if she'd dared to throw up the fact that but for Dougal Stalwart Blair's gambling she herself might have been Callum Mackinty's wife? Annie wondered briefly if she ever secretly regretted it, and knew there was no way she would ever know. Nor would she choose to. Some things were best kept eternally secret.

So three days later the three of them were seated in the Blairfinnan carriage with Siddons handling the horses, and on their way to Edinburgh. Already her weeks at Craggan seemed to be fading into the past, Annie thought. In her uncle's household they were never mentioned now. As far as Dougal was concerned it was as if they had never been.

The travelling would take all day, stopping for lunch and to water the horses at a wayside inn, and then continuing on their way. They would reach Edinburgh by sunset, and would have no trouble finding lodgings in an hotel near to Rob's quarters, as he had constantly assured them.

They jogged along in the carriage as the afternoon grew warmer and more sultry, the rumbling wheels on the tracks clearly sending Aunt Morag into a semi-somnolent state, while Dougal settled back to snore away the rest of the journey. Only Annie stayed wide awake, thinking that every turn of the wheels, like every beat of her heart, took her farther and farther away from the one place she really wanted to be.

Was she really so foolish not to take what was offered? Was she blind not to recognise that at least in the physical sense, Stewart wanted her with a man's needs? And perhaps emotional too, she admitted, remembering the times she had glimpsed more than just the urge for male domination in his pursuit of her.

She recalled something he'd once said to her. Her blue eyes revealed more than she wanted to show, while his darker ones hid his true feelings. But he couldn't hide the wild beating of his heart, matching hers whenever they were close. He couldn't hide the way his face lightened whenever she came into a room, nor the way he had paid no attention to any other woman on the night of her aunt's costume ball. To her knowledge, through the edict of her friend Trina Moray, he had rarely looked at another woman, despite the fact that they would all fall at his feet given half the chance. . .

So was it possible, even *remotely* possible, she thought tremulously, that she had been wrong about him all this time, and that he could actually feel something for her? Did all this attention mean that he loved her?

Even as the wildness of the thought filled her with joy, she dismissed it. If he loved her, why hadn't he told her so? And if he had, the irritating imp of reason queried, would you have believed him? Don't you prefer to disbelieve everything he says?

The carriage lurched perilously over a deep rut in the road and her uncle and aunt awoke simultaneously. Dougal released a string of mild expletives at the jolting, at which Aunt Morag tut-tutted once she had

201

re-arranged her bonnet and pretended she had been alert all the time.

'Begging your pardon about that, Sir,' Siddons called back. 'But we'll be nearing Edinburgh quite soon now, if the young lady cares to look ahead.'

He was always polite to Annie now, although she still couldn't quite forgive him for the way he'd betrayed her and Stewart. But she dutifully looked ahead to where the hazy sunshine and clear sky had given way to the deeper blue of the gloaming now. And soaring skywards, impressive and magnificent, were the battlements of a craggy castle on a high hill.

'That's Edinburgh Castle, Annie,' Aunt Morag said. 'They say that Castle Rock on which it's built was once the site of an Iron Age fort. You'll be interested in such things, no doubt.'

'Oh yes, of course!' she said. 'And in the city itself.'

Dougal snorted. 'Och, it's a hotch-potch of a place, all wynds and closes and courts, and no decent place for a lassie to be abroad of a night in some of the dark alleyways. The New Town's a better place than the old, with fine new buildings and the homes of writers and artists and engineers, I'm told. But there's been some dark history here over the years, and plague too, when one part of the city lost every inhabitant to the black death -'

'Dougal, you'll be frightening the lass if you go on so,' Morag chided him as he warmed to his tale.

'Aye, mebbe so, but since there's been no fear of plague now for more than two hundred years, you needn't get your dander up too much, woman.'

Annie was fully alert now, and intrigued by the sight of the city coming into view, etched in silhouette by the lengthening gloaming, but still visible enough to see its tall buildings, and the stout wall that ran around it like a fortress.

'And you'll have heard of the notorious Burke and Hare, no doubt,' Dougal went on.

'Oh yes,' said Annie, shivering as she remembered the tale of the body-snatchers her father had once told her.

'Dougal, she doesn't want to hear about such things, and neither do I,' Morag exclaimed as the carriage took them farther and farther into the city.

'Well, here's a softer tale to amuse her then,' he went on irascibly. 'Your English King George the Fourth came on a visit to the Palace of Holyrood House in 1822 and attended a ball. Fancying himself a wee bit, he attended in full Highland dress, but beneath it all he wore pink silk tights! What do you think of that for a sketch, eh?'

'I think you're making it all up, Uncle,' Annie said with a laugh.

'Not at all! You ask Rob if you don't believe me. 'Tis a well-known fact, lassie.'

Mention of Rob reminded him that they were almost at the part of the city where Rob had his quarters. He leaned forward to ask Siddons if he remembered the address.

'Oh aye, Sir, we'll be there in a short while now,' the man said. 'Will you be finding a hotel first?'

'Yes, I think so,' Morag said at once. 'I need to freshen myself up and change my travelling dress, I feel so stained. As soon as we see where Rob is quartered, we'll go to the nearby hotel and book our rooms. There's plenty time enough to call on him later this evening. It's early yet.'

'I hope he'll be at home,' Annie said suddenly. 'It would be awful if we've come all this way and he'd gone to the theatre or something.'

'Well, since we thought we'd surprise him with this visit, it's a chance we'll have to take,' Morag agreed.

They found the hotel easily enough, no more than a short walk away from Rob's quarters. Dougal dismissed Siddons for the night, after arranging for both the man and the horses to be given suitable accommodation. Annie looked around her. It was the first time she had ever stayed in an hotel, and she was finding the experience suddenly exciting. Who had slept here before, she wondered, eyeing the four-poster bed with its heavy drapes? A famous writer, perhaps? An artist? A politician? Or some *ingénue* like herself, visiting her cousin for the first time in the city? She laughed at her own thoughts, and splashed cooling water over her skin before she changed into fresh clothes and made herself presentable for visiting Rob.

She realised she was looking forward to seeing him again. They had an easy friendship now. They understood one other totally, and they each had the security of the documents they had signed. When the truth came out, as it eventually must, there would be no cries of betrayal on her part, no pining away on his.

She heard a tap on her door and Aunt Morag came into the room in answer to her call.

'I feel quite flustered in this splendid place,' she said to Annie. 'Rob never told us it would be so grand.'

Annie smiled at her with genuine affection. 'You need have no worries, Aunt Morag. You'd fit in anywhere. Though perhaps it's a pity you didn't bring your regal purple to wear at the dinner table!'

She said it teasingly, not expecting the words to send her instantly back to that night of the costume ball, when her aunt had been so magnificent, and Annie had worn her simple white, and had ended the evening in the arms of a dashing pirate. . .

'Your uncle's waiting for us, Annie,' she heard Aunt Morag say, and the images faded. 'It's just a short step as you saw, so we'll walk, of course. It's such a fine night for it.'

Dutifully, Annie gathered up her reticule and cape, and followed her aunt out of the room. Stewart Mackinty was miles away now, yet for the last few minutes his presence had been so real, so close, that she had had to force herself to remember where she was. She wondered fearfully if she was going mad. . .

'This city owes much of its fine architecture to Robert Adam, Annie,' Uncle Dougal informed her, with as much pride as if he was a personal confidante of the great architect. 'He designed the university which Rob attended, the north side of Charlotte Square, the Register house and so on. We'll be seeing some of those places tomorrow, if you've a mind to go sight-seeing.'

'Of course,' she said at once. She wanted to see something of the city. And besides, it would help to keep her mind off the one person who seemed to intrude into it when she least expected him to.

'We'll not spend hours walking around buildings though, Dougal,' Morag said. 'It's tiring at the best of times, and it's far too hot in late summer. The tenement buildings crowd in on me, and make me feel faint. You'll understand, Annie.'

Annie wasn't sure what she was meant to say, so she merely murmured her assent. It would seem a waste of a visit not to explore Edinburgh, but her aunt already seemed fatigued after the journey, and they must see how she fared tomorrow. Doubtless, the excitement of seeing Rob would soon raise her spirits.

'This is the place then,' Dougal said, stopping outside a tall crow-stepped house that seemed typical of many of the buildings here. He studied a plate outside the door, and spoke with renewed pride. 'Robert Stalwart Blair, Lawyer, Apartment 4.'

He pushed open the outer door and they began the climb up the central spiral staircase to the fourth floor. Morag was puffing by the time they reached it, and paused for breath, leaning against the handsome wrought iron banister. Dougal was already ringing the bell on the door inscribed with the elegant number 4.

After a few minutes it was opened, and Rob's astonished face looked at the three visitors on the landing.

'Mother – Father – and Annie too – what's happened –?'

Annie didn't know him well, but she had hardly expected this visit to disconcert him so much. He looked almost – she searched her mind for the right word – he looked *hunted*, that was it. It was so extraordinary a look to see on her normally composed cousin's face.

'Well, lad, are you going to ask us in, or do we stand looking at each other on the landing all night?' Dougal said heartily. 'Your mother's been looking forward to seeing you, and you might bid us welcome!'

'Of course you're welcome! I just wasn't expecting you, that's all.' He hesitated, and then opened the door wide. 'Come in, all of you. I've a friend here who you might remember from the night of the ball.'

From the reddening of his countenance and the slightly defiant way he said the last, Annie's feminine intuition told her the truth immediately. The friend was a female, and Rob was entertaining her alone in his rooms. It was enough to compromise any young lady. . .

'Perhaps we should come back tomorrow,' she murmured to her aunt, but it was too late. Dougal was already striding into the room, followed by Aunt Morag, and as Rob and Annie looked at one another, he gave

206

a little shrug of his shoulders and a desperate half-smile that told her everything.

'Oh!' Morag stopped short at the sight of the young woman seated on the sofa with a glass of wine in her hand.

She wore a gold-threaded gown of yellow silk, and some time previously she had kicked off her shoes, giving such an air of intimacy to the room that no-one could fail to notice it. Through an archway the visitors could see the remains of a meal still on the table, together with several empty bottles of wine.

The girl got to her feet with an easy grace, despite the stockinged feet, and smiled nervously.

'Mother, you will no doubt remember Miss Helen Fraser, who was one of my guests at your costume ball -'

'I remember her very well,' Morag began, though Helen had just been one face among many that night.

'What's the meaning of this little scene, Rob?' Dougal pushed past her and made no pretence at the niceties. He stood in front of his son aggressively. 'Are you in the habit of entertaining young women in your rooms? And what does the young woman's parents have to say about it, if indeed they know! Is this the way young lawyers behave in the city these days?'

Annie saw Helen blush a deep red, and felt very sorry for her. What of the times she and Stewart Mackinty had been alone together, she thought guiltily? What would her narrow-minded uncle make of that!

She saw Rob move quickly towards Helen, and draw her hand through his arm.

'Father, I'd ask you not to insult the lady who is to be my wife,' he said with stilted dignity.

Morag gasped, going white with shock and needing Rob to help her to a chair. But Annie noted that Helen showed no surprise at Rob's announcement, which seemed to prove that this was no impulse statement said to relieve the situation. It was genuine. She moved forward and caught at Helen's free hand.

'I'm very happy for you, Helen. Rob's fine man -'

'A fine man indeed!' Dougal found his voice and began to show his anger, taking no notice of Morag's attempt to shush him. 'He was to be the man for *you*, lassie. Have you forgotten that?'

Annie turned on him impatiently. 'I haven't forgotten that such an idea was all in your head, Uncle, and never in ours! Rob and I could never fulfil your plans for us, and we had the good sense to know it from the beginning. I'm sorry if that upsets your future plans, but people can't fall in love to order, and I can't think that you'd wish either of us to be pushed into a loveless marriage. I know Aunt Morag wouldn't!'

The oblique reference to their own circumstances was as far as she dared go. She wasn't meant to know anything of the way Morag had been won by a wager, and nor would she ever divulge it.

Whether her words had any effect she would never know, but after a moment Morag gave a slight nod towards her son and his lady, and her shaky smile embraced them both.

'If you're happy, then we're happy too, and it goes without saying that we welcome you into our family, my dear. Isn't that right, Dougal?'

They looked at him, wondering whether he would still bluster and object, and embarrass them all. His brows were drawn together as ever, but finally he nodded too.

'Aye, I can't deny that you look a well-matched pair,' he said grudgingly. 'So when's the wedding to be?'

'Oh, not for a while yet,' Helen said in her educated voice. 'My brother's abroad until next year, and I shall want to wait for him to return home. I couldn't possibly marry without him being there, and Rob agrees with that.'

'It's certainly to your credit to have such family feelings, lassie,' Dougal said, mollified.

'So, if we've settled all that, won't you please take some wine with us?' Rob said, throwing a more than relieved glance towards Annie.

And after Dougal had ascertained that Helen's brother was serving with a regiment in India, and that he sounded an extremely upright young man and of a suitable marrying age himself, Annie and Rob could hardly contain their laughter. To them at least, it was obvious that Dougal was match-making again, and was looking forward to meeting this young Fraser who would be escorting his niece at the kirk when the wedding of his son took place. He sounded a highly suitable young man. And who knew where such an association might lead?

'Meanwhile, we want to keep our plans private,' Rob was saying now. 'Helen's father's not too well at present and not up to any excitement. We don't intend an official engagement until Christmas, so I'd ask you all to respect that.'

'Of course we will,' Morag said, clearly enchanted at the thought of such a secret. 'But I hope we'll have the opportunity to meet your family while we're here, my dear?'

'Oh yes,' Helen said eagerly. 'I'll suggest that you all come to dinner at the house tomorrow evening -'

'And since I've no business to attend tomorrow, Helen and I will show you our city,' Rob put in. 'How does that suit?'

It was going to be a different visit from the one they had envisaged, Annie thought, but nonetheless enjoyable for all that. More so, in fact, because the prospect of herself and Rob as a couple could now be forgotten. She could rejoice in the sense of freedom from the pressure her uncle had put on her, and she had to admit that the recovered from his displeasure very well, and accepted the new situation.

But over the next few days, she found a new dimension creeping into her own feelings. The sight of Rob and Helen, so gloriously in love, and so eager to show the visitors 'their city', had the effect of making Annie unaccountably depressed. She was very happy for them, but it only emphasised her own position, especially as Dougal continued to make jocular remarks about Helen's brother Malcolm, whom Annie was sure to like.

She wished she dared tell him there was only one man in the world she could ever think of marrying. One man whom she already loved more than she thought it possible to love any man. She must do, she thought ruefully, after Stewart's attempt to seduce her in the vault at Craggan, and her furious discovery of no earthquake having occurred.

By their last night in Edinburgh, Annie was quite satiated with the manificence of the city and its treasures, its quaint wynds and closes, its ancient Palace of Holyrood House, its university and parks. She had met Helen's parents and younger sister, and seen the pleasure with which they accepted Rob as their future kinsman, and she envied their golden future with a fierce and quite unreasonable aching envy. She longed to be away from here now, and back to the normality of Blairfinnan. After a few days, the city had the effect of stifling her. As Stewart had said, she was a country lass, with country ways. . .

Chapter 12

'So we're to keep our exciting news to ourselves,' Morag said reluctantly when they were on their way back to Blairfinnan. 'It's such a pity. I'd dearly like to tell all my friends about Rob's plans. Every mother likes to brag about her son's approaching wedding –'

'But you mustn't do that, Aunt Morag,' Annie said, thinking Trina's mother was the very last person to keep anything to herself. 'We must all respect Rob and Helen's wishes, even though we may not see the need for it ourselves.'

'Aye, and you just remember that, Morag,' Dougal said keenly. 'You know how your tongue runs away with you at times.'

'And I'd remind you that I'm well able to keep it still when I've a mind to,' she said, just as tartly.

And knowing what she did, Annie kept her eyes ahead, not risking a glance at either one of them.

'Look back now, Annie,' Morag said suddenly. 'Did you ever see such a splendid sight?'

She turned obediently. They had travelled some distance away from Edinburgh by now, and the panorama behind them was of the great castle standing out in sharp relief to the rest of the city, as if all was subservient beneath it.

'Its truly wonderful,' she agreed. 'But for all that, I wouldn't choose to live there.'

She was almost surprised to realise it. Cities were so exciting, throbbing with a kind of energy the country didn't have, and yet there was a remoteness about it, an impersonal feeling that almost amounted to anonymity. In the country, everyone counted. Perhaps that was it. Annie couldn't exactly pin-point the feeling. She only knew that through that drowsily lovely day as they jogged along in the carriage, stopping for a mid-day meal as before, that the nearer the got to Blairfinnan, the more relaxed she felt.

It was more of a homecoming than on that first strange arrival from Devon, and in an odd way she had never felt so attuned to the ancestral home as she did today. In a way, she felt that today at last, she was finally able to shed the sadness of those last months of her old life, and was starting to feel as if she truly belonged. It was a feeling too emotional to share with anyone. . .

'We'll be seeing Rob again soon,' Aunt Morag was saying happily. 'He'll be home for the Earnlie Games in a couple of weeks' time, and he'll bring a party of friends with him, again.'

'The same friends who were here for the ball, I daresay,' Annie grinned, remembering how she had surmised then if one of the young ladies was Rob's special lady. And how he had asked what she thought of Helen Fraser . . . it had been little more than an idle question then, although she'd wondered at the time . . . but now, of course, the reason was crystal clear.

She thought it a good thing that Rob wasn't home too often. Otherwise, how could he bear not to mention Helen's name at every opportunity, since it was one of the things lovers wanted, needed, to do? But even if you couldn't speak of them you could think of them as constantly as you wished. Thoughts were your own and thank goodness it was so. . .

'Aye, Rob will be competing as usual,' Dougal said. 'He'll want to beat the Mackinty in the races this year.'

Stewart's name on Dougal's lips was so unexpected that Annie felt her heart jump.

'Did Stewart beat him last year then?' she said, wondering if she dare continue this conversation.

'He did, Annie,' Morag said. 'Whatever else you say about Stewart Mackinty, he's a fine athlete.'

Remembering the physique of the man, Annie never doubted that. He was not a brawny man in the cruder sense of the word, but he was powerfully built, with a strong muscular body and the strength to crush the lassie in his arms if he chose . . . she turned her thoughts away from Stewart's attributes with an effort and realised her uncle was still discussing him.

'Mackinty will have had more time to practise the running than Rob,' Dougal said sourly. 'I heard that some of the land at Craggan's Best has been given over to practice fields. They'll not go short in the awards.'

'Oh? And who have you been talking to about Craggan's Best?' Morag said, intrigued by this unusual reference.

'I don't recall now. It was probably just hearsay,' he said testily.

'I remember Kirsty telling me about the children dancing,' Annie said.

'Aye, that's right,' Morag said, her voice softening. 'And a pretty sight they look too, in their frilled white

213

blouses and clan sashes over their kilts. There's a platform erected specially for the dancing. The older ones compete for prizes, but the wee ones are all given a token at the end, and just dance for the pleasure of their mothers and fathers.'

And wee Kirsty had neither, Annie thought. . .

The next time she saw Stewart Mackinty, she exerienced a small shock. The Blairs turned up at Earnlie kirk for the Sunday morning service as usual, and the Mackintys were there before them. It was the habit for early arrivals to stand outside and chat on fine Sundays, before entering the kirk. And Stewart and his father were passing the time of day very amicably indeed with Catriona Moray and her mother.

'Annie!' Trina said, the moment she saw her. 'How lovely to see you all back. Did you have a wonderful time in Edinburgh? And how was Rob?'

'He was very well,' Annie said. 'And yes, we had a wonderful time. Rob showed us all around the city, which is very fine indeed. Do you know it at all?'

'I went there once when I was very young, but I don't remember it. I'm not much for cities,' she said. 'Neither is Stewart, I believe.'

'That I'm not,' he said, drawn into the conversation, although Annie realised that his eyes had been watching her ever since her arrival.

Out of some bravado she had dressed that day in her favourite dress, knowing she would be seeing him. It was in peacock blue sheerest muslin, the underpetticoats dyed a matching colour so as not to offend the eye and embarrass the wearer. It was a beautiful dress with a matching parasol, and she felt that she looked her best in it. She knew Stewart thought so too, his eyes saying what his words did not.

214

'So you enjoyed your visit with your cousin, did you, Miss Blair?' he asked sardonically.

'I did indeed. Why would I not?' *And I dare you to ask me if anything special was settled, she thought defiantly, and I'll tell you that it was, and you can make what you will of it!* Naturally he said no such thing, and she turned away from him.

With a small feeling of sadness she realised that Dougal and Callum were making no attempt to converse with one another, despite the fact that the older women-folk were chatting together. How did Morag see this situation now, Annie wondered? Or was it all too long ago for her to remember? She must have loved them both, or been wooed by them both, or at the very least, *wanted* them both. . .

'Where's Kirsty today?' she asked Callum now.

'She has a summer cold, and since any congestion always impairs her hearing slightly more, it's best that she stays indoors for a few days. She'll want to be well for the Games.'

'Of course,' Annie murmured, thinking that these Games, that she still supposed to be quite parochial, were assuming monumental importance.

'Annie, if you've finished your pleasantries, it's time we were going inside,' Dougal was saying now.

As she rejoined her family he nodded distantly to both Mackinty men, and the factions seemed to separate as smoothly as the parting of the Red Sea. Which would seem to be either a blasphemous or an entirely apt thought, Annie thought dryly, considering the day and the location.

Almost before they knew it, the day of the Earnlie Games was upon them. House-guests had been invited to stay at Blairfinnan for a few days, and Rob had arrived home with his friends. It was the same group as before, and immediately Lorn Thomson attached himself to Annie's side. She was both amused and slightly irritated by it. He looked at her with the soulful eyes of a puppy, and while such adoration might be appealing to some women, to Annie it was not.

She had greeted Helen with special warmth, and was full of admiration at the way she and Rob managed to merge in with the other house-guests, and yet retain a kind of coded message for themselves whenever the need arose. To any other watchers, Rob was equally attentive to all his guests, and to his cousin as well. It was only because she was looking for it now that Annie was aware of it. Without consciously aknowledging it, she was envious of those secret looks that made her feel alone, in a way she hadn't felt alone for some while now.

But this was no time to be melancholy when everyone at Blairfinnan was in party mood. Today was the day of the Games, and everyone was in high spirits. They were to start out for Earnlie early that morning, and just before they were all ready to leave in a convoy of carriages, Helen came to her room. Annie smiled at her, and bade her sit down a moment.

'How anyone can look at you and not know your secret, I can't think,' she said impulsively. 'The happiness just shines out of you, Helen.'

The other girl laughed softly. 'I know it. And what of you, Annie? You're not upset that Rob and I are going to be married? I know your uncle had high hopes of you and he –'

Annie shook her head positively. 'It was my uncle's fancy, not mine, and certainly not Rob's. We never had more than a family fondness for another. Besides –' she stopped quickly. There was a limit to how much she could or should tell this fiancée of Rob's. But Helen was more astute than she expected.

216

'Besides which, I have a strong suspicion you've already lost your heart to someone else. And that someone is certainly not Lorn Thomson! Dear friend that he is, anyone can see he's not half the man for you, Annie. And I think my brother Malcolm would come well down the line of prospective suitors, would he not?'

'There's hardly a line of young men on my horizon! Or is being in love making you especially intuitive?' Annie countered.

'Mebbe. Rob has also been telling me of your encounters with the family over the loch.'

'You mean my attempts to teach the little girl.'

'Oh aye, I can understand your fondness for the wee one,' Helen smiled. 'And there's also the man himself.'

Annie felt herself blush, and then the blush was replaced by a burst of anger. She twisted round on the vanity stool in front of her mirror where she was adjusting her bonnet.

'Has Rob sent you to find out how far the association between myself and Stewart Mackinty has gone? Is that it, Helen?'

'How prickly you are on his account! No, that's not it – well, mebbe it is, in a way –' she held up a hand as she saw Annie's indignation. 'But it's not for the reason you think, Annie, nor would he want to stop it in any way.'

'Well, that's extremely kind of him,' Annie said sarcastically. 'Does he think it's in his power to prevent me being friends with whomever I like?'

'But he doesn't want to prevent it! Oh, please don't be angry,' Helen said, contrite now. 'I'm being so clumsy about this, when I insisted on being the one to come to you rather than Rob. He can be rather a bull in a china shop when it comes to tact – like all the men in his family, I suspect. And now I've probably offended you again!'

217

'You haven't offended me.' She was too concerned with the extraordinary statements Helen was making, and wondering if she was being very dense or if she was rightly putting two and two together and making an incredible four.

'Are you telling me that Rob wouldn't object if Stewart Mackinty and I –' she couldn't say any more, because her throat seemed to be thickening up.

'That's right. If it meant an end to the feud and therefore the means for the families to be on amicable terms again, he'd welcome it.' She gave a slight reminiscent smile. 'Perhaps being in love himself has mellowed Rob a little. He's been telling me something about his young days here, and I gather he and Stewart Mackinty were once good friends.'

'Then why on earth don't they make up their differences like men?'

Helen gave a rueful laugh.

'Annie pet, I can see you've still got a lot to learn about men. They have their pride, you see, and neither one will lose face by giving in to other and being the first to make approaches.'

'So it's left to the women,' Annie stated.

'It always is,' Helen said dryly. 'You'll learn that in time too.'

'Then it seems to me it's high time things changed,' Annie said keenly.

'And I'd like to see the woman to do that! Though if anybody can change things, it would probably be you.'

But not by marrying Stewart Mackinty, unless it was for love. Not for his triumph over the Blairs, nor to salve her menfolk's pride in not being the first to make a move. If she married Stewart Mackinty it would be for love on both sides, and for no other reason.

And pigs would probably fly before that happened
. . . even though he'd already asked her, she remembered, with that jolt of the heart that happened
whenever his voice was in her head as she recalled
the way he'd said the words.

'Marry me . . .' he'd said softly . . . and it was a good
thing he didn't know she'd give the earth for him to say
it as if he really meant it.

'We'd better go down and join the others,' she said
briskly now, as they heard the sounds of voices outside
the house, and the rumbling of carriage-wheels as the
vehicles were brought to the front of the house.

'And you're not angry over what I've said?' Helen
said anxiously.

'Of course not –'

'There was one other thing, Annie. I want you to
be my chief bridesmaid when Rob and I are married.
Please say you'll agree to it, then I'll know you've
forgiven me.'

Annie kissed her cheek. 'There's nothing to forgive,
but I'll be delighted to be your chief bridesmaid, and I
feel very flattered that you've asked me.'

She felt unaccountably depressed too, which was
hardly the right way to feel at being given such an
honour. But Annie couldn't deny that every mention
of the future wedding and Helen's guaranteed happy
future, just seemed to underline how insecure was her
own.

The carriages from Blairfinnan were all lined up in the
stabling field at Earnlie now, the young village lads
paid for the occasion eagerly rushing about tying up
horses and bringing forth bags of feed and troughs of
water for their convenience. Rob had gone ahead to the
competitors' tent to ascertain the order of events, and

more lads and little girls in bright tartans were selling programmes to anyone who would buy.

The day was a blisteringly hot one, the excitement of the occasion accentuated by the wide-skirted dresses of the ladies and their gaily matching parasols. Across the field was the refreshment tent, and in front of it a platform for the dancing, while the main field was for the men's events, the caber tossing, the races, the pole-jumping, weight-lifting and the rest.

There were plenty of people to pass the time of day with the Blairs and their party, and they were soon joined by Trina Moray and her mother, with Geddes Cameron still noticeably hanging around, despite what Trina had said. Annie hid a smile, wondering if Trina was deliberately playing cool to keep his attention.

She found herself scanning the field for one particular face. There was really only one person she wanted to see, one person she would be egging on to win every race, at least in her mind. Ostensibly, in any race where the two men were competing, she must be seen to be willing Rob to win.

'He's over there,' she heard Trina say slyly at her side.

'Who is?'

Trina laughed out loud. 'Oh Annie, you know very well! You've hardly heard a thing I've been saying these past five minutes. Look there, with his father and the wee bairn.'

Annie saw him at once, in the act of giving Kirsty a hug before he strode off on business of his own. For a moment the two of them, the old man and the small girl, looked oddly vulnerable and alone, compared to the Blairs with a score of people chattering around them.

It was only a momentary illusion, of course. The Mackintys had as many acquaintances as the Blairs, but right then the urge to join them was too strong for

Annie to ignore. She turned to Aunt Morag before she could stop to think.

'Would it offend you terribly if I joined Kirsty and her grandfather some time today? I promised her that I would.'

'Then you musn't break a promise, my dear,' she said with no expression in her voice. 'Though I suggest you wait until we've had our picnic lunch so as not to offend your uncle.'

Annie had to agree to that, though it seemed an age to wait, while they watched the various morning events, and then ate their picnic lunch in the shade of the trees.

By the time she began making her way around the huge field in the early afternoon, Annie wondered just how Morag really felt about the situation. Did she too long to be sociable again with the family over the loch, as Helen had so quaintly called them? Did she ever regret not marrying Callum Mackinty, and throwing in her lot on the toss of a coin or the throw of a card, with the more irascible Dougal Blair? As far as Annie could tell, the marriage was a perfectly normal one, with no special highs or lows. And after so many years together, and allowing for Dougal's erratic moods, one that seemed remarkably content.

Annie decided she wasn't going to spoil her day by pondering on something that was no business of hers . . . and yet the Blairs and the Mackintys seemed piquantly unable to avoid making every problem a communal one. It was almost as if they simply couldn't let go of one another . . . as if the ties that bound them in bitterness and anger were every bit as strong and unbreakable as the bonds of love that had existed just as surely between them. Whether in love or in hate, the two of them couldn't seem to do without one another.

It took a long while to walk right around the huge field, and the sun was high overhead and prickling on her back by the time Annie reached Callum and Kirsty. By then, she had glimpsed the afternoon competitors coming out of their registration tent, and by an extraordinary trick of perspective, Rob and Stewart had seemed to be walking close together for a moment, before parting and moving in separate directions to their respective supporters. She reached Kirsty minutes before Stewart joined them.

The child looked up and saw her approach, and contrary to the whoop of pleasure Annie had expected, Kirsty clung to her grandfather's hand and turned her face into his side, refusing to look at her. Annie felt a great plummeting in her stomach at this reaction.

'Is this the way to greet a friend?' she said gaily, crouching down to Kirsty's level and touching her arm. To her dismay she felt the child pull away from her at once.

'*No. Want Granpa!*' she muttered harshly.

Annie stood up slowly, her eyes dark as she stared down at the child. Above her head she looked in bewilderment at Callum Mackinty, and saw him shake his head.

'Do you see now what you've done, Annie Blair? She's hardly bothered to speak at all since you went off in your tantrum,' Stewart's voice railed into her. She gasped, whipping around to see him glowering at her, arms folded aggressively across his chest.

'You can't blame me for that –' she said in a dry voice.

'No? You went away from her, just when she was finding herself and enjoying her learning. You've failed her, aye, and betrayed her too.'

'Now just a minute here,' she said hotly. 'I think you go too far, Mr Mackinty –'

'Do you now? Well, I do not,' he said, his gypsy eyes glinting with anger. 'The bairn was full of love and trust for you, and because of some whim of your own, you decided not to see her any more. Even when you knew she was full of misery with a cold, you couldna find it in your heart to visit and read to her. Shame on you, Annie Blair. You've no more compassion than the rest of your folk with their fairweather friendship. I suggest you get back where you belong, and I'll bid you good-day.'

She almost rocked back on her heels at the venom in his voice. She realised it was the first time his anger had been directed squarely at her and it had the effect of mentally knocking her off-balance for a moment. Was this really the man she purported to love? This arrogant man who clearly thought more of the child than the woman!

She dismissed the unworthiness of the thought, the sharp sting of tears behind her eyes telling only too well the bitter truth of her unchanged feelings. She dashed the tears away with a shaking hand, to find Callum looking at her, his eyes serious.

'You'll not begrudge him his anger, lass. He's a right to it, since he takes the wee one's frustrations to heart, and there's no reasoning with him when she's been hurt.'

Annie felt a lump in her throat. 'But I never meant to hurt her,' she said. 'It seemed best that I should stay away from Craggan – for so many reasons. And since my family wanted me to accompany them to Edinburgh, I couldn't have seen Kirsty then.'

'Aye, but she doesn't understand all that. All she knew was that she'd found a friend, and then the friend was gone.'

Annie looked at the child, still clinging to Callum, still refusing to look at her, let alone talk. Annie knelt down beside her again, uncaring of the grass or the bracken on

223

her fine blue striped dress, and spoke into Kirsty's ear, loud enough for her needs.

'I've come especially to watch you dance today, Kirsty, and I'd like to stay with you and your granpa and Stewart all through the Games, if you'll let me. We'll watch Stewart race together, and after we've seen you dance we'll all go to the refreshment tent and have some lemonade. Can I stay with you for that?'

For a moment she thought there was going to be no response at all, and then she saw one eye appear as Kirsty twisted her head a fraction to look at her.

'Dolly wants to watch too,' she muttered, bringing up the doll from the depths of her kilt.

'I could hold Dolly for you while you dance, if you want me to,' she said, feeling as if she was walking on egg-shells in her effort to win the child's confidence all over again.

Kirsty looked steadily at the bland china face of the doll and then gave a slow nod.

'Dolly says – yes,' she said, and Annie felt the most ridiculous, enormous relief.

For a second, she had wondered guiltily if she was seeking Kirsty's acceptance purely for Stewart's approval, but she knew deep down that it was more complex than that. Kirsty, Stewart, Callum, James Andrew and all those past Mackintys . . . they were all a part of it . . . just as she and Rob, her own rebellious father, Dougal and Morag and Miranda, and all the rest, were all part of the Stalwart Blairs too, and each faction was part of the whole. There was no separating them. There could be no separating them.

It was something she intended explaining to Stewart if ever she was given the chance. Something she suspected Rob already knew, but had too much of that masculine pride to aknowledge. But all during that long hot day when the races were won or lost, and the cheers or commiserations were handed out along with the trophies, Annie began to feel almost light-headed at the simple truth of it.

Her father had dared to break away, as others had done, but she had been drawn back despite herself. A Blair always came back sooner or later, and one way or another a Blair and a Mackinty were destined to be together. There was no winning or losing, only the continuation of what had been begun somewhere long ago in the mists of time.

'Are you keeping count, Annie Blair?' she heard Stewart's taunting voice say, startling her back to the present. 'Your cousin and myself are neck and neck, winning five heats apiece, and this next one will be the decider. Who's your money on now? Your lover or his rival?'

At least he sounded less angry now, she thought, though he clearly didn't expect a reply, and had merely come back to their position to douse his face and neck with a bottle of cooling water, the droplets glistening on his hair and skin.

'It depends which one of those you think yourself to be,' she retorted daringly, hoping no-one standing nearby would hear. Callum was already taking Kirsty to where the group of small girls were gathering for the dances, the older ones having finished their competitions. Stewart looked at her speculatively, as her fingers tightened around the child's doll in her hand.

'I'd advise you not to say such things lightly, lassie. Much as I ache to be your lover, a husband is a slightly more acceptable proposition between us. Or would be, if you believed in miracles.'

She wanted to say that she did, otherwise she wouldn't be here at all. Or Kirsty wouldn't be talking as well as she did now. Or Rob wouldn't have found his Helen out of all the women in the world . . . and Annie Blair and Stewart Mackinty wouldn't have been put on this earth at a marriageable age at the same time . . . but the time wasn't right for confessing, and he was already swinging away from her, arrogant and proud, and moving towards the starting-line, where he and her cousin Rob were to stand shoulder to shoulder by order of some wag of a linesman.

She caught sight of her family, bunched together on the far side of the field, and wondered with a pang if she should join them, and what they would be thinking at her defection. But the doll in her hand reminded her that Kirsty would be watching for her from the dance platform, and she dare not let the child down again.

The skirl of the pipes was loud in her ears now, and she turned away from the men's races to move towards the dancing. The little girls had arranged themselves in their sets, arms raised with fingers just touching, toes pointed for the reel. Annie smiled encouragingly at Kirsty, and stood at Callum's side as the performance began.

It was still continuing, the little girls weaving in and out of one another in the simple steps of the reel, when Stewart joined them, his breath still heavy after his exertions. Annie could smell the faint animal sweat on him, more aphrodisiac than offensive. . .

'If you'd taken the wager I suggested, you'd have lost,' he said softly in her ear, which gave her no indication at all of whether he or Rob had won the final heat of the men's races. She turned impatiently to ask him, and as she did so everything in her vision seemed to shake and slip sideways. The very ground beneath her feet seemed to be shuddering, and just as instantly she was aware of the pandemonium as the dance platform tilted sideways like a drunken man, and the children were thrown against one another, to fall screaming like a set of dominoes.

'Dear God, an earthquake,' Stewart said hoarsely and unnecessarily, for Annie didn't need telling that this was no trick, no staged performance. This was real, and the Earnlie Games were frighteningly caught in the middle of it.

Beneath the platform a narrow jagged crevice yawned open, snaking across the field and slicing through the earth as if with a mighty sword. Annie looked at in disbelief, unable to gather her senses for a moment. Everywhere people were shrieking in terror, clinging to friends and relatives. The news was quickly broadcast that the refreshment tent had collapsed, but only one person was hurt there, and it was the platform that had taken the brunt of it. There was dust everywhere, choking the lungs and blinding the eyes, and in the midst of it all Annie heard Callum's voice calling urgently for Stewart.

They rushed forward together. Callum was kneeling beside Kirsty, who lay flat and still on the ground. There was a large gash and an ugly lump on her forehead, and her eyes were closed in her chalky face.

'Lord in heaven,' Annie breathed, unwilling even to think how these two would react if anything really bad happened to Kirsty. Callum, who looked suddenly grey old, and Stewart, his face deep-etched with worry in less than a second. . .

'She's nobbut stunned, I think,' Callum said harshly. 'But where in God's name is the doctor?'

'He's coming through, man,' someone said, and seconds later Doctor Glenn was kneeling beside the child. He made a cursory examination, taking her pulse and smiling in relief as Kirsty's eyes slowly flickered open.

'There now, my wee one, you've a bump on your head but not much more than that. The wound will heal, though you'll have a sore head for a few days.'

'Like Ann-ie,' Kirsty whispered. The doctor looked startled for a minute, as if wondering if the blow had affected her mind, and then remembered how he'd attended Annie at Craggan when she'd been thrown from her horse.

'Will she be all right, Doctor?' Stewart said, as harsh as his father, which conveyed to Annie the depth of his feelings.

'Oh aye, after a few days in bed she'll be as good as new,' he said. 'Let her rest where she is for a wee while and then get her home and in bed with a warm drink and some home comforts. She'll need a bit of pampering, that's all.'

While he'd been speaking, there was a shivering in the earth below, and seconds later another that was hardly more than a ripple. He spoke cheerfully to Annie, like one who was well used to such a minor phenomenon, and disregarded it as no more irritating than a burr on a dog's back.

'That'll be the end of the quakes now, lassie, and I'm away to tend to other needy folk. Good-day to you, Mackinty.'

A crowd had gathered around them, but they began drifting away once the child was pronounced none the worse. A few still remained, and Annie suddenly heard her Aunt Morag's voice. Her head jerked up as she recognised it, and she caught her breath as she saw Dougal's weathered face behind her.

'How is the lassie?'

'She'll do,' Callum said. Morag nodded, and then spoke hesitantly.

'If there's anything we can do, you need only ask.'

Kirsty suddenly realised she was getting so much attention, and whether deliberately or instinctively, she decided to make the most of it.

'Ann-ie!' she shrieked. 'I want Ann-ie to stay. Stay, stay, stay!'

'Hush, sweetheart,' Annie said at once. 'I'm here with you now –'

'*No*! Stay with Kir-sty. Stay at Cragg-an!'

Annie's heart jolted. She looked helplessly at Stewart, who looked back at her stonily. She couldn't tell from his expression whether he wanted her at Craggan or not.

Dougal's gruff voice broke through her sudden misery.

'If it'll be any help to the bairn, then my lass can go back with you, Mackinty, providing you'll see she's brought safely back to Blairfinnan once the bairn's recovered.'

'You have my word on it,' Callum said steadily.

Annie was dumbfounded as the two men addressed one another quite civilly. Especially without even a predictable hint of sarcasm forthcoming from Dougal about the reliability of a Mackinty's word.

'Thank-you, Uncle,' she managed to say.

Her mind was in a complete whirl as Stewart gently lifted Kirsty in his arms and proceeded to carry her across the field to the Mackinty carriage. Clearly the Games had been abandoned now, and the major feeling was one of thankfulness that the few injuries incurred from the earthquake had been slight.

But reaction was setting in fast, and as she followed behind with Callum, all the spirit seemed to be draining out of her and leaving her numb. She was aware of people all around them murmuring words of sympathy, and expressing their relief when she and the Mackinty men told them time and again that Kirsty wasn't badly hurt.

By now all she wanted was to get right away from here. Anywhere, but especially not to Craggan . . . in essence Stewart seemed to have gone a million miles away from her, and the glorious feelings she'd felt towards him earlier seemed to have vanished like will-o-the-wisp. But as soon as they entered the carriage, Kirsty's small hands reached out for her, and it was obvious that she intended to cling to Annie for the entire journey back to Craggan.

'A moment of your time, Mackinty,' she heard a familiar voice say just as they were about to set off. 'You've forgotten something.'

She saw Rob approaching with his group of house-guests, and prayed that he wasn't going to make a fuss about her leaving with the Mackintys. This was not the time or place to start an argument, she thought wearily, and then her eyes widened as she saw him hand over a small trophy to Stewart.

'I'm obliged to you,' Stewart said briefly, and seconds later they were off, with Stewart handling the horses himself, careful not to jolt Kirsty any more than necessary.

'So you won?' she said quietly.

'Aye, however much it offends your filial feelings, I was the winner. And I wonder which of us you would have put your wager on, Annie Blair?'

Chapter 13

If she thought it was going to be easy to be back at Craggan, she was mistaken. Nothing was as it was before, Annie thought. Callum was more possessive of Kirsty than ever. The child herself was either tearful and clinging, or blatantly naughty. And Stewart was simply remote.

He was polite to her at meal-times, and seemingly joined in when Kirsty demanded that the three most important people in her life sat together in her room for the bed-time stories. Apart from that, he rarely spoke to her, and spent his days away from the house, examining the minimal damage the minor earthquake had done to Craggan's Best and organising the repairs.

She had to assume that Stewart had washed his hands of winning her over to that ridiculous Mackinty boast of taming a Blair lassie. The plain fact was, Annie thought, he just didn't want her any more. And that piqued her so much. . .

'What have I done to annoy you now?' she finally demanded after three days when she could stand his lack of communication no longer. His father had gone to bed with a migraine soon after the early evening meal, and Stewart had said shortly that he had work to do in his study, when she stopped him. He paused with his hand on the door-handle.

'I thought you knew,' he said. 'In fact, I'm surprised you could spare any time to come here at all, even allowing for your genuine concern for the bairn. Aren't you desperate to get back to Blaifinnan? You're free to come and go as you please.'

She looked at him in annoyance.

'I never did consider myself a prisoner here! But since you mention it, and since there's no-one here to share any intelligent conversation, I'll go over to Blairfinnan this evenig to see my cousin before he goes back to Edinburgh. I presume I have your permission for that?'

'You don't need my permission for anything. You've a strong enough will of your own,' he said, with a glint in his dark eyes.

'So I have,' she retorted. 'Thank-you for reminding me.'

She went to walk past him with her head held high, when he caught her arm. It was the first physical contact between them for days, and without warning Annie felt a shiver run through her veins. She looked at him impassively, trying to appear cool, in spite of the way her heart was suddenly racing. But if she thought he was about to embrace her, she was mistaken. His voice was savage with anger.

'Why did you not tell me you were betrothed to your cousin? Did you not think it was of interest to me?'

She was startled by the question, until she remembered how her uncle had bragged to Stewart that she and Rob were intending to marry.

'I hardly thought such news would make any difference to you,' she said witheringly. 'Doesn't a Mackinty simply take what he wants?'

'Not when it belongs to another man,' he said. 'There's been too much of that already.'

If he was referring to the fact that her Aunt Morag had been an unwilling pawn between her uncle and his father, it would seem to be a damning slight against Dougal Blair as the victor. And she couldn't allow that.

'I daresay the honours have come out even over the years,' she said icily. 'Though applying the word honour to certain members of either family seems hardly appropriate.'

'Indeed? And what gives you the right to come here with your soft southern ways and think you know everything about us?'

Her chin lifted. 'I have every right. My father was Dougal's brother, and I belong here just as much as you. I've also learned enough since I've been here to realise how stubborn and insular two families can become. My father did me a favour by moving south. He allowed me to see things as an outsider, and to see how petty all these family squabbles are.'

'So you dare to belittle all that my family has stood for all these years by calling our grievances petty squabbles, do you?' he was dangerously quiet now.

Annie felt alarm run through her now. He looked so angry, so large and aggressive, blocking her way through the door and therefore her escape to freedom. She dismissed the bizarre thought quickly.

'If I belittle your family, I belittle mine too, and I mean no disrespect to either,' she said. 'In fact, I wish –'

'What do you wish?'

She gave a heavy sigh. 'Just that all of it could end. It's so pointless, when we're destined to be neighbours for the rest of our lives –'

She spoke objectively, encompassing both families with her words, but Stewart clearly took them differently.

'I doubt that such proximity will bother you when you marry your cousin and go to live in Edinburgh. You disappoint me. I'd have staked my life on you being a country lass, but it seems the lure of the city and the man can turn the bonniest head.'

He had let go of her arm, and she fought with the conflicting thoughts brimming in her mind. He insulted her by his disparaging remark, and she could hurl insults back at him if she chose. Or she could tell him he was all wrong about her and Rob, and that her uncle had merely been indulging in fantasies of his own. She could even produce the document she and Rob had signed, and prove once and for all that there was no likelihood of marriage between them. Especially with the added information that Rob was to marry Helen, and that Annie had agreed to be chief bridesmaid when the time came. . .

'Well?' he demanded. 'Can you deny it?'

She felt her temper rise. 'I don't see that I have to affirm or deny anything to you,' she said. 'Now if you'll let me pass, I intend to spend an hour or so with my family, where I will certainly find the company more congenial than here.'

She pushed past him, and he made no attempt to stop her. It was over, she thought incoherently, hardly heeding the fact that nothing between them had ever really begun.

A short while later, she handed the reins of the pony and trap to Siddons, who had assumed an almost embarrassingly humble attitude where she was concerned. Annie was as impatient with such subservience

234

as with downright antagonism. Maybe there was something wrong with her, she thought with a deep sigh, to react with such irritation to everything nowadays. If this state of mind was caused by the misery of a one-sided love, then she would as soon have done without it. . .

She dismissed the uneasy thought and picked up her skirts to climb the front steps of the house in anticipation of enjoying her aunt's company. The evenings were still long, and an hour or so here would still enable her to ride back to Craggan before the short period of darkness prior to the dawn. It was one of the advantages of being so far north, she had discovered. Darkness only lasted a short time, and the days were deliciously long. . .

'My dear Annie, what an unexpected surprise!' she heard Aunt Morag say, coming forward to meet her and kissing her cheek.

'But not an unpleasant one, I hope,' Annie said, sensing an atmosphere she couldn't quite define. Aunt Morag was rarely ruffled, but tonight there was a heightened colour in her face and a brightness in her eyes that had nothing to do with her usual perkiness.

'How can you say that, dearie?' the lady protested. 'Come along in to the drawing-room and join your uncle and me. We were just having some hot chocolate, and you'll take some, I'm sure.'

'That would be nice,' Annie murmured.

Whatever the hour, and however hot the weather, the comfort of hot chocolate was always her aunt's panacea. They were walking into the drawing-room as she thought it, and when she saw her uncle's glowering face, she knew she'd interrupted some altercation. Pretending not to notice, she went straight across to him and kissed his cheek. She could feel the tension in it.

'So you've come home, have you, lass?' he said in a gruff voice.

235

'Just for a visit,' she said evenly. 'I wanted to see you and Aunt Morag, and since I'm such a little distance away it seemed silly not to take advantage of this lovely evening.'

'Oh aye. And what do your protectors think of that?'

It was such a ludicrous statement that she decided to be amused rather than angry.

'My *protectors*? We're not in the Middle Ages now, Uncle! I hardly think Stewart or his father would consider themselves in such a role.'

'And what role do they consider themselves?' he went on with heavy sarcasm. 'Abductors, mebbe?'

Annie looked at him steadily. 'I came to visit you and Aunt Morag because I care about you both and I wanted to see you again. I didn't expect to be treated to some kind of inquisition. Anyway, I thought you were quite agreeable for me to go to Craggan, considering the circumstances.'

'I presume you refer to the bairn's needs. But how long is she going to need you? Or is she just the bait by which the young Mackinty keeps you there?'

'Dougal –' Aunt Morag said warningly, but she was too late. Annie's eyes were already flashing with anger, but it was a cold anger now, and there were things that needed to be said.

'Nobody is keeping me anywhere against my will, Uncle Dougal. Not Stewart Mackinty – nor you. I seem to have become the pig in the middle amongst you all, and I resent it very much. I was assured that I belonged here, but in many ways I'm still an outsider –'

'That's not true, Annie!' Morag protested.

'It is true, and as an outsider I'll tell you what I see.' She took a deep breath. 'I see two foolish old men who are wasting the chance of a close companionship by keeping alive something that should have died out years ago.'

236

'You don't know what you're talking about,' Dougal snapped. 'There are things you don't understand.'

'Perhaps I know and understand more than you think,' Annie said, not wanting to divulge just how much she did know, with Aunt Morag's colour deepening. 'I even thought I saw something wonderful begin to happen at the disastrous Earnlie Games. You and Callum Mackinty almost forgot your differences. Can you deny it?'

In the small silence, Morag spoke softly.

'He cannot, Annie. It's just what I've been trying to tell him. It's time for the feud to end.'

'And I'm to be the one to eat humble pie, is that it?' Dougal said harshly. 'It takes two, woman.'

'But it only takes one to hold out a hand for the other to take,' Morag said.

'Why don't you just give it some thought, Uncle?' Annie said, thinking this conversation would do better to be mulled over rather than concluded here and now. They all knew that Dougal was not normally much of a thinker, preferring to rush in with hasty words and do his regretting later. But to her relief she saw him give a slow nod.

'I'll mebbe think on it, but no promises, mind. 'Twill take more than a handshake to blot out some of the past hurts.'

Annie wondered suddenly if he still felt guilt on Morag's account. Was there still an anguish inside him that even after all these years, she would admit she'd been wrong to go along with the wager, and that her true love had always been Callum Mackinty? Was there a dread that if the three regained their former friendship, Morag would even yet turn to his rival? As she wondered, she saw Aunt Morag go to him and drop a kiss on his gnarled cheek. She looked deep into her husband's eyes.

'You're an old fool, Dougal Blair,' she said in a soft, loving voice. 'But you're the only man for me, for all that.'

And that would seem to say it all, Annie thought a while later when she was on her way back to Craggan. A woman was fortunate indeed to know the only man for her, and doubly blessed to have his love in return. Her mouth trembled, knowing she'd give so much if she and Stewart could be that same situation.

The image of her uncle's reaction when Morag had reaffirmed her love for him remained in her mind. Contrary, aggravating, bombastic as he was, Annie had glimpsed a rare moment of tenderness in Dougal then, and the memory was enough to bring a lump to her throat. In that moment, no-one could have denied that here was a marriage that was rock-solid, and Annie had been both embarrassed and privileged to have witnessed it.

But the nearer she got to Craggan, the more restless she became. Before leaving Blairfinnan, she had gone to her room and retrieved the document between herself and Rob. Still caught up in the love story that was obviously Morag's and Dougal's, she had finally decided to bring it to Craggan, just in case . . . but the nearer she got to the Mackinty house, the less likely she thought it that she should show it to Stewart. Why on earth should she, when in effect by its production, she would be as good as offering herself to the man?

Everyone seemed to have someone, she thought suddenly. Morag and Dougal . . . Rob and Helen . . . even Trina Moray had her Geddes, for all that she seemed to be dangling him on a string . . . there were only the Mackinty men and herself who seemed destined to have no-one. But Callum was content within

238

himself, as long as he had the love of the child, and that left herself and Stewart. . .

'You've been gone so long I was about to send out search parties to bring you back.'

The object of her day-dreaming had materialised so suddenly she gave a small gasp. She had neither seen nor heard him approach through the long grasses of the glen until she heard the abruptness of his voice. She was startled enough for her own voice to sharpen.

'I assure you there was no need for that! I'm perfectly capable of finding my own way back, and it's far from dark yet. But I thank you for your concern.'

She saw his mouth ease into a small smile. Then with one swift movement he had leapt into the trap, squeezing beside her on the narrow seat, and taking the reins out of her hands.

'I'm naturally concerned that you don't desert Kirsty for a second time,' he said without expression.

The quick retort died on Annie's lips. She was so weary of all this antagonism. She looked at his strong and handsome profile, so splendidly Romanesque, so dear to her, yet so exasperatingly arrogant.

'Of course. I should have known it was on Kirsty's account that you fretted, and not on mine.'

'On the contrary. I'd fret about any living thing that was out and about at the onset of darkness. Even in the vicinity of my own house there are traps for the unwary, a stump in the grass, a hungry fox, even a canny rogue of the night intent on mischief –'

'Will you stop it, Stewart?' Annie said in a low voice. 'Why must you be like this?'

'Like what?' he turned and looked at her, and her heart stopped for a moment before racing on. There was no expression in his eyes, none at all. No love, no concern, just nothing.

239

'You know like what,' she went on relentlessly. 'You're as cold as charity towards me, and I've done nothing to deserve it! I came back when Kirsty needed me –'

'Aye, so you did, and I'm grateful for that, though on my own account it might have been better if you had not,' he said.

'And if you're only going to speak in riddles to me, then I'd rather you didn't speak at all!'

After a few minutes' brittle silence when they were almost at the Craggan stables, he spoke harshly.

'Just tell me one thing so that it's settled. Has your family set the date for the wedding yet?'

Annie knew the colour must be flooding into the cheeks now. And then she remembered something he'd said to her. He would never take that which belonged to another man . . . and he truly believed that she and Rob were to be married. If ever there was a time for disproving it, it was now. She knew very well that it would open the way for Stewart to start pursuing her all over again – if he chose – and she would still never know whether it was for herself or for the sake of the Mackinty boast. But she was so tired of subterfuge. She believed in the truth.

Slowly, she reached inside her reticule and brought out the envelope containing her copy of the document. She handed it to Stewart, and spoke in a voice that was choked.

'This should answer your question, but I'll ask you not to open it yet. I don't want to see that gloating look on your face when you realised what it means. Please do me the courtesy of waiting until I've gone inside the house.'

She got down stiffly from the trap, hampered by her full skirts, and considering the way her legs were shaking, she walked as coolly as she could towards the house. She trusted him not to open the envelope until she was safely inside, and she wondered if he would then come storming after her.

She waited downstairs for a time, uncertain if she expected him to make an instant declaration, and how she would react if he did. But he didn't come to her, and eventually she climbed the staircase to her bedroom, undressed with shaking hands and crawled into bed, with the feeling that she had been totally rejected.

She accepted that it was all her own fault. The situation between them could have been resolved weeks ago, and whether or not he wanted her for the right reasons or baser ones, the fact was that he had *wanted* her. Now, after reading the document, she had no idea whether or not he would even speak to her again, knowing she had kept such knowledge from him all this time.

She had lain in bed for a long while, dry-eyed and sleepless, when she heard her door-handle move. She turned her head in the dimness, thinking it would be Kirsty, restless in the hot summer night. And then her heart leapt, as she saw a tall shadowy figure pause by the door for a moment before starting to approach her bed.

'How can two intelligent people have been so foolish?' she heard Stewart's voice say huskily.

The blood was pounding in her veins, and she couldn't find any answer. Slowly he drew nearer until he was right beside her. She could hear the way his breathing was sharp and ragged, matching her own. His fingers reached out to stroke her cheek and then, as if they had a will of their own, she was holding out her arms to him, and he was folding her into him with an urgency that sent her spirit soaring to meet him.

'Dear God, but I love you,' he said savagely. 'Didn't you know it from the first, Annie?'

'I didn't know anything but the fact that you were the enemy,' she whispered wildly. 'They told me, and I believed them.'

He was kissing her eyes and her mouth, and his hands were on her breasts, and she wanted him with an exquisite need that was almost a physical pain.

'But I never wanted to be your enemy, my dearest lassie,' he whispered back. 'You and I were always destined to belong together.'

'I know it,' Annie said, trembling at the force of her own emotions. They seemed to have swept aside any thought of impropriety in an instant. Right or wrong, she was willing to submit to whatever he wanted of her now. Something stronger than herself was dictating that sense of belonging. Man and woman, two halves of the perfect being, herself and Stewart Mackinty. . .

Her eyes half-closed, half-dazed with the fury of passion that had enveloped them both in these last minutes, she suddenly heard him give a low oath, and she felt him move slightly away from her. She had never lain with a man before, but she had been fully aware of his arousal, and now she knew he was holding back, taking the essence of himself away from her and leaving her bereft. She was shocked at her own feelings, and the burgeoning sensuality she had never known existed in her.

He cupped his large hands around her face and kissed her gently on the mouth. The moment was so tender it brought the hot stinging tears to her eyes.

'Not like this, my dear one,' she heard him say. 'This is not the time or the way.'

His hands left her face, and seconds later he had left her. But he had left her wanting, and with an unreasoning fury mounting inside her. He had said he loved her, and she had been so ready to believe him, to surrender everything to him . . . and to her there could be only one explanation for his rejection. He was still enough in control of himself to adhere to the Mackinty boast. To tame a Blair lassie . . . to have her in his bed . . . did he imagine that she would go willingly to him now?

She swallowed dryly. To have what she desired the most snatched away from her like this was unbelievably cruel. And she still did not understand his words. Not like this . . . not the time or the way . . . it didn't make sense to her, when he must have known how pliant she had been in his arms . . . her eyes closed again, remembering how she had responded so eagerly and wantonly . . . what must he think of her now?

He was gone when she went downstairs the next morning, accompanied by Kirsty. The two of them ate breakfast with Callum, and Annie spoke slowly, having carefully rehearsed what she intended to say.

'It occurs to me that Kirsty might develop more quickly if she gets away from the house occasionally, Mr Mackinty. She's fully recovered now, and doesn't need me here all the time. I wondered if she could come to Blairfinnan several times a week, and I'd come here on other days to tutor her. What do you think?'

'You want to leave us?' Callum asked.

'My home is with my aunt and uncle,' Annie said, gently but quite firmly. 'You know this is only a temporary measure. But I've no wish to abandon Kirsty, and with my suggestion it would be a regular outing for her twice a week, and she would meet other people. It can only do her good.'

'Even if the people she meets are Blairs?'

'Even so.' Annie simply refused to be drawn into any argument, and they both looked to the child.

'What do you say to it, Kirsty? Do you understand what Annie's saying?'

It appeared that she did, and she agreed so readily that Annie was sure her instincts were right. The child was living far too insular a life here at Craggan. And it solved one problem very neatly. She intended to leave here today, and to be packed and gone long before Stewart came back from Craggan's Best. She wouldn't even allow herself the luxury of feeling that her heart was breaking. She had to give all her energies to making sure Kirsty didn't fret over her leaving once more, and understood that they would still see each other often. It was arranged that one of the older stable lads should take her back in the pony and trap, and before she left it was already arranged that he should bring Kirsty to Blairfinnan for the following afternoon.

She had spent an uneasy night in her old room. She had tried to face up to the fact that she'd probably never understand the complexities of a feud that had gained such strength over the years that a mere upstart of a young woman like herself could hardly hope to break its hold. And whatever Stewart's motive in coming to her room at Craggan last night, there must have been something deeper than desire holding him back. Some flicker of honour, perhaps, that wouldn't let him seduce her against her will after all. And her shame was in knowing that it wouldn't have been that way at all.

She took a walk through the glen that morning, trying to clear her head from the depression that enveloped her. She envied her cousing Rob so much, for no such complications had entered his life. His and Helen's future was set fair . . . unthinkingly she realised she had wandered almost to the edge of the loch, and she stopped abruptly. It was the last place she wanted to be, in the place where she had first set eyes on Stewart Mackinty.

The sunlight on the water dazzled her, mesmerising her for a moment. She could be almost light-headed, imagining she saw his face everywhere she looked, hearing his voice in every sighing whisper of bracken. . .

'Ann-ie! Ann-ie!'

Annie blinked, knowing that this was no phantom voice. It was Kirsty, and immediately after it Stewart shouted a warning. Annie's head jerked up to see the two of them in Stewart's boat in the middle of the loch. Kirsty was waving madly to attract her attention, jumping up and down in the flimsy craft in her excitement. The next minute the child gave a terrified cry as the boat rocked alarmingly and she over-balanced into the water.

After a heart-stopping moment when she remembered that Kirsty was afraid of the water and couldn't swim, Annie stepped into the cool shallow water at the edge of the loch and began wading out. Dimly from somewhere behind her, she heard Aunt Morag and Dougal calling her name, but she paid no heed as she heard Kirsty's panic-stricken screams.

'Hold on, Kirsty, I'm coming for you,' she heard herself screaming back.

'Go back, Annie,' Stewart shouted at her. 'The water gets very deep in the middle –'

She didn't listen to him. She was sure she could reach Kirsty. She saw him dive in after the floundering child, and she moved doggedly forward towards them. Suddenly there was nothing beneath her feet and before she could think what to do, her head was under water as the weight of her skirts and petticoats pulled her under, and then the terror was all hers.

She came up gasping and spluttering, to see Stewart swimming strongly towards her with Kirsty held tightly beneath his arm. She tried to tread water, but something seemed to be pulling her down into the dark depths of the loch . . . she felt utter panic. She was going to drown. She saw Stewart very close to her through the mists of water blinding her eyes, but she knew he couldn't save her. He was too occupied in saving Kirsty. . .

'Hold on to my ankle,' he snapped at her. '*Do* it, Annie.'

She floundered and gasped again, grasping hold of his limb as though it was a lifeline. Which indeed it was, she thought hysterically. The edge of the loch was such a short distance away, and yet it seemed to take forever as he swam so slowly towards it, hindered by her extra weight. Whatever had been dragging her down might even have been all in her imagination, she thought wildly, now that she knew she was going to be saved.

Once her feet reached the shallower waters she staggered ashore by herself, leaving Stewart to carry Kirsty carefully onto dry land where her aunt and uncle awaited them. She expected some word of praise from Stewart for her attempt to reach Kirsty, but to her fury he immediately rounded on her as she crawled onto the grass, utterly exhausted and dishevelled.

'Are you completely noddle-headed, to go into the loch when you're unable to swim yourself?' he said angrily.

'I was only thinking of Kirsty!' she said heatedly.

'Aye, and forced me to risk losing her by having to rescue two of you instead of one,' he snapped.

'Are you all right, Annie? That's the important thing,' Aunt Morag broke in anxiously.

'Of course I am. It's Kirsty we should be looking to,' she answered. The child was as bedraggled as Annie, but she looked well enough now the fright was leaving her eyes.

'She needs dry clothes and a hot drink,' Morag said. 'She'll come back to the house with us, and you can collect her later, Mr Mackinty.'

She glanced at Dougal, defying him to refuse the man entry. He seemed to be fighting with himself at that moment, then he gave a brief nod and spoke with his usual gruffness.

'Aye. I daresay you'll be wanting to retrieve your boat and go back to your own side to tell your father what's occurred. And when you come to collect the bairn, you can bring him with you, if he's a mind to come visiting. Tell him Dougal Blair issues the invitation.'

Annie tried to stop her mouth from dropping open. She had no way of knowing how long it was since Dougal had invited Callum to Blairfinnan, but it would obviously have been before the two men made their wager over Morag's hand.

'Am I to stay with you, Ann-ie?' Kirsty said eagerly, her damp hand held tightly in Annie's now.

'Just for a while, love, until your uncle and grandfather come to fetch you,' she said.

Was it too much to wish that this gesture on Dougal's part would mark the end of the feud? She hardly dared to hope so. She glanced at Stewart, as wet as herself and Kirsty, and felt a wild desire to laugh now that they were safe, though he still didn't seem to see the funny side of it. He was as dour and glowering as her uncle normally was.

'We'll be back in an hour or so then,' he said shortly.

'This afternoon will be soon enough,' Morag put in. 'The bairn needs a wee bit time to recover, and she's welcome to eat the mid-day meal with us.'

Stewart nodded and began to wade back into the loch before swimming the last yards to his boat with powerful strokes, and hauling himself on board. He raised one hand in salute to the group on the Blairfinnan bank, and Annie felt Kirsty's hand tighten in hers. She smiled at the child encouragingly, sensing that she was suddenly nervous at seeing her uncle depart.

'What a sketch we both look, don't we? We'd best both have a bath and make ourselves presentable, Kirsty.'

'And I'll see if I can find her some suitable clothes to wear in the costume gallery,' Aunt Morag said. The child's eyes lit up with excitement at this, and a few minutes later Annie tried to ignore the incongruity of Dougal Stalwart Blair carrying the Mackinty child in his arms back to Blairfinnan.

Once there a maid attended them both, and within an hour they were cosy in the drawing-room with hot chocolate, and Kirsty was beginning to enjoy the feeling of importance as this new family fussed over her. Even Dougal, Annie thought in some amazement . . . and thought for the first time that he'd make a wonderful grandfather.

By mid-afternoon she was becoming very nervous. She might not have been there at all for all the notice Kirsty took of her. She was enchanted with Morag and Dougal by now, and Annie wandered about, watching for a familiar face, alert for the first sound of carriage-wheels.

At last they came, and the two Mackinty men alighted, the one agile and strong, the other less nimble and looking his age. Kirsty ran to hold Callum's hand.

'Is she all right?' he said abruptly to Morag.

'She's fine,' Morag said, and Annie noticed how she had threaded her arm through Dougal's, as if in a brief reassurance of where she belonged. Annie felt her eyes prickle at the small cameo scene, the more so when Dougal spoke gruffly to Callum.

'Will you take a dram with me, man? It won't be Craggan's Best, but it will grace your palate just as well.'

Kirsty still held tightly to her grandfather, but she reached out to catch at Dougal's hand too, creating a link between the three of them. If anyone would bring them together, it would be the child, not herself and Stewart, however fanciful the idea. It was the bairn. . .

'You'll not be needing us just now,' Stewart said. 'Annie and myself have business of our own to attend to.'

'Do we?' she said.

'We do. But not here. We'll walk by the loch, and you'll not interrupt when I say what I have to say.'

She glanced at him, unsure whether he was angry. She couldn't tell. His gypsy eyes told her nothing. Nor did his striding walk that had her almost running to keep up with him as they'd done once before. She'd made him wait then. But now. The tingling in her veins told her the next minutes were going to be very important to them both, and she prayed she wasn't wrong.

They reached the cool seclusion of the loch-shore, where the grassy glen dipped down to the water's edge, and they were isolated from any prying eyes.

'Now then, Annie Blair,' Stewart said. 'You showed me a certain document, and I've another to show you.'

This wasn't what she had expected. Nor did she have any idea what he was talking about.

'What document?' she said, numb with disappointment. Hadn't he said he loved her? Hadn't he once asked her to marry him, however mockingly? And didn't he know how much she really cared, when he could read the passion in her eyes so readily?

He pulled out a parchment from the inside of his shirt and began to unroll it. 'The words are not originally mine, but were written by my ancestor James, and given to your Miranda. Today their meaning is for us as it was between them.'

Her throat felt so dry she could barely swallow. He spread out the parchment, and she glimpsed the date at the top, in flowery writing that had gone brown with age. October the twentieth, 1745. She remembered at once that it was the day James and Miranda were married.

'From this day on,' Stewart read slowly. 'I pledge to thee my love, my heart, and my life.'

For a moment neither of them spoke. The words seemed to hang in the air between them, the clear clean highland air that was as much a part of them both as those other two. However much they tried, in the end there was no separating any of them, Blairs or Mackintys, past or present.

For a moment more they stood apart, and then Annie was in his arms, where she belonged so completely. Where she had always belonged, she thought gloriously, throughout time and beyond.

His arms tightened around her more possessively, feeling her instant response.

'So, Annie Blair. Are you going to marry me?'

Her face was uptilted to his, and she almost laughed at the foolishness of the question, for hadn't it always been destined? And then she saw that the love in his eyes was hidden no longer, and the laughter died on her lips, for this was too sweet a moment to spoil.

'Just as soon as you wish,' she said huskily. 'From this day on, I pledge to thee my love, my heart, and my life –'

And then all time for talking was past.